P9-DFK-543

"Look, I'm not sure what you are expecting from this marriage."

Thomas took his hat off his head and wiped his forehead with the back of his hand. "But it isn't going to be a real marriage."

"We said vows, Thomas. Vows that I have been raised to keep." Now that they were alone, was this his way of saying he'd changed his mind? How could he do such a thing?

His gaze met and held hers. "I agree, but this isn't a real marriage, Josephine. The only reason I agreed to it was because I wanted you to be safe from your uncle and his evil plans. I have no intention of falling in love."

All Josephine could think to say was "All right." Inside she told herself she was happy that he harbored no desire to fall in love and live happily ever after.

Tension eased from her body. If he felt that way, then he couldn't expect her to love him, either. How could anyone love another when they weren't even sure they could trust them?

Still, a twinge of worry etched its way through her mind. "Does this mean you want to get out of the marriage?" She didn't want to not be married to him; she needed the protection of his name.

"No, we're married and you have the protection of the Young name, but that is all."

Rhonda Gibson lives in New Mexico with her husband, James. She has two children and three beautiful grandchildren. Reading is something she has enjoyed her whole life, and writing stemmed from that love. When she isn't writing or reading, she enjoys gardening, beading and playing with her dog, Sheba. You can visit her at rhondagibson.net. Rhonda hopes her writing will entertain, encourage and bring others closer to God.

Books by Rhonda Gibson

Love Inspired Historical

Saddles and Spurs

Pony Express Courtship
Pony Express Hero
Pony Express Christmas Bride

The Marshal's Promise
Groom by Arrangement
Taming the Texas Rancher
His Chosen Bride
A Pony Express Christmas
The Texan's Twin Blessings
A Convenient Christmas Bride

Visit the Author Profile page at Harlequin.com.

3 1526 04856361 0

RHONDA GIBSON

Pony Express Christmas Bride

HARLEQUIN LOVE INSPIRED HISTORICAL

If you purchased this book without a cover you should be aware that this book is stolen property. It was reported as "unsold and destroyed" to the publisher, and neither the author nor the publisher has received any payment for this "stripped book."

Recycling programs
for this product may
not exist in your area.

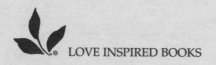

LOVE INSPIRED BOOKS

ISBN-13: 978-0-373-28386-6

Pony Express Christmas Bride

Copyright © 2016 by Rhonda Gibson

All rights reserved. Except for use in any review, the reproduction or utilization of this work in whole or in part in any form by any electronic, mechanical or other means, now known or hereinafter invented, including xerography, photocopying and recording, or in any information storage or retrieval system, is forbidden without the written permission of the editorial office, Love Inspired Books, 195 Broadway, New York, NY 10007 U.S.A.

This is a work of fiction. Names, characters, places and incidents are either the product of the author's imagination or are used fictitiously, and any resemblance to actual persons, living or dead, business establishments, events or locales is entirely coincidental.

This edition published by arrangement with Love Inspired Books.

® and TM are trademarks of Love Inspired Books, used under license. Trademarks indicated with ® are registered in the United States Patent and Trademark Office, the Canadian Intellectual Property Office and in other countries.

www.Harlequin.com

Printed in U.S.A.

To everything there is a season.
A time for every purpose under heaven.
—*Ecclesiastes* 3:1

A special thank-you to my family.
I love you all very much.
James Gibson, your support means the world to me.
Father God, thank You for the stories You place
on my heart and for being with me when I write.

Chapter One

Dove Creek, Wyoming
October 1860

Josephine Dooly lay low over her horse's back. She whispered soothing words in his ear, even though she felt sure he couldn't hear them over the yells of the bandits in hot pursuit of her. Her heart raced, adrenaline ran full throttle through her veins and pounding heart.

She doubted the bandits were after her money; they wanted the bags of mail in her possession, but if they stopped her, they'd get both and it wasn't in her to let them have either. She meant to keep the hard-earned money she had on her person—and her mother's locket. Josephine had a wedding trousseau to buy and a household to set up. Bandits out for the thrill of the steal were not going to alter her plans one little bit.

"Just a little farther, boy. We're almost there." The Pony Express station just ahead was Josephine's destination. Once she rounded the bend, she knew the men would stop chasing her. Ole Mac, the previous stock tender, had said so when he'd given her instructions about this part of her run.

Thankfully, this was Josephine's last ride for the Pony Express. She still couldn't believe that cutting her hair and shortening her name to Jo had gotten her employment with the Pony Express. But she thanked the Lord that it had. There'd been some close calls and a few lonely days, but she'd made it by the grace of God.

As promised, once she rounded the bend, the bandits turned back the way they'd come. She let out several loud whoops of her own and patted the horse's neck as she sped into the Pony Express station, where another rider waited to take her place.

She handed off the mochila and slid from the pony all in one motion. The other rider raced away, leaving Jo and the station manager standing in the yard in front of a tall barn.

The Pony Express station stock tender turned to look at her. "Boy, you look plum tuckered out." With a good-humored laugh, he slapped Josephine on the back and only her quick reflexes kept her from flying through the air and falling on her face.

He motioned toward a building a few feet away. "Welcome to the Young family home station. I'm Andrew Young. My brother Philip is in the bunkhouse. Head on over. He'll make sure you get something to eat and show you to a warm bunk, where you can bed down."

Josephine nodded. This was her first time at this station, but she knew that in another ten miles she'd be in Dove Creek—and that was her final destination. She'd hired on as a Pony Express rider simply to get here.

She lowered her voice to sound like that of a young

boy's. "Thanks, believe I will." Her legs felt as if she'd marched through mud and it had dried on her boots, weighing them down. She walked to the small bunk-house, happy for a little time to rest after her last run.

A smile tilted her lips. She'd made it to the Young Home Station. It had taken a couple of weeks, but she was here. And her uncle was none the wiser. She'd managed to escape his plans to marry her off to a distaste-ful gambler as payment of a large debt he owed. What kind of uncle did that to his niece? Apparently hers, as that was exactly what had happened. But she'd out-smarted him.

Answering Thomas Young's ad for a mail-order bride had been her saving grace. And the scariest thing she'd ever done in her young life. Well, that and sign-ing on to be a Pony Express rider.

Her forehead puckered in thought. What would Thomas's brothers Andrew and Philip think when she revealed that she wasn't a boy but their brother's mail-order bride?

Josephine hoped Thomas would be as happy to see her as she would be to see him. She'd not had the lux-ury of time to wait and see if he'd send her money to travel to the West, but had of necessity found her own way to Wyoming.

Josephine knew she'd had no choice. After her mother's death, her father had become depressed and one day just disappeared. Leaving her behind to fend for herself. At first her uncle had paid little attention to her, but soon he'd realized that she could become prof-itable to him. To escape her uncle and his plans, she'd signed on with the Pony Express and never looked back.

Josephine pulled her shoulders back and raised

her chin, readying herself to meet Philip Young. She touched her hand lightly against her chest, comforted by the warmth of her mother's locket. The jewelry was the only thing left of her mother, besides Josephine's memories, and she cherished it above all her possessions. Fortunately, her uncle hadn't known she possessed it or it would have been long gone.

She pushed the sad thoughts aside and entered the bunkhouse. She yawned and weariness filled her. Josephine knew that once she told Philip who she really was, she'd need a couple of hours' sleep before heading to the town of Dove Creek. She hadn't waited for Thomas's letter and now only hoped that she'd be given the directions to the relay station that he ran. If she understood correctly, it was a mere five miles on the other side of Dove Creek, so shouldn't be too hard to find.

Nerves warred with hunger as she thought about this new life she planned to carve out for herself. Josephine prayed once more that she'd made the right decisions in answering a mail-order-bride ad, joining the Pony Express to escape her uncle and then marrying a man she didn't know. Some might say she'd jumped out of the frying pan and into the fire; Josephine didn't know, but she was about to find out.

Thomas Young leaned against the stone fireplace, watching snow drift silently to the ground in light, fluffy flakes. Living at a Pony Express relay station was the perfect life. He and his brother Philip had everything they needed. They attended to the Pony Express station that rested on the far side of the Young Home Station, which was always their first and last stop on their rides. Their ma liked this because it meant she got to see her adopted sons at least once a week. The home stations offered a bed and meal, whereas their small station offered only a fresh horse and more miles to ride between home stations.

Thomas heard the bugle blow seconds before the young man came into sight. The Pony Express rider came in fast and hard. Not all the riders used the bugle, but this one did. Thomas pushed himself away from the fireplace wall. He hurried to the barn and pulled out the already saddled horse that the rider would exchange. He'd take care of the exhausted horse as soon as the Express rider was on his way.

The young boy rode low over his horse's neck. The powdery snow lifted from the horse's hooves like steam from an overheated kettle.

Thomas braced himself for the horse exchange. The boy practically leaped from one horse to the other in one motion. Thomas recognized him as Juan. *"Adios!"* he called after the retreating back. The pony beside him heaved. Juan had ridden him hard.

The rider waved and shouted back. *"Buenos Dias, Senor Young!"*

He smiled and then gently tugged on the reins of the spent horse. "Come along, boy. We'll have fresh oats in your belly in a few moments." Thomas took the horse to the small barn that housed six Pony Express horses. His own gelding was behind the barn in the lean-to it shared with Philip's horse.

The smell of hay and oats filled his nostrils. The warmth of the barn wrapped around his chilled body. Philip had been gone for almost four days. He'd planned to ride his part of the trail and then stop in at their adoptive mother's home station near Dove Creek.

As he worked, Thomas talked to the horses. "Philip should be home later today, boys. I've missed his constant chatter. How about you?"

One of the animals kicked its stall door in answer. Thomas laughed. "Well, at least one of you missed him, too." He took off the Pony Express–issued saddle and began rubbing down the horse that had just arrived.

"I see you are still talking to the animals."

Thomas turned to smile at the little woman who stood in the doorway. Hazel Gorman was short, round and full of wrinkles. Her hazel eyes twinkled as she looked at him. He wasn't sure of her age and had never been brave enough to ask. "Hello, Hazel. I didn't hear you arrive." He put the horse into a stall, where fresh oats awaited it.

She continued into the barn carrying a big basket. "With the way you and these horses were yammering on, I'm not surprised." There was a teasing glint in her voice that assured him she was joking.

"What's in the basket?" Thomas knew it contained some kind of eatable. Hazel was their nearest neighbor and enjoyed bringing them some form of baked good at least once a week. She also brought them canned goods and warm soups or stews.

"It's getting colder, so I thought you two boys might like a couple of loaves of bread, and I've also jarred up my favorite beef stew. It should last you a few days." Her wrinkled face crinkled up into a smile.

The old woman had more or less adopted Thomas and Philip and used the excuse of feeding them as a reason to come over and check on them. Thomas knew she grew lonely out on her place and, to be honest, he enjoyed her frequent visits.

"Well, thank you. Come on into the house. I just put on a fresh pot of coffee."

She fell into step with him. "When is Phil coming home?"

Thomas grinned. "Anytime now. He should have already arrived."

As if she heard the loneliness in his voice, Hazel grunted. "You two boys need wives to help you pass the time when the other is working."

He held the door open for her. Thomas didn't point out that he was working, too. And he wasn't about to talk about getting wives. Instead he said, "That stew smells good."

Hazel playfully slapped his arm as she passed. "You can't smell the stew. You're just trying to change the subject." She walked to the kitchen area and set the bread and jars on the table.

He closed the door and shut out the cold air and lightly falling snow. "Look, Hazel, I know you mean well, but Philip and I are doing just fine without wives."

She ignored him and moved to the cabinet that contained four tin mugs, the remainder of the clean dishes in the house. Hazel filled two of them with hot coffee and motioned for him to join her at the table.

Thomas sat down with a sigh. If he knew Hazel, and he believed he did, she was going to start a running conversation on the benefits of having a wife.

Hazel studied his features over the rim of her coffee cup.

He turned his face so that she could see only the right side. The last thing Thomas wanted was for her to focus on the scar that ran from his temple to his chin on the right side. It wasn't pretty and no woman should have to look at it straight on.

"You are a handsome young man, Tom. Look at me." She lowered her cup.

Thomas tried a teasing tone. "You are mighty pretty, too, Miss Hazel. Are you hinting you'd like to marry me?" He continued to keep his face tilted from her sight.

"You rascal. We both know I'm too old for you. Besides, I want a man who isn't ashamed of his looks." Her tone had lost its teasing tone.

Thomas didn't have a chance to answer. The door burst open and Philip came into the cabin. Cold air and a petite young woman followed him inside.

Without so much as a how-do-you-do, Philip blurted, "Hey, Thomas! Look what I brought home!"

This couldn't be good. Philip looked a little too cheerful. The pixie-looking girl beside him smiled shyly and clutched a worn piece of luggage in her small hands. She was a pretty little thing with big brown eyes, a mass of short red hair and the cutest turned-up nose he'd ever seen. Thomas didn't know how to answer his brother. He had no idea what was going on. "Um…"

Hazel got to her feet. "Did you up and get married, Phil?" She hurried forward and hugged him.

Shock filled Philip's face as he held his hands up like a bank robber in front of the sheriff. "No."

Hazel stood back and frowned. "Then maybe you should explain who this young lady is." She released him and crossed her arms over her ample bosom.

Philip reached behind him and pulled the pixie forward. "This is Josephine Dooly. Thomas's mail-order bride." His laughing blue eyes met Thomas's.

"What?" Thomas's and Hazel's shocked voices echoed each other.

The young woman seemed to have found her tongue. "I know I should have waited till you sent for me, but, well, under the circumstances, I came as fast as I could."

"What circumstances?"

Her cheeks reddened. "I told you in the letter." Small hands clutched the carpetbag as if she were afraid they'd take it from her.

"What letter?" Thomas stood and raked his hand down the side of his scarred face.

Philip looked as pleased as punch. His blue eyes danced with merriment as the scene unfolded before him.

Hazel's gaze darted between the three of them. She finally focused her eyes upon Josephine. "I'm Hazel Gorman. Let's sit down at the table and see if we can sort this all out." Her wrinkled hand waved toward Thomas and the chairs that remained empty behind him.

Josephine nodded. She sat her bag beside the door and walked toward him.

Philip shook his head. "I need to unload the wagon before the storm hits."

"It will wait." The steel in Hazel's voice stopped the young man. Wariness filled his eyes.

Thomas waited for the young woman to sit, then he did the same. Whatever was going on, it was obvious that Philip had a hand in it all. Thomas picked up his warm cup and cradled it between his palms as he watched his brother pull out a seat at the old wooden table. The smile on Philip's face set Thomas's teeth on edge.

Hazel set cups of coffee in front of Philip and Josephine. "All right, you two. Start at the beginning."

Josephine looked at Philip, who quickly began to study the surface of the table as if he'd never seen it before. She shrugged and said in a soft voice, "As Philip said, I am Josephine Dooly. I answered Thomas's mail-order-bride ad because my uncle is trying to marry me off to pay for his gambling debts. Mr. Grossman, my uncle's chosen husband for me, is three times my age and a gambler with no moral conscience. I'd simply be a servant in his house." She shuddered and inhaled before continuing. "When I answered Thomas's mail-order-bride ad, I explained that I wanted to get away from my uncle and start somewhere fresh. Thomas wrote back and said he'd send me money for passage out to Dove Creek as soon as he could afford to. I couldn't wait, so I took a job as a Pony Express rider and brought myself to Dove Creek."

She took a deep breath and looked to Philip, who still studied the tabletop. A sigh escaped her lips before she pressed on. "I met Philip at the home station and he said he was Thomas's brother and would take me to him. So while he completed his Express run, I went into town and bought a couple of dresses, shoes and other things I knew I'd need to start a new life and home with Thomas. My things are on the wagon."

Thomas shook his head. "I never placed a mail-order-bride ad."

Josephine's chocolate eyes flared with new brightness. "I wrote to you and you answered."

Hazel focused on Philip. "What do you have to say about all this, young man?"

He finally looked up. "Well, I got to thinking about

what you said." Philip paused, but Hazel's lips only grew thinner. "You know, about how lonesome Thomas gets when I'm off on my rides for the Pony Express." He paused again. Still no response came from the older woman. "So I placed the ad." He held up his hands at the flash of anger that entered the older woman's eyes. "Now, Hazel, don't get all riled up. You are the one who said he needed a wife." Philip crossed his arms over his chest and tilted his chair back. "I got him one."

Josephine gasped. From the look on her delicate features, this was news to her, too.

Thomas wanted to knock the chair right out from under Philip. He lowered his voice and said, "Philip, this has to be the stupidest thing you've ever done. I don't want a wife. You marry her." He pushed away from the table.

Philip dropped the chair back onto four legs and stood, also. "I'm not the one who is moping around here like a lost puppy."

Anger flared through Thomas's blood. "I haven't been moping and I don't want or need a wife." He waved his hand toward Josephine.

Josephine was on her feet in an instant. "I will not marry him!" she said, pointing at Philip with a shaky finger. "He's a liar and can't be trusted." She turned toward Thomas. "You, on the other hand, I have to marry and I have to do it quick."

"Why me?" Thomas demanded through gritted teeth, not liking that he felt as if he were being pushed against the wall.

Hazel spoke calmly but firmly. "Sit down, all of you." When all three did as she said, Hazel sighed. "Philip, this is a mess and it's your fault." She turned to look at Josephine. "I'm sorry you got involved with these two's tomfoolery."

Josephine's big brown eyes filled with tears. "I have to marry Thomas. My uncle could find me at any time and force me to marry Mr. Grossman. I don't want to get married, either, but it's my only escape."

Thomas studied the girl. She had a heart-shaped face surrounded by short, fiery red curls that came to her jawbone. Brown eyes as big as pie plates were filled with the bare glistening of tears. Small freckles were sprinkled over her pert nose. She certainly was a pretty little thing.

Josephine's eyes blazed into his as she huffed and visibly stiffened, gaining her nerve, it would seem. "Look, I realize this isn't what you want, but I have to get married and *you* are the one I am going to marry." She swallowed hard, lifted her chin and boldly met his gaze.

The show of strength and the determination in her voice took him by surprise. What had happened to the young woman who moments ago had trembling lips and tears in her eyes? Was her situation so desperate she'd marry a scarred man like him?

The wind whipped around the cabin windows. Hazel looked at the swirling snow outside. "I have to get home, but I refuse to leave this young woman alone with you two." She pushed her chair back. "Josephine, you come home with me and we'll sort this out tomorrow."

Josephine pushed herself to a standing position and raised her chin with a cool stare in Thomas's direction. "I expect to get married tomorrow." With her head held high, Josephine picked up her bag and followed Hazel out onto the front porch.

Thomas's gaze followed her. She couldn't be more than five feet tall. Such a tiny woman for such a big attitude.

Josephine turned and looked at Philip. Her hand clasped something under her blouse as if she were seeking strength. "You will pay for this, Philip Young." Then she followed Hazel off the porch and into the swirling snow.

Thomas looked at his brother's stricken face. Had he not been so upset with Philip, he'd have laughed outright. For once in his life, Philip actually looked afraid. Josephine Dooly might be small, but she'd put the fear into Philip.

Renewed anger at what his brother had done turned Thomas's tone to grit. "I'm going to follow Hazel home. I'd hate for them to get trapped in this weather. You need to get whatever is in the wagon and bring it into the house."

Seeing Philip's horse standing beside the porch, Thomas decided to take it for the short ride over to Hazel's small farm.

Hazel and Josephine sat side by side on Hazel's wagon bench. The two women were bundled up and heading down the rutted road. Thomas followed. What was he going to do now? He didn't want to get married, but the fear he'd seen in Josephine's eyes had been real.

If he understood her correctly, Josephine's uncle intended to sell her to his gambler friend to pay off his own debts. No one deserved to be held in servitude to another, and if what the young woman had said was true, Thomas knew he'd never allow anyone to marry her off like a piece of property.

Deep down, Thomas knew he'd marry her to save her from her uncle and the gambler—even if this wasn't the path he would have chosen for his own life.

Chapter Two

Josephine trembled with anger. She'd been lied to. Again. What made men act the way they did? Were there no honorable men left in the world? Josephine pulled the locket from under her dress and held it in her hand. In the past her mother's necklace had given her a sense of hope. Now it only felt like a weighted piece of jewelry.

"Are you cold, dear?" Hazel used her right hand and tucked the blanket tighter around Josephine's legs. Snow drifted easily about them.

"Not really," she answered as she tucked the necklace back inside the neck of her dress. How did she explain that she trembled from fear? Her plans had seemed so simple when she left St. Joseph. She'd get to Dove Creek by traveling the Pony Express trail, then once she arrived, find her mail-order groom and get married. But that wasn't how it had worked out. Now her future looked vague and shadowy. She tried to force her confused emotions into order, but sadness enveloped her along with the ever-constant and pulsating fear.

"Angry?" Hazel ventured.

Josephine looked at Hazel in surprise and nodded. Philip had been the one who had placed the ad and answered her letter. He'd lied to her. Like all the men in her life, he'd turned out to be a deceiver. First her father had deserted her shortly after her mother's death, then her uncle had betrayed her by using her to pay off his gambling debts and now Philip had tricked her. Men couldn't be trusted. "Very," she admitted.

"I don't blame you one bit. Phil doesn't always think before he acts. I'm sure it never dawned on him that his meddling in Thomas's life would put you in danger." Her aged hands slapped the reins over the horses' backs to speed them along.

The snow continued to fall heavily in big, puffy flakes. Josephine didn't correct her by saying she'd been in danger long before Philip's deceit. Instead she asked, "Why would he do such a thing?"

Hazel shook her gray head. "I might be partially to blame. I've been telling those boys for months that they needed wives. It gets lonely out here, but I never imagined Philip would go off and do a harebrained thing like this. I'm sorry, Josephine."

"Miss Hazel, it's not your fault. Philip is the one who placed the ad and encouraged me to come. He's to blame." Josephine looked over her shoulder. She could see Thomas trailing them, riding Philip's horse. Had he really not known what his brother was up to? Maybe he hadn't. His green eyes had shone with confusion when she and Philip first entered the old shack.

If Hazel heard the bitterness in Josephine's voice, she didn't let on. "They are both nice young men," Hazel said, turning down another lane.

Josephine didn't want to argue with the older woman,

but right now she just didn't see it. Philip had lied to her and pretended to be his brother; at least, he had in the letter he'd sent. And at no time during their trip out to the way station had he said anything about Thomas not knowing she was coming. As for Thomas, he might be nice, but he didn't want to get married and she didn't know what she'd do if he didn't marry her.

The wagon slowed to a stop in front of a farmhouse. "It's not much, but it is home," Hazel said, setting the brake and preparing to dismount from the wagon.

Josephine looked at the small house and smiled. She watched as smoke curled upward from the chimney into the late-afternoon sky. Its warmth beckoned to her. "It's perfect." Weariness weighed heavily upon her shoulders as she climbed down from the wagon.

Thomas pulled up beside them. His cowboy hat covered most of his head, but light brown hair could be seen around his ears and neck. A light beard covered his face. "Hazel, it looks like we are in for a heavy snow. Can I cut more wood for you?"

It seemed now that he wasn't filled with shock, his voice had lowered a degree. Josephine found herself looking up at him. She liked the warmth in his expression.

Hazel answered, "No, thank you, Tom. We're set for a few days." She carried her basket up the steps.

A few days? Josephine hadn't planned on staying with the woman a few days. She needed to get back to Dove Creek and to the preacher who could marry them. Her gaze moved from the old woman back to Thomas.

His green eyes searched hers. "Do you mind talking for a few minutes?" he asked, swinging down from the saddle.

"Come on inside, both of you. You can use the sitting room to have your visit," Hazel ordered as she entered the house.

Josephine didn't know exactly when or how she'd let the older woman take over her life, but it seemed Hazel had done just that. She turned her attention back to Thomas. "I need to talk to you, too." If she could make him understand why she needed to get married as soon as possible, then maybe he'd agree.

He nodded and followed her into the house. Josephine stopped inside the doorway. She hadn't expected to see a plush settee and large chair in the small home. A beautiful rug rested on the floor and colorful paintings filled the walls.

Hazel came out of a door to the right of the room. "Josephine, you can sleep in there tonight." She indicated the room behind her and then continued on to the kitchen. "I'm going to make hot coffee. Would either of you like a slice of spice cake to go with the coffee?"

Thomas answered, "I can't stay long." He took his hat off and worked the brim with his hands.

"I'd love a piece," Josephine replied as her stomach growled.

Hazel nodded and left the room. Josephine moved to the settee. "Would you like to sit?" She set her bag down.

Thomas nodded. "I'm sorry that Philip lied to you."

"Me, too. But that doesn't help me now."

"No, I suppose it doesn't." Thomas looked to the doorway where Hazel had gone.

Was he wishing he'd followed her? Josephine sighed. "Was that all you wanted to say?"

He looked back at her. "No. Were you telling the truth? Is your uncle going to force you to marry someone to pay off his gambling debt?"

"Yes." Her voice trembled. Had he heard the fear she felt?

Josephine prayed she could make him change his mind about marrying her. "The man my uncle wants me to marry is old, smells like rotting food and is willing to take me as payment for my uncle's debts." She stopped, her gaze met his and she involuntarily shivered at the thought of someone like the gambler ever touching her. "He makes my skin crawl when he looks at me," Josephine admitted.

Thomas moved his hand to the right side of his face, where a faint line ran from his temple to his chin, and asked, "And marrying me would be better?"

Josephine smiled at him. "Well, you aren't old and I can't smell you from here. So I think so." When he didn't smile back, she sighed. "Look, I just need to be married. I'm not asking you to be a real husband. I can take care of myself. In a few months I'll be twenty-one and out of my uncle's and Mr. Grossman's reach. But until then, I need to be legally married so that my uncle will no longer be my guardian."

He continued to study her. "What Philip did wasn't right." Thomas cleared his throat and said a little louder, "Hazel, would you join us, please?"

She immediately entered the room, carrying a plate with a slice of cake on it. "The coffee is taking a little longer to brew, but Jo can start with the cake." She handed the plate to Josephine.

Thomas grinned. Was he grinning because Hazel had shortened her name to Jo? Josephine had noticed the woman had shortened both Thomas's and Philip's names, too. Maybe this was her way of showing affection to the people around her. As long as she didn't call her Josie, it was fine.

"Thank you." Josephine set the plate down on the table in front of her. "I'll wait for the coffee."

"Hazel, can Josephine stay with you for a few days?" Thomas asked.

Disappointment and fear hit her like a sack full of apples. Josephine pleaded, "Thomas, I don't have a few days. If you aren't going to marry me, I need to move on. My uncle is probably already halfway here."

Hazel nodded, ignoring Josephine's outburst. "She is welcome to stay as long as she likes."

Thomas nodded. "Good. Who knows how bad this storm may be, but if we can, we'll head to town tomorrow."

"So you are going to marry her?" Hazel asked with a wide grin.

"I am," Thomas answered. He stood to his feet. Looking down at Josephine, he said, "This storm may last a few days. If that happens, we'll go to town and find the preacher as soon as the weather clears. The good news is that it will stop your uncle from coming for you right away."

Relief flooded her. She was getting married just as she'd planned, but for some reason, Josephine couldn't feel happy about it. Could it be because Thomas was only marrying her since he felt forced to do so? Was it possible Thomas would change his mind after he'd had a little time to think about it? The prospect of marrying a complete stranger didn't appeal to her, either, but what choice did she have? She shoved the fear down that trickled up her spine and into her hairline. No, she'd not borrow trouble. But pray that Thomas was a man of his word.

The snow fell continuously as Thomas rode home. Philip's horse snorted and pranced toward the barn. Thomas let the horse gallop as he thought about the past few hours.

Thanks to Philip, Thomas would be marrying a girl he hardly knew. Thomas had to admit the prospect didn't rankle as much as it had at first. He didn't know when he'd seen a prettier girl. Her red hair looked soft enough to touch, but he hadn't dared. Her pretty brown eyes revealed every emotion that flowed through her. Was she aware of how expressive her eyes were?

Josephine had said that all she wanted was his name and the right to claim she was married. Would that be enough? She'd also said she was almost twenty-one, two years older than him. But she was still young enough to want someone she could love. Still young enough to want a house full of children someday.

He'd never be someone she could love. His scarred face had caused girls to giggle and laugh at him. While living in the orphanage, he'd been tormented because of the scar. At the age of eleven, he'd had a crush on one of the girls, only to have her scorn him with cruel words. *You're so ugly, no one will ever want to adopt you.* Those words had stuck with him and they could still do damage if he dwelled on them.

If Philip, who'd been his best friend at the orphanage, hadn't said that Rebecca and John Young couldn't adopt him unless they took Thomas, too, then he would never have been adopted.

He dismounted in front of the lean-to, where his own horse waited to be fed. Philip's gelding hurried into the warmth of the small shed. Thomas fed both horses and unsaddled Philip's.

Besides the fact that he bore a hideous scar on his face, Thomas also dealt with the fact that he'd never know who his real parents were or where they had come from. He had no idea who he really was. Would any of that matter to Josephine someday?

His fingers moved to the scar. The caregivers at the orphanage had said he'd been dropped off on the doorstep with no identification and the wound on his small face. How was it that a baby of a few months could get such a gash?

Rebecca Young said that the scar was hardly visible, but Thomas knew it was there. He could feel the light groove with his fingertips. Earlier, Thomas had sensed Josephine's gaze on it and he figured that she thought the scar was revolting. She'd shivered just looking at him.

Thomas knew he'd marry Josephine and stay married to her for as long as she wanted. But he vowed he'd never allow himself to believe that she'd care for him. With that thought in mind, Thomas headed for the house.

The snow continued its slow, mesmerizing drift to the ground. In a couple of months Christmas would arrive, and from the looks of the weather right now, it might be a white Christmas. It was hard to believe that he'd spend the holidays as a married man.

Thomas shook the snow off his collar. He stomped his feet on the porch to remove the packed slush from his boots. The question tore through him again. Was he out of his mind agreeing to marry a total stranger?

What would it be like to spend every day with someone other than Philip, especially a female? Would she expect him to be at her beck and call?

He opened the door and entered the warmth of the cabin. It really was more of a shack, but he and Philip had gladly called the place home. Now he wondered if it would be good enough for Josephine. Would she hate it? Think it ugly? Would she soon be demanding they get a place of their own?

Philip turned from the stove. His eyes danced. "Sorry I sprung her on you like that. I meant to talk to you about her before she arrived," he said, dishing up a plate of Hazel's stew and fresh bread.

Thomas took his gloves off and stuffed them into his pocket. He calmly hung his coat on the nail by the door. His hat was last to come off. "Philip, you have done some stupid things, but this takes the cake." He turned to face his brother. "What were you thinking?"

Philip placed a second plate of food on the table. "Well, at the time I simply thought you needed someone to be here with you when I'm off riding the trail."

"Why? Do I seem like the sort who needs constant companionship?" Thomas pulled a chair out and sat down.

Philip added a plate of sliced bread to the table, then turned for the coffeepot and two cups. "Hey, between the two of us, you are more sensitive. I get lonesome, so figured you did, too." He sat down.

Thomas bowed his head, said a quick prayer before speaking again to Philip. "Then why didn't you get a bride for yourself instead of one for me?"

"I'm not the marrying kind," Philip said, then tucked into his dinner.

Thomas laughed bitterly. "And I am?" Didn't his brother realize that of the two of them, he, Thomas, was the less likely to have a woman fall in love with him? After all, he was scarred both inside and out.

Chapter Three

The next day, after taking care of the morning chores, Thomas made his way through the falling snow across the back pasture to Hazel's farm and knocked on her door.

The whole way over he'd prayed Josephine had changed her mind about getting married. Maybe Hazel had talked some sense into her. After all, would marrying him really keep her uncle at bay?

"Good morning, Tom. What brings you out in this weather?" Hazel asked, stepping to the side to let him in.

He took his hat off. "I just wanted to make sure you two were all right."

She shut the door. "Why wouldn't we be?"

Thomas shrugged, then followed her to the warm kitchen. Josephine sat at the table cradling a coffee cup in her hands. Red curls framed her face; they looked damp, as if she'd just washed her hair. Wide brown eyes met his and he saw weariness in their depths. Or maybe it was just acceptance of the situation she found herself in.

"Sit down. I'll make you a cup of coffee," Hazel said. She walked to the stove. "Would you like a warm biscuit with butter and honey?"

He grinned in her direction. "I'd love one. You make the best biscuits around." Thomas pulled out a chair and sat.

In a soft voice Josephine asked, "Did you come to tell me you've changed your mind?" She stared into the cup instead of looking at him.

This was his chance. He could say yes and she'd probably understand, but something in the way she sat and looked into the coffee stopped him. It was as if she expected him to back out. She tucked a curl behind her ear.

If nothing else, Thomas Young was a man of his word. He straightened his shoulders and answered, "No, I just wanted to come by and see if Hazel would like for me to milk the cow this morning. It's pretty cold out there." He took the plate Hazel handed him.

Hazel pulled on her work boots and grabbed her coat off the hook by the kitchen door. "Thanks, Tom, but I think I'll run out and milk her. You kids probably have stuff to talk about." Hazel hurried out the door, not giving him time to protest.

Silence hung in the air between them. Thomas wasn't sure what to say. He breathed a silent prayer for the right words. After he'd finished his biscuit, he asked, "What did Philip write to you about me?"

Josephine rocked the cup back and forth in her hands. "Not much. Just that you lived in an isolated place, but that we could meet in Dove Creek and we'd get married there."

He picked up his own cup. "Well, before we get

married, we should get to know one another." Thomas set the cup down. "I'll start. I was raised in an orphanage not far from here. My parents or someone dropped me off on the doorstep as an infant. I have no idea who my parents were or why they abandoned me like an old, torn-up shoe." He heard the bitterness in his voice and pressed on. "When I was twelve, Rebecca and John Young came to adopt a boy. Philip and I had grown very close. They picked Philip, but he refused to go with them unless they took me, too."

Once more he stopped. Philip was his best friend, but that didn't excuse what he'd done this time. "I know Philip did a stupid thing by luring you here, but he's my brother and cares about me." At her doubtful glance, he pressed on. "Anyway, Rebecca talked John into taking us both and they became the only parents I've ever known. Not only did they adopt Philip and me, but five other boys, and they had a little girl, Joy, so I have a big family." He paused to see her reaction.

She sat with her chin resting on her hands. "How did you end up out here in the middle of nowhere?" The softness of her voice and the way her eyes searched his sent a warm feeling through him.

He grinned. "Before he died, John had talked to his friend who worked for the Pony Express and they'd decided that the Young farm would be a Pony Express home station and that we boys, all six of us, would be riders. Ben is the baby boy and too young to ride." Thomas still missed his adoptive father. "After John died, Rebecca married Seth Armstrong, and Philip and I learned that the relay station manager here quit, so we took over for him. We both still ride for the Pony Express, too."

"How did you meet Hazel?" Josephine asked. Her brown eyes bored into his, and for a moment Thomas had the strange thought that he could lose himself in them if given the chance.

He cleared his throat. "She came over the first day we arrived. Introduced herself as our neighbor and has been a friend ever since." Thomas grinned.

Josephine sipped at her coffee and nodded. "She's treated me with nothing but kindness, also." She traced the wood grain on the table, then looked back up. "I suppose it's my turn now."

Thomas tipped his own cup and drank the luke-warm coffee, glad for the liquid that washed through his overly dry mouth. He waited as she scrunched up her face and gathered her thoughts.

"My mother died when I was fourteen years old. My papa loved her dearly, and when she died, my uncle said Papa couldn't stand to look at me because I look just like her. About four years later, Papa left me in my uncle's care and never came back."

She looked up at Thomas, and tears filled her brown gaze. "Uncle continued to take care of me, made sure I kept up my studies and that I was raised as a true lady, but last year Uncle started gambling." She swallowed hard. Thomas noticed that she put her hands under the table. "Things in the house started disappearing—paintings, rugs, the good silver and china. At first he accused the hired help of stealing them. Then he fired them all using the excuse that they were thieves, but the truth was he could no longer afford to pay them. Then he blamed me. Out of money and ways to acquire enough money to pay his debts, Uncle noticed Mr. Grossman's interest in me."

Thomas felt the need to gather her into his arms and protect her from the life she described. "You don't have to continue, Josephine."

She nodded. "But I do. I want you to understand why I need you to marry me." Josephine pulled her hands out from under the table. She clasped them together, but not before he saw the trembling. She continued, "Uncle explained that he owed Mr. Grossman more money than he could ever afford to repay. Mr. Grossman had threatened to have Uncle put in prison if I didn't marry him. I asked for a month to prepare for the wedding. The next morning while reading the paper, I saw your ad—well, Philip's ad—for a mail-order bride. I realized it was my means of escaping marriage to Mr. Grossman. He's far older than me and has been married three other times, each time his young wife died suddenly and under suspicion. And each time he's managed to escape the hangman's noose. I know deep in my heart that I am not safe marrying the likes of him. I wrote to you, I mean Philip, and he wrote back saying he'd send money for my passage out here as soon as possible. But I couldn't wait. My time was running out. So I cut off my hair, stole a pair of my uncle's work pants and a shirt, and went to the Pony Express office to apply for a job." She took a deep breath.

"So you told them you were a boy?"

Josephine shook her head. "No, I just asked if I could apply for the job. When the man asked my name, I told him it was Jo. He asked for a last name and I told him my name was just Jo." Panic filled her eyes. "I couldn't tell him my full first name or he would know I was a girl, and if I'd given the man a last name and if my uncle happened to ask him about me later, Uncle would know immediately where I'd gone."

Thomas searched her face. Didn't she realize she had lied by omission of the truth? She'd led everyone who worked for the Pony Express to believe that she was a boy. That was the same as lying to them. He understood why she'd done it, but it was still deceitful.

"After I got the job, I had to continue letting everyone think I was a boy. It was wrong, but I felt for my own safety I had to continue with the lie. I've asked the Lord to forgive me and I believe He has." She looked at him, waiting for his response.

Thomas didn't know what to say. It wasn't his place to judge her, and if she'd confessed to the Lord her wrongdoing, well, that was between her and her Maker. He nodded and saw relief wash over her face. "So you got here by being a rider for the Pony Express?"

"I did."

Riding for the Pony Express was dangerous work. How had she managed to make the rides? Had she run into bandits or Indians?

"I knew that if I could make it to Dove Creek, I'd find you and you'd save me from my uncle and Mr. Grossman." Her hands trembled as she ran them through her curls.

Thomas knew the danger she'd put herself in by coming to him. "I'm glad you made it here safely." He also knew now, without a shadow of doubt, that he'd marry Josephine to keep her safe. "As soon as the snow clears, we'll ride into Dove Creek and get married."

A smile trembled on her pink lips. "Thank you. I promise I'll be a good wife. I can cook, clean and help out around the station."

The back door blew open and Hazel followed the cold wind inside. "Peaches sure was glad to see me this morning." She held up a pail of fresh milk and shut the door.

Thomas noted that her cheeks were red from being out in the wind. He should have gone to milk the cow and felt bad that the older woman had gone out in the cold to do it. He stood. "Hazel, I'm sorry. I should have done that for you."

"Nonsense. I've been milking Peaches for several years now, winter and summer." She set the pail of milk on the counter and stood by the stove for warmth. "I trust you two had plenty of time for your talk."

Josephine nodded.

Thomas answered, "We did." He put his hat on his head. "Thank you for the coffee and grub, Hazel. I best be getting back to the station." He turned to Josephine. "My run is tomorrow and Thursday. When I get back, hopefully the snow will have cleared enough to get to town. Stay with Hazel and stay inside. If your uncle is about, I don't want him to see you before we get married."

Josephine frowned but nodded. She looked sad, dejected and weary. His heart went out to her. As he left the house, Thomas silently vowed to protect Josephine from her uncle and from Mr. Grossman.

Realizing how much her emotions affected him, Thomas told himself that she might become his wife, but he'd never allow himself to fall in love with her.

Josephine watched him leave. "He really is a nice man, isn't he?"

"That he is," Hazel answered. She rubbed her hands

together over the stove. "You know, I've been wanting to make a quilt. Maybe you and I can piece the top together while we wait for his return."

Josephine nodded. "Is his word good?" Josephine felt a frown pull at her brow. She wanted to believe Thomas would keep his promise and marry her, but she worried that after a couple of days in the saddle with lots of time to think he'd change his mind.

Hazel chuckled. "His word is good. Thomas will marry you, but I don't know that he'll trust you. You'll have to earn that."

"Why wouldn't he trust me?" Josephine asked.

Hazel poured hot coffee into her cup. "Those boys don't trust anyone very much. Probably because they were orphaned at an early age."

Josephine nodded. She'd been deserted by her father and the hurt still lingered. Truth be told, she didn't trust easily, either. What kind of marriage would she and Thomas have? She'd promised to be a good wife. Could she uphold her promise?

Josephine had no intention of falling in love and living happily ever after. Men couldn't be trusted. They deserted, lied and thought of women as personal property.

Nope, she wasn't about to fall in love with her future husband or anyone else. No man would ever hold her heart. Thomas Young was a handsome man, but Josephine vowed not to let that sway her into trusting him.

Chapter Four

As the saying goes, Thomas felt as if he'd been ridden hard and put up wet. He had to admit the past two days had been grueling, but riding through the wet snow on an ice-packed trail wasn't completely to blame for his weariness. Thankfully, his return ride had ended at the Pony Express home station in Dove Creek. The farm of Rebecca and Seth Armstrong, his adoptive mother and stepfather.

Andrew Young slapped him on the back. "Welcome home, little brother."

"Thanks, Andrew." His gaze moved to the house. Rebecca stood on the front porch and he smiled.

"She's been waiting all day for you." Andrew gave Thomas a little shove. "Better not keep Ma waiting."

Thomas walked toward the front porch. He'd never had a mother until Rebecca took him in. She wasn't that much older than him, but her wisdom and motherly love offered a comfort no other woman had ever filled. His boots thudded as he stepped up onto the porch. "Hello, Ma."

Rebecca wrapped him in a big hug. Excitement filled

her voice and she said, "I'm so glad to see you." She released him and stood back to look up at him. "I've missed you." Twin dimples and blue eyes smiled up at him.

"I've missed you, too." Thomas knew his words rang true. He missed her easy smile and the light touch of her hand upon his face.

Rebecca lowered her hand and then pulled him inside the house. "I wish Seth was here. He's been worried about you and Philip, but unfortunately he and Clayton had to go into Dove Creek for supplies. When Philip passed through here the other day, he assured us you were fine, but parents want to see for themselves."

"Thomas!" his little sister, Joy, squealed as she ran to him.

Thomas caught her in midair. He hugged Joy close. The sweet scent of vanilla filled his nostrils. "Hi, squirt!"

Joy's happiness at seeing him shone in her blue-green eyes. Thomas realized he'd stayed at the relay station too long. His family missed him and he missed them, too. He lowered Joy to the ground.

His gaze moved to Fay Miller and Emma Jordan, who stood together by the kitchen door. They were as much a part of his family as his brothers and adoptive parents. Fay had moved in with Rebecca after his adoptive father John's death to help out with their little sister, Joy. Emma Jordan was like a sister to him. She came to the family as a slave of one of the stage coach riders. Thanks to the stage being robbed, she and her owner had had to stay longer at the stop, and during that time, he and his adoptive brothers had helped Rebecca and Fay buy the young woman from her owner.

Emma was immediately given her freedom papers and now lived with the family as a free woman.

Fay smiled at him. "It's good to see you, Thomas. Are you hungry?"

Thomas yawned and nodded at the same time. "I'll get him a plate, Fay." Rebecca hooked her arm in his and walked to the kitchen.

Fay patted his arm as he passed. "I believe your mother wants you to herself for a few minutes." She grinned at Rebecca.

The two women had a special bond. After her husband died, Fay had been cast from her house in town and Rebecca, being the kindhearted woman that she was, had offered her a home. Then the two of them had taken in Emma.

His gaze moved to the young woman. Emma had been sold as a slave by her father to pay his debts. Much like Josephine's uncle was attempting to do to her. What was wrong with those men? Didn't they realize how important family was? He shook his head to clear his thoughts.

As if she could hear those thoughts, Emma said, "Joy, let's get your room clean before your pa gets back." She grasped the little girl's hand before she could protest and pulled her to the back of the house.

Thomas laughed when he heard Joy's protest. "I don't want to clean my room. I want to talk to Thomas." Joy wasn't much for talking around strangers, but with her family and Emma, well, the little girl was very verbal.

Fay gave him a parting grin and then followed Emma and Joy from the room. She called out, "We'll talk to Thomas when your mother is done catching up with him. I imagine the quicker you get that room clean, the quicker you'll get to see that big brother of yours."

Rebecca pulled him into the warm kitchen. "I hope you don't mind me hogging you to myself. It's a mother's prerogative to be able to learn all about her son and what he's been up to in his time away. Don't you agree?"

Thomas wasn't about to argue with her. "Of course I don't mind. I wanted to talk to you in private anyway." He sat down at the table. What was Rebecca going to think of his news?

Rebecca moved to the stove and dished up a large bowl of beans and ham. "Sounds serious," she said, placing a big hunk of corn bread on a plate and then adding a bowl of hot stew.

"It is." There was only one way to find out how she would feel about him getting married. *Just blurt it out, Thomas ole boy*, he said to himself before doing just that. "I'm getting married."

She squealed. "That's wonderful news, Thomas." Rebecca slid the food in front of him and sat down. Her eyes were bright and curiosity filled their depths. "Who is she? Where did you meet? No wonder you haven't come to visit us. You've been too busy courting."

This wasn't the reaction he'd expected. Thomas had thought Rebecca would be giving him advice and telling him that maybe he should wait, but instead she stared at him with big blue eyes and a broad smile, waiting for answers to her questions.

He swallowed, then answered, "Her name is Josephine Dooly." He picked up his spoon and dipped it into the bowl.

"That's a pretty name. Now, where did you meet?"

Her excitement both amused and perplexed him. "Philip brought her home."

"What?" She jerked backward and gave him a stern look.

That was better. To prolong her waiting, Thomas happily took a bite of the beans. Their meaty flavor tasted good on his tongue. He swallowed. "Yep, brought her home and said she was my mail-order bride."

Gone was the joyful look that she'd had earlier. "Maybe you should start at the beginning." Rebecca leaned forward once more. Now she looked more like the mother he'd grown to love.

Thomas laid his spoon down and told her about the past few days. He assured her that Josephine was staying with Hazel and not in the house with him and Philip, at least not until they were married.

Rebecca nodded in all the right places. She frowned as he told her about Josephine's uncle and the need to marry quickly. "It's funny that Philip didn't mention her." She chewed on the tip of her fingernail.

That was curious. Philip had told him that Josephine had ridden in as a Pony Express rider. She'd told him who she was and asked if he was Thomas's brother. The two had planned their trip back to the relay station. He'd left for his run. Upon his return, two days later they headed to town, where she'd gussied up like a girl and bought things she thought she'd need in her new home. Why hadn't his brother told their parents about Josephine? Had Josephine continued to act like a Pony Express rider while his brother was away? So many questions swirled in his mind and he made a mental note to ask Philip about them when he returned home.

"Do you really want to marry this girl, Thomas? Have

you prayed about it?" Her questions pulled Thomas from his inner thoughts.

He focused on his mother's face. Would she understand? How could she? Thomas wasn't sure he understood what he was doing himself. "I feel like I need to marry her. I've asked the Lord to have His way and He hasn't given me any signs or feelings to make me change my mind." Thomas pushed his plate back.

In a soft voice Rebecca asked, "Do you love her?"

Thomas wanted to laugh but didn't. "Love her? No, I haven't known her long enough to love her."

"I see." The frown on her face indicated that she didn't approve.

He shook his head. "Josephine doesn't love me, either, Ma. It is to be a marriage in name only. She needs an escape, and since Philip sent for her, I feel obligated to marry her."

Rebecca pushed out of her chair. She walked to her teapot and poured herself a cup of tea. "Mark my words, one of these days, Thomas, your soft heart is going to get the best of you. I just hope this isn't that time." She paused, then continued, "Why doesn't Philip marry her?"

Thomas shook his head. "Josephine doesn't trust him and who can blame her. And Philip says he's not the marrying kind."

He carried his plate and bowl to the washtub, then poured himself a cup of coffee. Thomas sighed. "I know it isn't normal to marry like this, but when I look at her and see how afraid she is, I feel that I have to help her."

Rebecca cradled her cup in her hands. Her eyes betrayed the worry she felt. "What happens after her uncle finds out she's married? Once he realizes he can't force her to marry, will you stay married?"

"I'm not sure, but until I do know, I'd like to keep this between you and me." Thomas drained his coffee. "And Philip, of course."

"You don't want the family to know you are getting married?" Rebecca shook her head. "I don't know, son."

"Please, Ma. I just don't want them to know until Josephine and I have had time to decide how we are going to handle her uncle. Then we'll get married and tell everyone." He searched her face.

Rebecca returned his gaze. "All right. I feel the family should know that you are getting married and be able to attend."

He put the cup in the washtub with the other dirty dishes. Then Thomas walked to her and enfolded her in his arms. "I understand your feelings, Ma." Another yawn escaped him and he laughed. "I really need to get a couple of hours' sleep and then head home."

Joy ran into the room. She stopped just inside the door. "Now, Ma? Please. Now can I talk to Thomas? I've missed him so much."

Thomas knew he'd not get any sleep for a while. Fay and Emma followed Joy into the room. He would enjoy his family and worry about sleeping later.

He released Rebecca and nodded his consent to stay and visit with Joy, Fay and Emma. Rebecca's eyes expressed the worry she felt for him. Would Seth and his brothers feel the same way as Rebecca? Or would they understand his odd feelings of protectiveness toward the young woman?

Josephine slipped out the kitchen door into the backyard. The water well stood several feet away and she walked slowly to it. So far Hazel hadn't noticed that she'd left the house. After spending three days indoors, Josephine relished the fresh air, even if it was icy cold.

Her fingers were sore from sewing the quilt blocks she and Hazel had begun piecing together. Working on the fabric had helped to keep her busy, but still she'd longed to be outdoors.

She loved the way the log cabin quilt was shaping up. Hazel had said that the red fabric came from one of her late husband's shirts. It was fitting that the red was the center of each block, since Hazel said her husband had been the center of her world for as long as she could remember.

Josephine hadn't asked Hazel for more details than that. The older woman's eyes had teared up, so Josephine had changed the subject. It was obvious that Hazel had loved her husband very much. What did a person do to have a love like that? Was there some formula? Could it be a family secret passed down through the generations? Aggravation twisted her gut. A girl should have a mama to instruct her in things of this nature.

She leaned against the cold stone of the well and sighed. Thoughts of her future husband filled her mind. Would she ever be able to trust him enough to have that type of love? Josephine shook her head. Probably not. Her distrust of men ran too deep, and Josephine knew that her heart couldn't take it if Thomas decided this marriage wasn't for him.

Her eyes searched the road. Darkness kept her from seeing past the barn. Thomas should have been back this morning, but as the day had worn on and the evening shadows lengthened, Josephine realized he wasn't coming. She sighed again.

"That bad, huh?"

Josephine jumped at the sound of Thomas's voice and gave a small squeal. Her hand covered her heart. "You pert nigh scared the life outta me." She protested a little louder than she'd intended.

He rested his arms along the rim of the well. "You were so deep in thought, your uncle could have walked right up to you."

The accusing tone of his voice set her teeth on edge. She wasn't a child and she didn't need him reminding her of the danger she'd put herself into coming out for fresh air. "Thankfully, you aren't him." Josephine looked out into the darkness, lightened only by the white of the snow.

Thomas laughed softly. "You have spunk, Josephine Dooly. I've never heard of a woman riding the Pony Express. And now here I find you outside when you know it could be dangerous."

Josephine turned her gaze back on him. Had she misheard him a few moments ago? The warmth in his laugh drew her like a kitten to fresh milk. Was she so used to her uncle treating her like a child that she expected Thomas to treat her the same way? She searched his face. "You aren't angry with me."

"No, I'm not. I am concerned that you take risks, but I am not your keeper. You can come and go as you wish." He pushed away from the well. "I came by to tell you that tomorrow we'll go into town and get married, if you still wish to do so."

Josephine exhaled. "I do, but what about my uncle?"

"I've been thinking on that. I don't think there is anything he can do after we're married. And as your new husband, I will keep you safe."

Relief filled her. "Thank you." She swallowed.

He nodded. "Can I walk you back inside?"

A longing to stay out in the fresh air battled with wanting to please him and go inside. The cold air nipped at her cheeks, helping her to make the decision. Josephine nodded and led the short distance back to the house.

His boots crunched through the snow as he followed her to the kitchen door. She stepped up on the porch but then turned to face him. He deserved an apology and she didn't want to offer it in front of Hazel. As it stood right now, she would have to apologize to the older woman, too. "I'm sorry. I should have done as you asked and stayed inside."

He reached up and brushed a wayward curl from her face. "I understand your need to come outside. I'm not sure I could stay inside for three whole days, either."

The light touch of his fingers against her cheek surprised Josephine. Her gaze met his. Dark circles surrounded his eyes. Had he rested or come straight to her after his run? She felt the urge to lean her face into his warm palm. He smiled and pulled his hand away. Thomas yawned. "I best be heading back to the house. I'll see you tomorrow."

As he turned to leave, Josephine called out, "Thomas."

He stopped and searched her face.

"I'm glad you are home." She smiled as her mind went blank. She could think of no more words to retain him.

His lips twitched into a grin. "Good night, Josephine." And he walked into the shadows.

She stepped into the kitchen but turned to watch Thomas climb onto his horse and head into the darkness that now enveloped the world. It seemed she was forever watching him leave.

Tomorrow they'd be married. Would they be compatible? Or would he soon tire of her and want to go on with his life, without her? She didn't know why, but the last thought troubled her.

Chapter Five

Josephine looked at her reflection with apprehension. Her short red hair curled about her face and ears in a wild array. She didn't feel like a bride. She wasn't sure she even looked like a bride.

Cutting her long red hair had been a big sacrifice and made her look like a boy. The store-bought dress she wore was too big and hid all her womanly curves. Weariness filled Josephine's eyes where joy should reside.

"You look beautiful," Hazel said as she slipped into the room.

"I don't feel beautiful." Josephine ran her hand down the pale green dress that hung on her slim body.

Hazel grinned. "Well, you are."

"I should have tried the dress on last night. Then I'd have known it was too big and could have taken in the sides." She sighed, wishing for another dress but knowing that the only other dress she had fit just as this one did.

Store-bought dresses never fit right. If only she'd had the foresight to buy material, but she hadn't. At the time she'd bought the two dresses, Josephine hadn't cared how they would look on her, but after just a few days around Thomas, she did care.

Josephine sighed. He deserved a pretty bride. Last night as she lay thinking about her wedding day, she realized that Thomas really was a good man. The fact that she was pretty sure he'd given up sleep to check on her made Josephine want to please him. It had been a long time since anyone had thought of her and put their own needs aside.

Hazel studied her a moment, then snapped her fingers. "I have just the right thing." She returned a few moments later with an exquisite belt made of soft, supple leather with lace overlay and a dainty gold buckle.

Josephine let out a long, audible breath. She fingered the belt reverently. "Oh, Hazel. It's lovely."

"Well, put it on, girl. Let's see what it does for you."

Josephine buckled the belt about her waist, then turned to look in the mirror. The belt pulled the material snugly over her shoulders, accentuating her womanly curves and tiny waist. Of its own accord her smile broadened in approval. Hazel tugged here and there in the back and then met her eyes in the mirror. "Are you about ready to go? Thomas and Philip arrived a few moments ago. They are hitching up the wagon now." She touched one of Josephine's many curls.

Butterflies took up residence in her stomach. She placed her hand over the flutters. "As ready as I'll ever be." Josephine picked up her handbag and hat, then turned to the older woman. "I know I'm getting married today, but it doesn't feel the way I thought it would."

Hazel opened the door. "What did you think you'd feel?"

Josephine knew she was being silly. Growing up,

she'd fantasized about the perfect wedding, with her papa by her side and the man of her dreams standing at the church altar waiting for her. Her white dress would flow about her instead of the green dress she now wore with a belt to take up the slack. The thoughts saddened her. As a child, she'd dreamed of love and romance.

She picked up the green cloak that matched her dress. "Never mind, it doesn't matter." Josephine put on the cloak and then stepped around Hazel. With her head held high and her stomach in knots, she walked out the front door.

Thomas turned in the saddle to look at her. What did he see? She felt her cheeks grow warm under his steady gaze. His eyes no longer looked clouded with weariness, and for that she was thankful.

"Green is a pretty color on you," he said, swinging down from the horse.

He was just being kind. Still Josephine answered appropriately as she made her way to the wagon. "Thank you."

He helped her up onto the wooden bench and did the same for Hazel. Josephine busied herself tucking a blanket around her cold legs. The older woman scooped up the reins and smiled. "It might be cold, but the sun is shining. A perfect day for a wedding."

Philip laughed and swung his horse around. He led the way down the muddy road that led to town. Thomas brought up the rear.

Josephine wished she could see Thomas's face. Was he as nervous about today as she was? Or was this simply a chore that he needed to get done and over with?

It was at times like this that Josephine wished her mother were still alive. She pulled her mother's gold-plated necklace out from under her dress. Her hand wrapped around it. If her mother were here, Josephine knew, she wouldn't be marrying Thomas Young. She'd be home preparing to become the wife of a man of stature. Not a Pony Express rider who, thanks to his brother's meddling, felt obligated to marry her.

Josephine glanced over her shoulder. Thomas was looking to the left. She took the brief moment to study the side of his face. Even with the faint scar that ran from his temple to his chin, he was probably the most handsome man she'd ever seen.

Thomas swiveled in the saddle to find her gazing at him. Embarrassed to be caught staring, Josephine quickly turned her head to face forward once more. She worried her lip between her teeth as they rode in silence.

This was the day she'd been waiting for. The day when she'd finally have freedom from her uncle and his evil intents. It was supposed to be the happiest day of her life.

Josephine sighed heavily. If only it were a happy day. Instead the four people heading to town all looked as if they were walking to the gallows.

Was she making the biggest mistake of her life? Would marrying Thomas turn out worse than marrying an old, fat gambler? Could she ever trust Thomas? Probably not.

As soon as her uncle found out she was married and left, Thomas would be finished with his need to help her. She'd be alone. Josephine raised her chin and looked straight ahead. *Don't fall in love or trust this man*, she told herself.

Thomas felt her rejection as strongly as if she'd slapped him. Oh, she said their vows and acted like she'd meant them, but earlier he'd seen the way she quickly turned after staring at his scarred face. He wasn't fooling himself into believing that Josephine would ever grow to love him. If anything, she'd put up an invisible wall.

"You may now kiss your bride."

What? Kiss your bride? He'd forgotten all about this part. Should he have discussed it with Josephine before the ceremony? He looked into Josephine's upturned face. Her eyes were closed as she waited for his kiss. A kiss he was sure she'd despise.

Philip slapped him on the back. "Go on, kiss her," he encouraged a little above a whisper.

Thomas leaned in and gently touched his lips to hers. A soft shock tickled his lips. He opened his eyes to find her looking into his with an emotion he'd never seen there. Had the spark between them surprised her, too? He pulled away.

Hazel grabbed Josephine and hugged her fast. "Congratulations." Tears filled her eyes.

His new wife's soft voice responded with a quick "Thank you."

Thomas thanked the traveling judge and quickly paid him for his services, then followed Hazel and Josephine from the small office.

Philip clasped an arm around his shoulders. "I wish you a lifetime of happiness, little brother."

"I'm only a month younger than you, Philip," Thomas answered, shrugging Philip's arm away.

They stepped out into the sunlight. Thomas squinted his eyes. His gaze quickly found Josephine. She and Hazel stood beside the wagon. They'd parked it under a tree off to the side of the sheriff's office, where the ceremony had taken place. His horse was tied to the gate of the wagon along with Philip's.

"Tell Ma and Seth I said hello," Philip said, falling into step with him as he walked toward the women.

He sighed. "I wish you could come with us."

Philip chuckled and dropped his voice. "Why? Afraid of your new bride?"

Thomas glared at him. "Never mind. On second thought, I'm glad you aren't coming."

"Yeah, me, too. When Ma finds out you got married without her, she's going to skin you alive." Philip shook his head in mock sorrow and then hurried on toward Hazel and Josephine.

Thomas pushed air from his lungs. Philip was right. He should have given the family time to come to the wedding. But on the way home, he'd remembered how afraid Josephine seemed and he'd only wanted to protect her and get married as soon as possible. Now that he was sure her uncle could never hurt her, Thomas knew it was time to tell the rest of the family and his mother that they'd gotten married. Philip looked to Hazel. "Hazel, are you ready to get back to your place?" he asked as he untied his horse from the wagon.

"Just about. Since we aren't going out to the Young farm, I'd like to stop in at the general store and pick up some thread before heading home. If it wouldn't be too much trouble."

"What's going on?" Josephine asked, looking from one of them to the other. Confusion filled her soft features.

Hazel looked at her and grinned. "Philip and I decided to let you and your new husband go to his parents by yourself." She smiled as if this was a wonderful gift that had just been bestowed on them.

Josephine's expressive brown gaze met his. "I didn't realize we were going to your parents."

"I'm sorry. I forgot to tell you last night."

"Thomas, I didn't pack for an overnight trip." Reproach laced her indulgent words.

He hadn't thought of that, either. Where was his head? His thoughts had been so wrapped up in getting them to town safely and keeping a lookout for trouble from her uncle that he'd not considered what would be important to her. "Um, we can go to the general store and buy what you need." Thomas congratulated himself on his quick thinking.

But one look at her face and he could tell she wasn't impressed. So far her wedding day had been a total disappointment. He'd seen the way her face had dropped when they discovered that the preacher was out of town but that they could be married by the traveling judge. And now she had to face his family without Hazel's steady comfort and her personal belongings.

Hazel patted Josephine's arm, drawing her attention from him. "This is my fault, too. In all the excitement of getting ready, I didn't notice that you hadn't packed a bag this morning. I'm sorry, Josephine."

Philip pulled himself up into his saddle. "I don't see where there is any harm done." He turned his horse toward Main Street. "Other than that ragged carpetbag, she didn't arrive with anything personal to start with."

Thomas wanted to strangle his brother. Philip had the sensitivity of a grizzly bear. Josephine touched the necklace that rested on her chest. She pulled her shoulders back and nodded. Her eyes still sparkled with what

Thomas could only estimate to be anger or perhaps unshed tears. He quickly looked away.

Hazel hurried to the side of the wagon and climbed aboard. "I have a better idea. Josephine and I will run over to the widow Ring's house. Her dresses will fit Josephine better than those store-bought ones."

"But I don't have any money with me, Hazel." Josephine ignored Thomas's offer to assist her up to the wagon seat. She pulled herself up and smoothed her skirt about her legs.

Thomas quickly assured her. "I'll pay for whatever you need."

Philip's deep chuckle irritated him. He frowned at his brother while untying his horse from the wagon. Thomas pulled himself into the saddle.

"Of course you will. You're married now. Whatever Josephine wants, you will pay for," Hazel reminded him. She snapped the reins over the horse's back, setting them into motion.

Thomas nodded. Nothing he said or did today was right. He clamped his lips shut, determined not to say the wrong thing again.

"Why don't you boys go wait for us at the general store? I'd like a little time with Josephine before you two take off for your parents'. We'll meet you there in an hour." Hazel wasn't really asking them to leave; her tone told them to go.

Thomas heard his brother's snort of laughter again. This was all Philip's fault. If his brother had just minded his own business and not written an advertisement for a mail-order bride, neither he nor Josephine would be in this situation now.

Hazel turned the wagon down Elm Street and left the men staring after them.

"Looks like we have an hour to kill. What do you want to do now?" Philip asked. He rested his arms on the saddle horn and looked across at Thomas.

"I'd love to strangle you. But since that's against the law and I'd have to answer to Ma if I did, I suppose we can go to the bakery and get a slice or two of sweetbread while we wait." He turned his horse toward the small store.

Thomas hoped a hot cup of coffee and sweetbread would calm the troubled waters of his stomach. He felt as if he'd just fought a mighty battle and lost. Josephine was angry at him and they hadn't been married even a half hour. Would they forever be at odds? Or was this about to become normal life for him?

Chapter Six

Josephine sat beside Thomas on the wagon seat. She wanted to smile knowing she had two beautiful new dresses, undergarments, a nightgown and a new pair of shoes in the basket at her feet. Much more than what she'd need for an overnight stay at the Young farm, but they all fit.

Mrs. Ring's goods were as wonderful as Hazel had described. The dresses fit perfectly on her small frame. The widow woman had a real talent with needle and thread. Something that Josephine hoped to accomplish someday, as well. Her fingers were still sore from working on the quilt blocks with Hazel.

The shoes were a soft tan and had come from the general store. Unlike her boots, they hugged her feet and made her feel like a woman again, instead of a Pony Express rider.

She cut her eyes and looked at Thomas under her lashes. The question that burned in her mind, but she'd never ask, was—had he felt that little spark when he'd kissed her? Josephine had tried to push that thought, that memory of their lips touching for the first time away all morning. But now, secretly admiring her husband, she couldn't keep it at bay any longer. Still, she tried by thinking of other things.

Hazel had said that Josephine needed to learn to trust her new husband. That was easy for the older woman to say. Hazel had never been abandoned by her father, almost sold by her uncle or lied to by her new brother-in-law. Hazel had confessed to having a wonderful marriage that had lasted almost forty years.

Thomas stared straight ahead. He hadn't said much since leaving town. Josephine wondered about the faint welt on his face and had to stop herself from reaching up and tracing it with her finger. How had he gotten the scar? He seemed very aware of it, and even now his jaw clenched under her observation.

She felt more than saw him guide the horse to the side of the road. Josephine waited as they came to a complete stop.

He set the brake on the wagon, then Thomas turned to face her. A deep sigh released from his chest as he said, "Well, we did it."

Josephine nodded. She tried to add a teasing note to her voice as she answered, "We sure did."

His face remained serious. Thomas wasn't in a bantering mood. Her new husband had something important to tell her. His jaw clenched, and then Thomas said, "Look, I'm not sure what you are expecting from this marriage." He took his hat off his head and wiped his forehead with the back of his hand. "But it isn't going to be a real marriage."

"We said vows, Thomas. Vows that I have been raised to keep." Now that they were alone, was this his way of saying he'd changed his mind? How could he do such a thing? Bitter bile rose in her throat.

His gaze met and held hers. "I agree, but this isn't a real marriage, Josephine. The only reason I agreed to it was because I wanted you to be safe from your uncle and his evil plans. I have no intention of falling in love."

All Josephine could think to say was "All right." Inside she told herself she was happy that he harbored no desire to fall in love and live happily ever after.

Tension eased from her body. If he felt that way, then he couldn't expect her to love him, either. How could anyone love another when they weren't even sure they could trust them?

Still, a twinge of worry etched its way through her mind. "Does this mean you want to get out of the marriage?" She didn't want to not be married to him; she needed the protection of his name.

"No, I married you before God. I just want you to know that there will be no children and no romance. We are married and you have the protection of the Young name, but that is all." His Adam's apple jumped in his throat as he swallowed.

Josephine lowered her eyes. Would her uncle be content with this sort of arrangement? Could he take her away if he knew they were sharing a name and nothing more? She hadn't thought of this before because she hadn't wanted a real marriage any more than Thomas did. Josephine still didn't want a real marriage and prayed that her uncle would be none the wiser.

The warmth of his hand enveloped her shoulder. "Look, no one else has to know our personal business. Ma knows why I married you, but none of my family knows." He grew silent for a moment, then continued, "Well, that may not be entirely true. I'm sure by now she's expressed her concerns to Seth."

So his adoptive parents knew. "I see." She raised her head and looked at him. "Are we keeping it a secret from everyone?"

Thomas sighed. "No, tonight we'll tell my family and make sure that they know how important it is to keep our secret. That this isn't something we want shared with the world. My family will understand."

The warmth of his hand seeped through the fabric of her dress. The comfort it offered wasn't enough to keep the cold fingers of fear away. "I know you trust them, Thomas, but I don't." She placed her hand on top of his. "Trust isn't something I offer easily and I'm scared. What if one of them lets it slip to my uncle or Mr. Grossman that we're married in name only? Could he have the marriage annulled if he knew?"

"I don't think so, and even if he wanted to use that as an excuse, it could easily be rectified." His hand moved to touch one of the many curls that surrounded her face. "Would it make you feel better if we didn't tell the others?"

Hadn't she just said that? Josephine sighed. "It would."

He jerked his hand from her hair and turned back toward the front. "All right. I'll talk to Ma and Seth when we get there." Thomas flicked the reins over the horse's back and then set them on the road and headed to his family farm. "Philip knows, also. I told him to move his things into my room before we get back. You'll be staying in his room."

So he'd already made arrangements to move her

into another room before he'd spoken to her about it. Josephine wondered how Philip had taken the news that he no longer had his own bedroom. "Was Philip all right with the move?"

Thomas shrugged. "He's fine with it. He'll have the room to himself two days a week."

"What about the rest of the week?" Josephine asked out of curiosity.

"He'll be on the Express trail two days a week and the other three we'll share the room." Thomas glanced over at her. "Don't feel sorry for him. He brought this on himself." His gaze returned to the road.

Josephine hated that Philip had invited her to marry Thomas, and she hated that she'd had to come, but most of all she hated that both men had to change their way of life for her. It hadn't been fair to either of the men and yet there was nothing she could do about it now.

"Thomas?"

"Yes?"

Josephine took a deep breath. She wanted to make up for his lost freedom and way of life. "I'm sorry you are upset, but I promise I'll be a good wife. I can cook and clean, and I'm learning to sew."

He grinned but continued to face forward. "I'm sure you will be."

Josephine heard the doubt in his voice. Did he expect her to fail at being a wife?

She'd failed at being a good daughter. Why else would her father have abandoned her after her mother died? What made her think she could be a good wife? Maybe Thomas was wise to doubt her abilities.

Josephine turned away from him. She didn't want to

fail. With hard work, she'd prove she'd be a great wife and Thomas Young would be glad that he'd married her. She clutched the chain of her necklace and fought the tears that threatened to spill from her eyes. This day just continued to get worse and worse.

Thomas pulled into the front yard of his parents' house. He jumped from the wagon and helped Josephine down. She'd remained quiet the rest of the way to the farm.

Rebecca hurried out of the house with a smile on her face. "Thomas! I can't believe you've come back for a visit so soon." She turned her blue eyes on Josephine. "You must be Josephine. Thomas has told me all about you." She hugged Josephine quickly.

Thomas wished she hadn't said that. It was bad enough that he'd not told Josephine anything about his family. Now she was going to be angry that he'd told Rebecca all about her. "It's nice to meet you, Mrs. Young."

His mother looked from Thomas to Josephine.

Thomas handed Josephine her basket. "Ma's last name is Armstrong. She married Seth not too long ago," he explained.

"Oh, I'm sorry." Josephine glared at him.

He thought he'd told her Rebecca's last name was now Armstrong. Maybe he should have mentioned it again. Thomas touched Josephine's arm. She pulled away from him. "I'll take the wagon to the barn and be right back." He climbed back on the wagon and turned the horse toward the barn.

Rebecca's soft laughter filled the tense air. "No harm done. Call me Rebecca. Mrs. Armstrong makes me sound old. Come on inside, Josephine. I can't wait for you to meet the rest of the family," Rebecca said, wrapping her arm in Josephine's.

He was in big trouble, Thomas thought. He had no idea how to act around his new wife. He should have told her more about his family. Thomas jumped from the wagon and unhitched the horse.

Andrew stepped from the barn. "I see you brought a woman home to meet Ma."

"Not just any woman, my wife." Thomas looked to his older brother.

"Wife?"

"Yep, we got married this morning." Thomas leaned against the wagon and crossed his arms.

Andrew whistled softly. "Congratulations. I can't believe you got married." He shook his head and then looked sharply at Thomas. "Does Ma know?"

Thomas groaned. "No." He'd sent his new bride inside and hadn't mentioned they were married. Would he be facing two angry women when he went back to the house?

The front door slammed as Benjamin, Thomas's youngest brother, ran out onto the porch. He yelled, "Thomas! Ma wants you in the house." He leaped from the porch and continued running toward them.

Andrew slapped Thomas on the back. "Don't look so stricken. I doubt your new wife has had time to spill the beans just yet."

Benjamin stopped a few feet from them. "Miss Josephine says she's your new wife. Did you know that?"

A laugh spilled from Andrew's lips. "Of course, I could be wrong." His older brother moved to the head of the horse and said, "Beni and I will take care of the horse for you."

Thomas pushed away from the wagon with a groan. "Thanks. This day just gets better and better," he grumbled.

Chapter Seven

Thomas entered the house quietly. He figured the women would be in the kitchen. What was he going to say? How angry was Ma?

Laughter filled the house. The sound came from the kitchen. Thomas frowned. Maybe he'd read too much into Ma's summons to come inside. He walked the short distance to the kitchen.

Rebecca saw him in the doorway and pushed away from the table. She hurried to him and gave him a hug. "Josephine tells us that you two got married this morning." Blue eyes looked up at him. There was a smile on her face, but disappointment filled her gaze.

"We did. I meant to tell you but got sidetracked," he offered in the same manner he'd done as a boy when he and Philip had gotten themselves into trouble with her.

"Would you like a cup of coffee and a couple of cookies? Joy baked them." Rebecca turned from him and walked to the stove.

He smiled at his little sister, who stood beside Josephine. "I'd love one of Joy's cookies."

Joy grinned proudly at his words. "They are sugar

cookies." She cut her eyes to look at Josephine. "I like to use lots of butter in my cookies."

"I noticed that. They are especially yummy." Josephine smiled at the little girl.

Thomas walked to the table and sat down beside his new wife. "I love sugar cookies." He scooped up Joy and hugged his sister close.

Josephine watched them with a soft grin. "I'll have to borrow your recipe, Joy."

Joy's shyness filled her voice as she said, "It's really Ma's recipe. She just lets me use it."

"I'll be happy to write it out for you, Josephine. But I have to warn you, Thomas will eat them all if you don't watch him closely." Rebecca sat a dessert plate in front of him with two cookies on it.

He snatched one of the cookies up and made a big show of taking a bite from the treat. "Mmm, these are good." Thomas prayed he'd make it through the day. Both of the women in his life seemed as prickly as porcupines and he was the one who seemed to rub them both the wrong way. All he could do was pray.

Watching Thomas with his brothers and sister, Josephine envied his large family. After they'd told them about Philip's sending for her as a mail-order bride and her uncle's treachery, Josephine began to enjoy their laughter and teasing. During the meal, she observed Joy's shyness but realized that Joy's brothers did not have that affliction. They were all very easy natured and outgoing, from the youngest, Benjamin, to the oldest, Andrew.

She handed Rebecca the almost empty bowl of mashed potatoes. "What else can I do, Rebecca?"

"If you want to dry, you are more than welcome to do so." Rebecca smiled at her.

Fay and Emma exchanged puzzled looks. "Um, then what are we supposed to do?" Emma asked.

"Whatever you want." Rebecca grinned over her shoulder at them. "I'd like to get to know my new daughter-in-law over the dishes."

Josephine swallowed. What did Rebecca want to know? She dreaded the questioning that would soon take place.

"You don't have to tell me twice." Fay walked from the room. Emma giggled and followed.

The rest of the lunch crowd fled the kitchen, including Rebecca's husband, Seth. Rebecca laughed. "I guess I didn't have to tell them at all."

Josephine wanted to thrash her new husband. He'd been the first to leave the room.

Rebecca turned to face her. "Well, now that we're alone, let's get to know each other." She offered a sweet smile and began to wash the dishes.

Josephine took a cup from her and asked, "So what do you want to know?"

"Anything you want to tell me." Rebecca's dimples showed as she looked at Josephine. "I just want to get to know you. I'm not your judge. I want to be your friend."

Just like that? All she had to do was share a little about herself and Rebecca would be her friend? Josephine focused on the cup in her hands. "I'm not sure where to start." Stalling, that was what she was doing, stalling, pure and simple.

"How about telling me where you are from?"

"St. Joseph, Missouri." She set the dry cup aside and reached for the next.

"It must have been hard to leave there."

Josephine thought about that for a moment. "Not really. Mama died seven years ago and Papa ran off four years later. I really don't have any other family except my uncle and I don't miss him at all."

Rebecca placed another clean dish in the drying bucket. "What about friends?"

She shrugged. "I don't have any."

"I'm sorry to hear that."

Josephine laid the dishrag to the side and faced Rebecca. She didn't want her mother-in-law's pity. "I know this sounds strange to you, coming from this big family and all, but I really don't have anyone who cares about me. No family, no friends, nobody." She heard the crispness in her voice and almost wished she could take it back. But maybe this was just what Rebecca needed to hear. Not everyone had the perfect family.

Rebecca turned so quickly that Josephine took a step back from her. Her blue eyes blazed and her cheeks turned bright pink, anger laced her words. "Let me tell you about me. I grew up in an orphanage and had one brother. He was forced to leave me at the age of twelve and brave the streets alone and in the cold of winter. He froze to death. I was sent here to this farm to help my late husband John's mother and father, not as a daughter but as a hired hand. John saw me, liked me and married me. Mainly to please his mother and father. We grew to love each other and we built this family. After John's death, Seth arrived here as a Pony Express station manager. We fell in love and have kept this family together."

Josephine opened her mouth to say she was sorry, but Rebecca held up her hand to silence whatever she thought Josephine was about to say. "During that time,

I met Fay. Her husband had died and the owner of the house they were living in kicked her out. Emma came here as a slave. Fay and I, with the boys' help, figured out a way to save her from her owners."

Rebecca placed her damp hands on her hips. "We all have had a hard life, except maybe Joy. All of these young men that I call my sons were orphans. So, no, I don't find your situation strange. What I do find strange is your need to lash out at someone who is offering you the hand of friendship and the chance at a new life."

She deserved that. Josephine licked her lips and nodded. "I'm sorry. I shouldn't have assumed your life was any easier than mine has been."

Rebecca pulled her into a tight hug. "Josephine, Thomas sees something in you that he likes. Believe it or not, I see it, too. The fact that you don't trust anyone hasn't gone unnoticed, but let me assure you, you now have a family and friends, if you will allow myself, Fay and Emma to get close enough to you." She released Josephine and looked into her eyes.

Josephine wanted to believe her. She wanted to trust that they were all offering her the hand of family and friendship. But when her uncle had begun selling off their property and firing their help, her so-called friends had all distanced themselves from her. She had quickly learned the only one she could depend on and trust was herself. "I'll try." And she would, but it wouldn't be easy.

"I'm sorry I lost my temper. It doesn't happen often."

Josephine smiled. From the shame-filled look on Rebecca's face, she knew Rebecca meant her apology. "I was feeling sorry for myself, but I don't anymore. I needed to hear about your past and will try to tell you more of mine without feeling sorry for myself as I do so."

Rebecca nodded and then turned back to the wash-basin. "We better get the rest of these dishes done before it's suppertime."

Josephine picked the drying towel back up and asked, "Has Thomas told you why we got married?"

"He did. I was hoping he'd wait until his family could attend the service." Rebecca's hands flew as she washed dishes.

"I'm sorry."

Soft laughter filled the air. "It's not your fault. Thomas could have told me yesterday when he was here that he was getting married today, but he didn't. That's not your fault, it's his."

Josephine didn't argue. She spent the next hour telling Rebecca about her childhood, her mother's sudden death and her father's abandonment. They put away the last of the dishes and Josephine felt as if maybe she and Rebecca could be friends. She still had trouble trusting the other woman completely and knew she'd never trust Thomas. For now, it was nice knowing that his family was trying to befriend her.

They spent the rest of the afternoon with his family. Fay and Emma both thanked her for doing the dishes. Josephine learned that each household member had chores and that Emma and Fay were responsible for the lunch dishes, among other things.

Thomas's brothers Andrew, Clayton and Benjamin were funny and kind. They didn't hang about the house but left shortly after lunch to "get back to work," as they all said. She liked them all, even Noah, who was the quietest and most serious of the brothers. Benjamin had told her that his other brother Jacob had moved to California and he missed him very much. Josephine felt sure that he was just as friendly as his other brothers and looked forward to meeting him someday, too.

While Fay put Joy down for a nap, Emma and Josephine talked on the front porch. Emma was a little shy and her eyes often searched the barnyard. Josephine couldn't help but wonder if she was sweet on one of the Young men.

"I'm glad you married Thomas." Emma picked at a piece of lint on her skirt.

Josephine smiled. "I am, too."

Where had her new husband and his mother gotten off to, anyway? Was Rebecca telling him about their talk in the kitchen? Was she scolding him for marrying without inviting the family?

The sound of horse hooves pounding the ground drew her attention to the barn and yard in between. Clayton sat on a horse waiting for the Pony Express rider to arrive.

Her heart picked up speed as she remembered waiting for the mochila, a leather bag that held the mail, to be passed to her. The mochila had to be kept safe at all times and moving down the trail. What important letters and messages were in this particular mochila? That question ran through her mind every time it was passed to her.

Clayton caught it in midair and sped away. His horse knew its job and jumped in its hurry to continue on carrying the mail. The young man who had come to the end of his ride slid from his horse, much like she'd done several days before. His shoulders drooped and he slid to the ground.

He's hurt. The words thundered in her mind. "Get Rebecca," she yelled at Emma. Josephine raced off the porch to his side.

Andrew was already there. "Bill? Can you hear me?" He was picking him up with an arm around the man's waist. Josephine moved to the other side and helped to lift him.

The young man didn't answer.

"Should we carry him to the bunkhouse?"

Andrew looked at her, his eyebrows raised, but he simply nodded. "That's probably for the best."

Josephine grunted as the rider's weight shifted more onto her when Andrew had to release him to open the bunkhouse door. Within a few moments they had him lying down on a bunk.

Bill groaned and his eyes fluttered open. "Thanks, Andrew." He turned his head and looked at Josephine. "Thanks, pretty lady." A crooked smile spread across his face.

Andrew groaned. "Billy, are you hurt? Or not?"

The young boy, who looked as if he were fourteen or younger, pulled his buckskin jacket back, revealing a bloodstained shirt. "Shot." His eyes fluttered closed once more.

Josephine opened his shirt up further. "Yep, he's been shot, all right. Turn him over, Andrew, we need to see if it went through or if he has a bullet in him."

Rebecca and Thomas hurried into the bunkhouse. Thomas immediately helped Andrew in turning the young man onto his side.

"How is he?" Rebecca hurried to the cot.

Josephine saw that the bullet had gone completely through and sighed with relief. "I think he's going to be fine. The bullet went all the way through. Gently turn him back over." She looked up into her husband's admiring eyes.

"Praise the Lord," Rebecca said, leaning against the doorjamb.

Josephine walked to the water basin and thoroughly washed her hands. "Do you have any carbolic acid?"

Rebecca straightened from the doorway, then walked toward her. "What's that?"

"It's a wound care salve. Keeps out infection, eases pain and stops bleeding."

"No, we don't have that, but I sure would like to get some. Where do you purchase it?"

"In Missouri, most any feed and seed store will have it. I assumed they would have it here, too." Josephine wet several cloths she found hanging on a line near the water basin. They felt damp, indicating that someone had washed them earlier. The moist cloths would have to do.

She eased the shirt from the boy's wound and wiped the bloodstains. The rider had managed to stanch the blood flow with his bandanna. Josephine left it in place till she had thoroughly cleansed the area. She glanced up to see Thomas and Rebecca watching her closely. "Do you have any honey?"

"Yes, we do." Rebecca whirled around and left the bunkhouse.

Josephine looked to Thomas. "Do you have anything we can use as bandages? I'll need at least two to cover these holes."

He nodded and soon both mother and son returned with a jar of yellowish-red honey and clean rags to use as bandages.

"Can you guys help me get his shirt off?"

Both men nodded. Andrew lifted the boy into a sitting position while Thomas helped Josephine pull Billy's shirt over his head. Then she removed the bandanna and quickly poured a small amount of honey directly into the bullet hole. The boy grunted but continued to sleep. The blood that had begun to ooze immediately stopped and she placed a bandage against the hole on top, and then she repeated the action in the back.

Lastly, Josephine ripped the entire bottom of the boy's shirt away and used it to tightly tie the back and front bandages around his body. "There. That should fix him right up."

"How can we ever thank you, Josephine?"

Josephine heard the respect and admiration in Rebecca's voice and couldn't help the tiny burst of pleasure she felt. "No thanks needed." Josephine stood and walked to the washbasin. She started to wash the cloths she'd used to clean the wound, but gentle calloused hands placed over hers stopped her.

"Someone else will do this." Thomas's voice was low and tender, almost a murmur. He dried her hands for her, the roughness of the towel scraping against her skin. Lightly gripping her elbow, he escorted her from the bunkhouse.

Back in the house, everyone spoke at once. The thing that had Josephine twisted up in knots was the many times she found Thomas's gaze on her. At one point when asked questions by four different people at exactly the same time, without thought she reached for his arm as if needing his support. She looked up to find him regarding her with amusement. He inclined his head and his breath stirred the curls near her ear, but what he whispered curled her toes.

"Let's get out of here."

She nodded, not trusting herself to speak. Josephine tried to answer his family's many questions, but Thomas took over. She listened as he said their goodbyes, fielding more questions and accepting several packed bags of goodies from Rebecca, Fay and Emma.

They loaded the wagon, accepted three extra blankets and a beautiful quilt, and then they were on their way. Josephine sat close on the seat next to Thomas. Moonlight shone upon the well-traveled trail instead of the road they arrived on. As soon as they were away from the farm, Josephine scooted over. She could still feel the heat from Thomas's body, but now they weren't touching.

"Where are we headed, Thomas?"

"Home, eventually. We'll camp a mile or so down this trail, then in the morning we'll travel the main road and be home before lunch."

Home. The word echoed in her ears. She welcomed the sound, knowing it wasn't a real home, but that it was a safe place. "That sounds good to me."

They rode awhile in comfortable silence. The air about them began to get colder and Josephine wished she'd thought to grab one of the blankets and wrap it around her legs.

"Where did you learn to treat a gunshot wound like that?" His voice lulled her into a relaxed mood.

"From the time I was a child, all things medical have interested me. Our cook taught me about herbs and spices that healed and my mother often filled in as nurse to our town doctor. I learned a lot from going with her on rounds."

"You must miss her very much."

Josephine's hand sought the locket around her neck. "To say the sunshine went out of my life the day she died would be putting it mildly."

Thomas guided the wagon off the path onto a flat spot. Josephine heard the gentle trickling of a creek nearby. She missed the sound of frogs croaking. They were hibernating for the winter.

"We'll camp here for the night."

Josephine's stomach growled, loudly.

"Why don't you see if there is something in one of those bags to quieten down that beast in your belly," Thomas teased.

She laughed and searched the bags from Rebecca, finding enough food to feed them for days.

He started to climb down from the wagon, but she grabbed the sleeve of his coat. Thomas turned questioning eyes on her.

"You want a slice of pie before we settle down?"

With a grin, Thomas sat back down. "That would hit the spot for sure."

Josephine handed him a good-sized slice of sweet-potato pie and took a piece for herself. They ate in silence for a few minutes, then she surprised herself by asking him a personal question. "Do you regret marrying me?"

"What do you mean? We've been married exactly eight hours, give or take a couple of hours."

She laughed at his words. They'd been married for about ten hours, but who was she to correct her teasing man? "True, but surely by now you're feeling the responsibility of caring for another person seven days a week?"

He shifted on the seat beside her but said nothing. Those moments of silence were the longest Josephine had ever experienced. In the moonlight she noticed a muscle quiver at his jaw. But when he spoke, his voice held an infinitely compassionate tone.

"I haven't felt responsibility yet. I did before we were married, but since this evening, you've more than accepted my big family and all their oddities. You patched up one of the Pony Express riders, proving you can more than take care of yourself, and quite possibly have been the best camping companion I've ever had." He exhaled a long sigh of contentment and aimed a grin of amusement down at her uplifted face.

Was he really feeling content? She studied him a moment before returning his smile, enjoying the shared moment. Her despair of the past month or so lessened and she experienced a strange comfort. Her gaze traveled his handsome face.

He jerked as if she'd slapped him and then jumped from the wagon. "Well, I'll settle things for the night. You make a bedroll here in the wagon."

Confused by his sudden change of mood, Josephine blurted, "And where will you sleep?"

"I'll pitch my bedroll under the wagon."

He set the brake on the wagon wheels, then wedged them with a big rock. Josephine wondered why the extra precaution, since they were on flat land, but chose not to ask. Seemed to her there'd been enough questions for one night. She spread the blanket on the hard wood of the wagon bed. "Are you sure you don't want to share the wagon?" she asked.

"I'm sure," Thomas answered. He walked the horse to a grassy spot beside the small stream.

Josephine shivered. The night was cold. Colder than she'd thought it would be. Thankfully the snow from the days before had melted, but the ground was frozen and Thomas would be cold.

That had been her reasoning in offering to share the wagon bed. They could both have snuggled down in their own blankets and he wouldn't have to sleep on the hard, ice-covered ground.

Thomas patted the mare as she drank from the cold water. When the horse had drunk her fill, he walked her back to the wagon and tied the lead rope to the side-boards. "Thanks for not fussing about heading home tonight." He pushed his hat back.

"I'm glad we did. As much as I like your family, I didn't want to lie to them and I couldn't see how we could get out of sleeping in the same room if we'd stayed." She pulled her coat tighter around her shoulders.

"No, Ma is stubborn, and even though she knows this isn't a real marriage, she would've insisted that we stay together tonight. If for no other reason than because the rest of the family would expect it." Thomas leaned against the wagon's sideboard, facing Josephine.

She looked down at the makeshift bed she'd just prepared. "I'm not sure I like the idea of you sleeping on the ground," Josephine admitted.

Thomas laughed. "I've slept on the ground many a night, Josephine. Some nights were a lot colder, too. I'll be fine."

His mood had swung again, back to the teasing man she'd enjoyed earlier. Men were a fickle bunch. Josephine handed him a quilt and a blanket. To fill the quiet, she said, "It was nice of Rebecca to give us bedding as a wedding present."

He nodded. "I wonder if she knew you'd give me the pretty quilt to use on the ground tonight."

Most women would give their husband the thickest bedding to use. Rebecca must have thought that Josephine cared for Thomas and would have done the same as women for generations had been doing. "She's a smart woman. I'm sure she did," Josephine answered.

Thomas spread the quilt under the wagon. "That she is." He lay down and tucked the blanket around his body.

Satisfied he was settled for the evening, Josephine settled on one thick blanket and covered herself with another one. Immediately warmth began to seep into her cold body. She looked up into the starry night. This wasn't how she imagined her wedding night would be.

"Thomas?"

"Um?"

Josephine smiled at the sleepy sound. "Are we still on the Young farm?"

"Yep."

She listened to the sound of a cow lowing in the distance. The horse stomped its foot. Were they safe here? Josephine had been chased by Indians, bandits and wolves when she rode the Pony Express trail. She knew that any or all could be lurking in the shadows.

"This was one of my favorite camping spots when I was a boy," Thomas said in a hushed voice. "Philip and I would beg Ma to let us come here to camp."

Josephine smiled. "I imagine you two were rascals when you were younger."

He chuckled warmly. "That we were. What we didn't

realize at the time was that she'd make either Papa John, Andrew or Jacob follow us and keep watch all night."

She yawned. "When did you find out they were watching you?"

"We were about fourteen years old and one night we saw a campfire in the distance. We'd noticed it before, but this night we sneaked around to see who else was camping out here and it was Jacob. To be honest, we both slept much better knowing he was watching over us."

Josephine listened as he shifted positions. "Did you ever tell him you knew he'd followed you?"

"Yeah, that's when Jacob said that he, Andrew and sometimes Papa John followed us. But he made us promise not to let on to Ma that we knew." His yawn filled the night.

"So to this day she doesn't know?"

Thomas chuckled. "Nope. And she's still up to her old tricks."

Josephine turned onto her side so that she could see between the cracks of the wagon bed. His arms were tucked under his head and he lay faceup. "What do you mean?"

He grinned. "See that light on the hill to your right?" Thomas pointed as if she didn't know her right from her left.

She raised her head and looked in the direction he was pointing. "Yes."

"That's Andrew and my brother Noah's camp."

Josephine had met all the Young men and knew that Noah was next to the youngest of Thomas's brothers. She gasped. "They followed us?"

"Yep. Ma was worried about us heading out after dark and asked them to."

She eyed the flickering light in the distance. "You sure it's them and not someone else?"

His gaze met hers through the slats in the wagon. "Yep. Andrew told me before we left that she'd asked them to follow us."

"So they are watching out for us." It was a statement and she didn't expect an answer. What would it be like to have brothers who would watch out for you? Being an only child, Josephine didn't know.

He grinned at her. "Yep, and if I know Noah, I could probably throw a rock and hit him, he's so close."

Josephine lowered her voice. "Really?"

Thomas yawned again. "Yep."

"He's twelve years old?"

He shook his head. "No, he's thirteen now. Had a birthday last month."

"Still, that's young. Why didn't Andrew come closer?" Josephine knew she was asking a lot of questions, but it all baffled her. Not just what they were doing but their reasons for doing it.

"Andrew likes his sleep. Noah enjoys the night and is the best shot of all of us. If anyone comes close, Noah will fire off a warning shot."

Josephine raised up on her elbow and tried to find Noah in the dark. She yawned again. Where was the little boy? Noah wasn't very big and could be hiding anywhere. She couldn't believe that Rebecca would send her sons out into the night like this.

"Josephine, get some sleep. We're safe."

She lay down. "When you say he'll shoot off a warning shot, who will he be warning? Us or the bad guys?"

"Both. Now go to sleep. I want to get an early start in the morning." He yawned again.

Turning onto her back, Josephine looked up at the night sky once more. The stars twinkled down on them. Within a few moments Josephine heard Thomas's soft snores.

She lay awake thinking about Thomas's family. They'd been warm and welcoming when expressing their congratulations on marrying Thomas. Did that mean they thought of her as family? Josephine longed to be a part of a loving family that really cared about her.

Doubt and mistrust crept about her like a morning fog. No matter how badly she wanted to be a part of a family that she could trust, Josephine knew it was impossible. Her marriage wasn't a true marriage, so therefore Thomas's family would never be her true family.

No, it was better to forget such silly thoughts and do as he said and go to sleep. Still, Josephine wanted to hang on to the dream of having people in her life whom she could trust and love.

Chapter Eight

The next morning Thomas knelt by the small fire he'd built and warmed his hands. The cold night had turned into an even colder morning. His gaze searched the hill for his brothers.

Within a few moments, Andrew stepped out of the tree line.

Thomas motioned that Josephine was still sleeping in the wagon.

Andrew whispered, "Good morning. I brought breakfast." He held up a rabbit that had been cleaned and positioned on a stick.

"Just one rabbit?" Thomas asked. He'd really hoped his brothers would supply breakfast this morning, but if all Andrew had to offer was one rabbit, it was going to be a skimpy breakfast.

Andrew's shoulder shook as he silently laughed, and then he mouthed, "I didn't say I brought breakfast for you. This is mine."

Thomas shook his head and looked about for Noah. His younger brother always brought home enough for everyone. If he didn't, Thomas knew he'd have to borrow one of their bows and arrows and get breakfast for both himself and Josephine.

Noah came from the woods holding up three more skinned rabbits. His bow was slung over his shoulder and he grinned, obviously pleased that he'd killed enough for everyone.

Thomas placed his finger over his lips in a motion to be quiet and waved toward the wagon once more. He watched as Noah looked in Josephine's direction and nodded his understanding.

Noah walked the rest of the way to them and handed Thomas two of the speared rabbits. Andrew had already begun to turn his over the fire.

In a low voice Thomas said, "Thanks. At least one of my brothers thought about us this morning." He playfully scowled at Andrew. Thomas then positioned one of the rabbits over the fire and placed the other to the side, making sure not to get it in the mud.

"Hey, it's my day off. I can hunt for whoever I want."

In a quiet voice Noah asked, "Who are you going to hunt for today?" He indicated he'd killed the rabbit that Andrew was carefully turning.

"Just because I didn't shoot this one doesn't mean I can't," Andrew answered with a sheepish grin.

Thomas laughed quietly. He missed his brothers and the playful banter they shared. Working with Philip had been a dream come true until his brother had decided he needed a wife. Now things would never be the same.

"Why so gloomy?" Andrew whispered across the fire at him.

Thomas looked up. Had his face betrayed his thoughts? From the way his brothers looked at him, he realized it must have. He smiled. "Who says I'm feeling gloomy?"

Noah muttered, "Your face says it all."

"Oh, and what does it say, smarty?" Thomas shot back as he turned the rabbit over the fire. Did it tell them how unhappy he was with Philip? How out of control he felt over his own life? But a tiny voice reminded him that last night it had felt good to share his time and thoughts with Josephine.

Even so, that didn't take away his feelings of anxiety. What would his life be like now that he was married?

Josephine turned on her side and watched her new husband's face as his brothers confronted him. She'd been awake the moment Thomas had crawled out from under the wagon. At first she'd stayed put because her pallet was warm and the early-morning air was cold. Then she'd seen the brothers come into their camp and didn't feel right intruding on Thomas's time with them.

Even with his voice lowered, Josephine heard Andrew answer. "It says you were in deep thought and not very pleased with those thoughts."

Andrew's back was to Josephine and she couldn't tell if he teased Thomas or if he were serious. She held her breath as she waited for his answer.

"I was just thinking about Philip."

Andrew chuckled. "Yep, he makes me scowl, too."

Thomas shook his head. "I just can't understand his need to find me a wife."

"I don't know why you're complaining. Josephine is beautiful," Noah said as he looked into the woods away from them.

She felt her face flush at the compliment. Noah was young, so what did he know about beauty? Still, his comment made her feel good.

Andrew nodded. "I have to agree with Noah. And, after meeting her, I'd say she's probably just as pretty on the inside, too. Not to mention how clever she is. I've never seen a woman fly into action the way she did when she saw Billy hurt."

"Who said anything was wrong with Josephine? I was trying to figure out what Philip was thinking by ordering a mail-order bride for me." He shook his head and tested the meat with his fingers. "Sometimes I think he has peas for brains."

The other two brothers laughed.

Josephine had asked herself the same question. Why had Philip placed the mail-order-bride ad? She looked to the east, where the sun had just begun to peek over the mountain. The sky was a soft pink, looking as if God had randomly swiped His paintbrush over the heavens.

Thomas called out, "Josephine, breakfast is ready."

She turned her head back to look where he sat. He'd gotten to his feet and was smiling. The smell of the roasted rabbit filled her nose. Her stomach growled. Josephine sat up and stretched. "You should have woken me sooner." She pushed the blanket back and climbed out of the wagon. Digging in the bags, she found linen cloths that they could all wipe their hands on when they'd finished their breakfast. Josephine looked forward to unpacking the bags when they got home. So far she'd loved all the things Rebecca, Fay and Emma had given them for wedding gifts. "I thought you wanted to get an early start."

"It's not late. Come get this while it's still hot."

Josephine rubbed her arms. Her breath led the way to where the men knelt beside the flames. She looked about the campfire. There were no rocks to sit on. She handed each of the men a cloth and then took the stick from Thomas's hand. "Thank you."

Thomas nodded and picked up the other rabbit. He handed it to her. "Would you hold this over the fire for me?"

"Of course." Josephine took the stick and began turning it slowly over the flame.

Andrew and Noah shared a grin. Thomas seemed to ignore them and hurried to the wagon. He quickly returned with a blanket. Folding it, he laid it on the ground and then took his rabbit back from her. "There you go, a nice comfortable place to sit."

"Thank you." Josephine sat down. She pulled a leg from the rabbit and then tugged on Thomas's pants leg. When his gaze met hers, she smiled and offered him the leg.

He took the meat with a grin.

Andrew shook his head but didn't say anything. Noah continued to watch the sunrise. They all ate in silence. Josephine didn't know what to say. She wished that Thomas had left her in the wagon and continued sharing the morning with his brothers. It was her presence that had caused them all to be as quiet as church mice.

Her gaze moved to the sunrise that Noah was so intent on watching. "It's beautiful, isn't it, Noah?"

He glanced over at her. "It is."

Thomas looked to the sky. "That is one thing about Wyoming. We have beautiful sunrises and sunsets."

"And hills and valleys," Josephine added.

"Oh, we have mountains, too, in the north part of the state. Not many people have settled there yet." Noah seemed excited about that. His voice rose a notch and for the first time he appeared eager to talk.

Josephine smiled. "I tried climbing a mountain once. In Colorado. The higher I climbed, the more difficult it was to breathe."

"Did you give up?" Noah asked the question, but Josephine noticed the interest his brothers had in their conversation.

"Of course not. It took me a little longer than my cousin, but I finally made it. The view from the top was amazing. Totally worth the effort it took to get there."

"That's a good lesson for you, Noah boy." Thomas tossed his stick onto the fire, then licked one of his fingers before thinking to use the cloth Josephine had provided.

Noah mimicked his older brother by tossing his stick but finished by swiping his hands down the sides of his pants. Josephine barely bit back a grin.

"And what lesson would that be, oh bigger and wiser older brother?"

"That the good things in life are worth the effort it takes to achieve them."

Josephine stared at Thomas in wonder. What a great thought to add to her mountain climbing story. She'd have to remember that and teach it to her children one day. *What children?* a voice in her head mocked. In a marriage like hers, there would be no children.

Once more silence fell over the group. Josephine finished what she wanted of her rabbit and handed the remainder back to Thomas. "If you gentlemen will excuse me, I think I'll go wash my face."

She heard their soft laughter as she left. What was so funny? Were they laughing at her? Josephine looked over her shoulder at them. All three of the Young men watched her with varying expressions. Quickly she turned back around and headed to the riverbed. More laughter followed her retreat.

Josephine didn't see what was so humorous about her going to the river to wash her face and hands. Men could be so immature, she huffed to herself. The river gurgled past as she knelt down beside it. She dipped her cloth into the icy water.

Ringing out the moisture, Josephine once more pondered the sound of the men's merriment. She washed her face and neck with the cold rag and then readied herself to go home.

Would it ever be home? She pulled her shoulders back and walked to the wagon. *I'll make it a home*, Josephine thought. *It may not be the perfect house, but it will be a place that Thomas will be happy to return to each evening.* She nodded sharply as if to assure herself that her thoughts were true.

Chapter Nine

◦◦◦

They arrived back at the Pony Express relay station just as the riders traded horses. No matter how many times Thomas saw it, his heart always hammered in his chest as if he were the one speeding off to deliver the mochila to the next rider. His gaze cut to Josephine, who sat next to him. She'd been quiet all morning, but as she watched the Express rider speed away, her eyes glistened with excitement.

"I never get tired of watching the exchange," she said. "Makes me miss my horse even more."

"You had a horse of your own? Before you joined the Pony Express?"

She grinned. "Yes, her name was Mistletoe, and she was solid black except the white star on her nose. Papa gave her to me for Christmas."

"What happened to her?" He waited to hear, hoping the horse hadn't died.

Josephine's smile turned into a frown. "Uncle gave her to Mr. Grossman to pay part of his gambling debt." Sadness filled her voice and he wished he'd not asked.

"I'm sorry to hear that." Thomas pulled the horse

and wagon to a stop in front of the barn. "Welcome home," he offered.

Philip came out of the barn. "You two made good time."

Thomas jumped from the wagon. "That we did." He turned to help Josephine down but found that she'd crawled over the seat and was even now pushing boxes to the back of the wagon.

She smiled at Philip. "Hey, Philip. Look what all Rebecca sent."

"Nice," he muttered.

"Yes, it was, and I've been thinking. Since you like helping Thomas so much, you can carry these boxes in for us while Thomas unhitches the horse and I go inside and decide what to do with it all." She climbed down from the wagon. Without commenting on his stunned features, Josephine marched to the house.

Once she was safely out of hearing range, Thomas roared with laughter.

"Who does she think she is? Bossing me around like that. I'm not her husband, you are." Philip didn't budge from where he stood in the barn door.

"No, but you are the one who sent for her. And I do believe Josephine plans on making you regret that day." Thomas unhitched the horse. "I suggest you get used to it."

Philip shook his head. "She can't make me haul boxes or do anything else." He folded his arms over his chest.

Thomas stood up taller. "No, but I can."

A teasing glint came into his brother's eyes. "You think so?"

Hardness filled Thomas's voice. "I know so."

Philip's face turned from teasing to confusion. "You are serious?"

Thomas wanted to throttle his brother for the trouble he'd caused. "Yes. After what you did to her, doing what she asks for a while is the least you can do."

"I got her married to you. Now all her problems are solved," Philip argued.

"No, you made it impossible for her to find someone who will love her the way she deserves to be loved." Thomas pulled the mare into the barn.

Philip followed him. "She'll grow to love you. I read once that parents used to arrange their kids' marriages all the time and they did just fine." He leaned against the door of the stall Thomas had just entered.

"You read that, did you? Well, most things you read in books are fictitious, meaning not pertaining to real life."

"I know what fictitious means," Philip snapped.

"Then clearly you didn't ponder your actions or you'd never have meddled in two people's lives as you did. Now the least you can do over the next several weeks is graciously accept whatever she throws at you."

Thomas saw by Philip's expression that he warred with his choices, so he decided to seal the deal for him. "And I also need you to help me keep an eye out for any strangers that come to town. We need to be vigilant so that Josephine is protected at all times, and being forewarned in this case is our biggest advantage. Who knows what her uncle will do when he finds her."

Thomas knew he had Philip's full attention now and he added, "And since you're the one that lured her away from her home, you're the one that needs to make the transition work for her."

"And how in Sam Houston am I supposed to do that?"

"You can start by carrying in those boxes and then I think there's the matter of a small debt you owe."

"Huh? What debt?"

Thomas knew it was wrong to enjoy getting one up on his brother, but he couldn't deny the satisfaction this gave him. He all but rubbed his hands together in glee. "You told her you'd send her the fare to get here, so fork it over. She can use the money for personal things."

"But," Philip stammered, "she made it here on her own steam. She didn't require any money."

"True. And at any moment she could have been killed. And how would you like that on your conscience?"

"All right. All right. But this means I'll have to start saving my money all over again to buy that new saddle." Philip's sour look told Thomas he'd won this round but Philip didn't like it one bit.

Thomas felt his grin tip both sides of his mouth when Philip slammed the barn door behind him on his way to the wagon. Then he laughed out loud. Revenge tasted a little sweet today, but he figured he'd pay for it later.

This new life he and Josephine were creating would be full of good times and bad. Thomas shut the door to the stall and headed out to the yard. He prayed they'd have more good than bad.

Josephine looked about her new home with fresh eyes. The one and only time she'd been in the house had been the day Philip presented her to Thomas as his mail-order bride, and her mind had been occupied with worry and stress about her future. Though she still felt stressed, it was of a different kind. She sighed. Did the men not know how to clean?

Philip brought in the last box. "It's a mess. Sorry about that." The smirk on his face said he wasn't sorry at all.

"Yes, it is a mess." Her gaze ran over the two rockers that sat by the fireplace. The outline of where someone sat showed through the dust or dirt, she wasn't sure which. A table sat against the far wall, with a bench on one side and a chair at each end. The kitchen washbasin was piled high with dirty dishes.

A tiny bit of confidence spiraled upward inside her and she felt an indefinable feeling of rightness. This was now her home to do with as she saw fit and that she would do. She struggled to keep from laughing out loud and twirling round and round. Being free from her uncle and having her own home gave her incredible joy.

She walked to the room closest to the door leading off to the right.

"That's our room," Philip informed her. "Your room is right off the kitchen."

Josephine turned around. "Oh, well, good. You can help me carry those boxes in there." She walked to the boxes and lifted one. It wasn't as heavy as she thought it would be and she grinned as she passed him.

Philip scowled but did as she said.

Josephine entered her new bedroom. It was small. A bed rested under a window. There were no sheets on it, so she was grateful that at least one of the boxes held linens. A small table stood at the head of the bed with a kerosene lamp on top of it. That was it. No rug, no washbasin or chamber pot.

Philip dropped the boxes he carried right inside the

doorway and left as quickly as he'd arrived. Josephine sat down on the bed. This room would need work to make it feel homey. She would have liked to have had a comfortable chair and a chest to put her clothes in. Her gaze moved along the wall and saw several nails. She assumed they were used to hang up her dresses.

This would never do. A smile pulled at her lips as she began to think of all the things Philip could make for her, provided they had wood to do so. She turned around and looked out the window. The barn came into view.

"I'm sorry it isn't a very big room."

Josephine pulled her gaze from the window and looked at her new husband. Thomas leaned against the doorjamb. "It's fine. With Philip's help, I'm sure I'll have it looking great in no time." She grinned.

Thomas laughed and she loved that he understood her. They were on the same page. It had been a long time since Josephine felt that with anyone.

The warmth of his pleasure caused her to giggle. "I thought I'd see if he could build me a closet. Nothing fancy, just something I could hang my clothes in. Do we have any wood?" she asked.

He shook his head. "No, but we could make a trip to town and get some at the sawmill. What else would you like?"

Josephine stood up and looked about the small space. "Maybe a table for a washbasin?" Her gaze searched his. Was she asking too much?

Thomas nodded. "What else?"

"Would a small bookshelf be asking too much?"

He grinned. "Not at all."

Josephine twirled around. "I'd really like a comfortable chair so that I can read in here."

Thomas rubbed his chin. "We might have to order that at the general store."

"Well, if you think that it would cost too much, it's not that important." Josephine tried not to show her disappointment.

Philip entered the room carrying Josephine's basket from the wagon. "Do you want this in here, too?" he asked her.

"Yes, thank you." Josephine hurried to him. She didn't want him dropping it on the floor like he had the boxes. For now, she'd use the basket to hold her few clothes.

"Philip, were you going to give something to Josephine?" Thomas asked his brother. He blocked Philip from leaving the room.

Philip frowned. "I don't have it with me."

Thomas stepped aside. "Then go get it."

Philip huffed and walked out.

There was a gleeful gleam in Thomas's eyes that caused Josephine to wonder what he was up to. He seemed quite pleased with himself. "What was that about?"

"Oh, you'll see in a moment." Thomas propped against the wall facing the door, his face a study of expectancy and pleasure.

Philip returned and walked over to Josephine. "Here is the money I promised to send for your fare out here." He handed her a fistful of bills. "There is a hundred dollars there. That should have been enough to get you here."

Josephine protested. "I can't take this."

Thomas pushed away from the wall. "Yes, you can. That will get you that comfortable chair you wanted and pay for the lumber you'll need." He slapped Philip on the back. "Isn't that right, Phil? You don't want her to give it back now, do you?"

Philip shook his head. "No, it's only fair that you keep it." He turned on his heel and left them standing there.

Josephine lowered her voice. "Thomas, I don't feel right taking his money. I know what he has to do to earn it." She tried to give him the money.

Thomas gently folded her fingers around the bills. He held her hand closed and looked deeply into her eyes. "No, you should keep it."

Josephine felt breathless. He was standing too close. She'd felt this strangeness when he'd kissed her after they'd said their marriage vows the day before. Taking a step back, she pulled her hand from his. "All right."

Thomas nodded and then said, "I need to go feed the horses and I'd like to check on Hazel. Do you want to ride over with me?" he asked.

"Not today. I'll go see her tomorrow. I think I'll unpack these boxes while you are gone." Josephine put the money into her dress pocket and knelt down near the closest box. "Tell Hazel hello for me."

"I'll do that." Thomas walked out the door.

Josephine leaned back on her heels. What had gotten into her? She laid her hand over her pounding heart. *Get a hold of yourself, Josephine Dooly.* The thought that she was no longer Josephine Dooly but now Josephine Young only accelerated the pounding of her heart. *You cannot fall for Thomas. He might be nice, but he's a man. And men can't be trusted.* But strangely, her thoughts on the matter had lessened in strength. When she had time, she'd ponder on that a bit, but right now she had a household to set up and miraculously it appeared she'd get to do it alone. That was icing on the cake because who knew how many times she'd have to move things around to get them just right.

Josephine found a straw broom in the corner by the fireplace and set to work in her bedroom. There were layers of dirt on the wood floor, so she dampened the edges of the straw so that the sweeping wouldn't stir up so much dust. As she worked, Josephine silently prayed. She hadn't done much praying lately, but now she breathed a prayer of thanks for things working out for her so nicely.

Four times with a rag mop she cleaned the floor, adding a drop of linseed oil to the last bucket of water. The outcome was a clean smell as well as a bit of a shine on the floor. Moments later she could actually see through the window and, taking a deep, fortifying breath, she stepped to the door and looked back into the bedroom. She exhaled a long sigh of contentment.

Whether it was the hard work or the fact she had her own home, Josephine experienced an unusual strength shiver through her. For the first time in her life, she felt in charge. Thankful for her home, her new life and the man who would be sharing it all with her, Josephine whispered, *"Lord, is this how it feels to be in Your will? If so, this is where I want to stay."*

A smile tugged at her lips. Josephine dug through the boxes till she found the sheets and bedspread. The lavender soap she'd put in the same box had made the sheets smell good and the bedspread quilt from Rebecca added just the right feminine touch.

She couldn't wait to show it to Thomas. She hoped he would be proud of her.

Chapter Ten

After assuring himself that Josephine would be happy to be left alone, Thomas had pulled his gloves back on and headed out to the lean-to. Both his horse and Philip's snorted when they saw him. He patted Philip's on its velvety nose and then went to his own gelding. "Ready for a ride?" he asked.

The horse stomped its front leg as if to say, "I've been waiting all day."

Thomas opened the gate and led the horse to be saddled. He looked about for Philip. Not seeing him, Thomas went into the barn. Was Philip hiding from both him and Josephine? Had he been too hard on his brother and best friend? He really didn't think so. Philip had brought this upon himself. He grinned at the thought of telling Philip that he'd soon be building furniture. Not seeing his brother, Thomas returned to his horse.

In record time he had the horse saddled and was on his way to Hazel's. Thankfully there wasn't another Pony Express rider coming through the relay station tonight, so he could take his time visiting.

He tied the horse up to her front porch and then knocked on Hazel's door.

"Well, hello, Thomas. When did you get back?" Hazel held the door open for him to pass.

"We arrived about an hour ago. The wagon's unpacked and Josephine is putting stuff away," he answered, whipping his hat off as he entered the sitting room.

"How about something to eat?" Hazel asked. She shut the door and headed for the kitchen.

Thomas wanted to eat, but he wasn't sure how Josephine would feel if he ate with Hazel. His new wife hadn't said she'd be cooking dinner, but Thomas thought she probably would fix something. "I best not spoil my appetite."

"Oh, I should have realized Jo would fix dinner for you." Hazel turned to face him. "Do you think she'd mind if I sent a few slices of pie home with you?"

"Not at all."

Hazel laughed. "I don't think you know what she'd mind."

He chuckled with her. "Nope, but I want pie."

She waved him to the table. "How about a small slice now with coffee and I'll send more home with you?" Hazel's eyes twinkled at him.

"That sounds even better." Thomas sat down and laid his hat on the floor at his feet.

"How was your visit with your family?" Hazel placed a plate and fork in front of him. The scent of apples and cinnamon filled his nostrils.

"It went well. They are all good." He waited for her to return with a cup of coffee for the both of them.

"What did your ma think of Josephine?" She sat

down with her cup and took a sip. Hazel motioned for him to eat.

Thomas picked up his fork. "I think they liked each other." He shrugged. "Ma isn't happy that we got married without her being there and I think Josephine wasn't too pleased with the wedding, but they both seemed to like each other." He took a bite of pie and savored the sweet flavors that coated his tongue. He'd never tell her, but Ma's apple pie didn't hold a candle to Hazel's.

"And how are Josephine and Phil getting along?"

He stopped eating and looked across at her. Did she know something he didn't? "They seem to be doing okay. Why?"

She rotated the cup in her hands. "Phil wasn't too pleased to have to move out of his bedroom." Hazel watched the liquid swirl in her cup.

"Well, he shouldn't have ordered me a bride. Now he has to share my room so Josephine can have some privacy."

"I see."

Thomas didn't like where this conversation was going. Even Hazel had known from the beginning that this wasn't a love match, so why did she sound as if she disapproved of him?

He laid his fork down. "What do you see?"

Hazel placed both hands around her cup and blew on the hot liquid. "I thought you two would give up on this idea of a marriage of convenience." She held up her hand as if she thought he'd interrupt. "In my day we had arranged marriages and the husband and wife slept in the same room."

Thomas squirmed. "Well, Josephine and I are different. We agree that this isn't a marriage of love."

She huffed. "Arranged marriages weren't marriages of love, either. But they stuck and some even turned into love."

He didn't want to argue with her, so he filled his mouth with pie. Hazel just didn't understand. Thomas chewed slowly and pretended that the pie still tasted sweet. Her talk of love had ruined the enjoyment of his dessert.

"I should just mind my own business," Hazel muttered.

Thomas swallowed. He glanced up to see the older woman's countenance fall; a look of tired sadness passed over her features. In a polite, gentler voice he said, "Look, Hazel, I know you mean well, but Josephine and I just aren't meant to have a real marriage. It's not what either of us would have wanted or dreamed of, but it is what it is."

"That's too bad. She really is a sweet girl and you are a nice boy. I think if the circumstances were different and you'd met on different terms, you both would have fallen head over heels in love with each other." She smiled at him to take the sting out of her words.

"Possibly, but I don't think Josephine trusts men very much and I don't feel like she could ever stand having romantic notions with a man like me."

"Why not? What do you mean, 'a man like me'?"

He ran his finger down the scar on his face, and quicker than a bullet, she caught onto his meaning.

"Because of that little scar on your face?" She grunted in disgust. "You are making more out of that than needs be."

Was she right? No, he'd caught Josephine staring at his face several times and each time she'd quickly looked away. "Maybe." He'd agree with Hazel, but only because he respected her.

She shook her head. "Don't patronize me, Thomas Young." Hazel smiled at him. "I'm old, not stupid."

Thomas pushed his empty plate away. "No, ma'am. No one can call you stupid." He cradled the coffee cup in his hand. "Is there anything I can do for you while I'm here? Milk the cow? Chop some wood? Sweep the snow off the porch?"

Hazel reached across the table and patted his hand. "Naw, I can do all that for myself, but thank you for offering."

"I don't mind."

She smiled. "I know, but if I let you do all that, what would I do to entertain myself once you go home?"

"Read? Sew?"

"Oh, there is plenty of time for that." Hazel picked up the plate and carried it to the washbasin. She poured herself more coffee. "Would you like for me to top you up?"

Thomas looked into the almost empty cup. He should probably get on back to the relay station. "No, I'd better get back to the house before Josephine works Philip to death."

She frowned. "What do you mean?"

He laughed. "Josephine has decided that since Philip wanted her here so badly, she'd put him to work."

"Uh-oh. How does he feel about that?" Hazel asked.

"Well, at first he refused, but I straightened him out."

"You boys didn't come to blows, did you?"

"No, ma'am. I simply reminded him that he's the

reason she's here and he needs to do as she asks." Thomas chuckled. "I even talked him into giving her the money he'd promised to send her to get out here."

"You're kidding. That boy can squeeze blood out of a coin, he holds on to it so tight." Hazel placed her cup in the washbasin. Her chuckle had him grinning from ear to ear.

Thomas handed her his cup. "I just knew he'd buck up and refuse to pay her the fare, but nope, he gave her a hundred dollars."

Hazel whistled. "Well, I'll be." Her brow wrinkled and her eyes took on a faraway expression.

He didn't know what she was thinking but decided now was a good time to head home. "Thank you, Hazel, for the pie."

His words seemed to pull her from wherever she'd gone to. "Oh, let me get those extra slices for you." Hazel quickly scooped the pie onto a plate and covered it with cheesecloth. "You going to be able to get this home safely?"

Thomas grinned. "I believe so."

She handed him the plate. "Don't break my dish."

"I'll do my best not to." Thomas walked to the front door. "Josephine said to tell you hello." He opened the door.

"Tell her I said howdy back and to plan on coming over and helping me with that quilt."

Thomas set the pie on the porch railing and walked down to his horse. "Will do." He swung into the saddle and reached down to grab the plate. "Thanks again for the pie."

"You're welcome." She sounded sad.

Was Hazel lonely? Thomas waved and then headed

home. Would the old woman like a dog for a companion? Maybe while he and Josephine were in town, he'd see if anyone had a puppy or dog they no longer wanted. The thought of Hazel being lonely saddened him. It would be nice if she and Josephine would become close friends. Perhaps a dog would deepen that friendship.

Josephine began to fret over Thomas's absence. Where on earth was he? What was taking so long? Hunger pangs tightened her stomach and she searched the food basket Rebecca had given them.

She found a packet of tenderloin and put it on to fry. There were eggs and cheeses and relishes of all kinds. She cut several slices from a loaf of bread and nibbled at a piece. Its soft, fresh buttery taste had her stomach begging for more. She'd have to ask Rebecca for her bread recipe the next time they went to the Young farm. She hummed happily as she scrambled eggs and dropped pieces of cheese into them.

Josephine had just finished warming the bread slices when she heard a horse ride into the front yard. Josephine hurried to look outside and saw that it was Thomas riding to the barn.

Thinking to finish their dinner, she turned back to the kitchen only to see her reflection in the silver pie plate hanging by the fireplace. Her eyebrows rose in horror. Her hair hung in sweaty strings against her face. There were black smudges on her chin and arms.

He couldn't see her like this. Josephine started to the bedroom, then stopped. She had no water for her pitcher and she'd not unloaded the washing cloths. Did she have time to get the water and the cloths?

The sound of boots clopping across the front porch

filled her with dread. Josephine gulped hard, trying to hold back tears of disappointment. The door opened and he occupied the doorway.

Shock filled his voice as he said, "What in the world has happened to you? You look like you've been rolling in the pigpen."

Seeing herself through his eyes, Josephine knew she looked like she'd been put through the wringer. Dirty and disheveled, she resembled one of the waifs off the streets. She stared wordlessly across at him, her hands clinched against her stomach.

Unable to control her tired emotions, Josephine felt her face crumple. To hide her tears, she ran for her room. The door slammed with a harsh bang.

Josephine's heart felt as if it had just been shattered. He hadn't noticed the work she'd done at all. All he'd seen was his ugly wife.

"Josephine, may I come in? Please?"

Was that regret in his voice? Even if she'd wanted to, Josephine couldn't answer him. Tears choked her and then began to flow down her cheeks unbidden.

The sound of the doorknob turning told her he was coming in without her permission. She stood with her back to him. Frantically she wiped at her eyes with the tail of her apron. Josephine didn't want him to see that his words had hurt her feelings.

"I'm sorry, Josephine. I can see what you've been doing. The place looks better now than it did when we moved in."

Did he mean it? Hope flared.

Thomas gently turned her to face him. "I never dreamed the house could look or smell this nice. I didn't realize how filthy the place was until I saw what you've done." He took the apron bottom from her and finished wiping the tears from her face. "I really am sorry. Can you forgive me?"

She found herself nodding. His gentleness touched something deep within. A place she'd meant to keep away from him. Her voice trembled. "You really like what I've done?"

He tilted her face upward and smiled at her. "I could not be more proud of my new wife."

Weren't those the words she'd been longing to hear? Just moments earlier she'd prayed Thomas would like what she'd done to the house. She smiled. "Are you hungry?"

"Starving."

Josephine stepped back but reached for his hand, pulling him along behind her. She pointed to the chair at the head of the table. "Sit there and I'll dish it up for you. It's just eggs with cheese, and tenderloin that your family sent, but I didn't know where to find anything else."

She handed him the plate and utensils and watched as he studied them quietly. A furrow creased his brow. Josephine held her breath but then couldn't stand his silence a moment longer and asked, "What's wrong?"

Thomas held up his fork and swept a hand over the plate. "Are these new?"

Now it was her turn to feel puzzled. "No, they were here already. I just washed them."

He burst out laughing. "I don't think I've seen these in six or seven months. After all the dishes became dirty, Philip and I just washed what we needed from the top of the pile. These must have been at the bottom."

Josephine didn't know whether to laugh with Thomas

or shake her head at him. Instead she chose to ask, "Will you say the blessing, Thomas?"

He stared at her for several long moments. She watched his Adam's apple bob. Then he did as she'd asked and prayed over the meal.

After he'd said amen, Josephine asked, "How was Hazel?" She moved to the stove and dished up her own meal.

"She's the same as always." He snapped his fingers. "That reminds me. Hazel sent us pie for dessert." Thomas got up and walked to the mantel over the fireplace. He picked up the plate of pie and returned to the table.

"Hazel makes the best pie." He scooped up eggs and stuffed them into his mouth.

So now she'd need to get Hazel's pie recipe. Josephine was beginning to think she'd need to create a cookbook for all the recipes she'd soon be writing down.

Thomas made a satisfied noise, then said, "Josephine, these eggs are wonderful. I love the cheese in them."

"Well, thank you."

The front door opened once more and Philip entered the house. "No one called me for dinner," he protested.

"Oh, I'm sorry, Philip." Josephine stood up and waved him to a chair. "I'll make you a plate. It's not much, just scrambled eggs and tenderloin."

Thomas chuckled. "That's what she told me, too, but just wait until you taste these eggs."

Josephine hurried to get another plate and silverware. How could she have forgotten Philip? "Would you like water or coffee?"

"Do you have coffee made?" Thomas asked around a mouthful of tenderloin.

She shook her head. "No, but I can make some."

"We'll just have water. Come eat your dinner." Thomas waved his large calloused hand toward her chair.

Josephine thought about arguing with him, but her stomach growled. Instead she handed Philip his plate and hurried to fill three glasses from the water bucket. "I'll make the coffee as soon as I finish eating."

Philip tucked into his meal as if it were his last supper. Around a mouthful of eggs, he asked, "Got any more of these eggs, Josephine?"

She frowned. "No, but I can make some more."

Thomas interrupted. "No, you eat yours." He looked to Philip. "Eat the rest of your dinner, and then we'll have pie with coffee in a little bit."

Josephine watched the brothers finish their meal. She chewed slowly.

Where had Philip been all evening, anyway? It didn't take long for that question to be answered, when he looked at Thomas and said, "Brother, we have meat for the winter."

Thomas looked up from his plate, his eyes alight with interest. "What did you bag?"

Philip squirmed with excitement, then blurted out, "A deer. It's huge, Thomas. There should be enough meat for us and to share with Hazel."

The more they talked about cutting and storing and salting, the more tired Josephine became. There was no way she could hold out long enough to help them. Her spirits drooped as well as her eyelids. She would fail at her first job of providing for her family.

"Did you store it where other animals couldn't get at it till we can work it up tomorrow?"

She glanced up at Thomas's question, hope brightening her thoughts. If they weren't going to work the meat tonight, she'd have new energy in the morning to help.

"Yes, I hung it from a tree limb in back of the barn, covered with a sack full of snow. We'll pack it again before bedtime."

"Good. We can start on it first thing in the morning." Thomas all but clapped his hands.

Half in anticipation, half in dread, Josephine asked, "What can I do to help? I've never put up fresh meat before."

Both men looked at her as if she'd lost her mind. Finally, Thomas answered her, "Well, I don't rightly know what you do. We cut the meat up and put it in the washtub and bring it in the house. I guess you wash it and cut it into smaller-sized pieces. Then Philip and I will salt it down and store it in the smokehouse."

Josephine swallowed hard. She had to handle fresh raw meat with blood and guts attached? A suffocating sensation tightened her throat. Just how could she get out of this?

Chapter Eleven

Thomas plonked the washtub down on the table, relieved to let go of the weight. "We went ahead and cut the meat down to proper size so you wouldn't have to do any cutting. If you'll wash each piece to remove any bone fragments or dirt, we'll salt it down and hang it in the smokehouse."

Josephine swallowed and reached a shaking hand toward the tub. She seemed to be gulping air. Her brown eyes wide.

"Josephine?"

"I can do this," she stated emphatically, then asked weakly, "Can't I?"

In spite of himself, Thomas chuckled. "There's not much I've seen that you can't do."

She was a study in contradictions. Thomas had to admit, he had a growing fascination with her. She stood before him now, her face white beneath her tan. The corners of her mouth turned down into a frown and she clasped her hands together tightly against her apron front. This was the girl who had braved the West as a Pony Express rider amid Indians and bandits.

"Thomas?"

"Yes, Josephine?"

"You might want to stand here with me while I learn how to do this."

"I'll be right here."

Her mouth firmed and the set of her chin suggested a stubborn streak he'd seen the first day he met her. She poured hot water in a basin, then added a bit of cool well water. She washed her hands thoroughly. Earlier that morning he'd had her wash and sterilize all available pots and pans. She readied a pitcher of lukewarm water and, taking a deep unsteady breath, lifted the first hunk of meat.

She gagged.

Thomas could not look away.

She gagged again and almost lost her grip. He took an abrupt step toward her, but she lifted her shoulder in a defensive move, so he backed up. And then the meat was in the water. She rushed to the basin and washed her hands and he wondered if she realized the water was unclean. Apparently it didn't matter to her, because she dried her hands, shook her head and grabbed the hunk of deer meat. Josephine scrubbed for all she was worth and within moments had that piece of meat drying on the wooden cutting board.

He stood mesmerized. What determination. She imposed an iron control on herself. He'd never seen anything like it. What a woman he had married.

"Well." Her voice drew him back to the present. "What are you standing there for? Get the rest of the meat, please."

While he'd been woolgathering, she'd washed all four body portions of the deer. Next would come the leg quarters and he felt confident his new bride would be up to the challenge.

By the time they finished packing the meat in coarse salt and black pepper, she had regained her color and even made a few jokes about the size of the deer's legs. She helped them hang the meat from the rafters in the smokehouse, then served them leftover ham and beans.

Thomas leaned back on his chair legs, a piece of straw between his teeth. Tired but exhilarated over a job well-done, he rested, enjoying the company. Not only had they gotten the meat put away, but he'd learned a little more about Josephine. And what he'd learned, he liked.

"You're proud as a peacock, aren't you?" Philip teased Josephine.

Thomas raised his eyes to find her watching him. "She has every right to be proud. Ma has Fay and Emma helping her, yet Josephine did it all herself."

"I had both of you to help me." She brought her hand up to stifle a giggle. "You should have seen your face, Thomas."

"My face?" He heard the incredulousness in his voice. "What about yours? I thought you might swoon."

"Oh, phooey." She pushed back a wayward strand of hair. "I'm a Pony Express rider. I don't swoon." Thomas noticed she rubbed her arm in a circular motion. "How long will that meat last us?"

Thomas answered, "Should last past Christmas. We'll share with Hazel."

"That's very neighborly of you, Thomas. I'm happy that you're doing so."

"That is, if you don't burn it when you're cooking it," Philip teased.

She waved her hand in a gesture of dismissal. "Don't you fret your head about that, Philip. If I do burn it, you'll be the one eating it."

Thomas liked that she gave tit for tat. He thought about the long, lonely evenings he and Philip had spent before she entered their life. In less than a week, here they sat, laughing and enjoying great food and fellowship. If Hazel were with them, there'd also be some wild storytelling. And that reminded him of his earlier thoughts on getting the older woman a dog.

"I've been thinking."

"Whoa. Stop the presses." At Josephine's words, Philip roared with laughter. She made no attempt to hide from Thomas that she was teasing him.

Thomas narrowed his eyes at her and warned, "Bad things happen to those that sass."

"Mmm-hmm. But you'd have to catch me first."

Thomas liked the sound of that a bit more than he expected. To his interested amazement, a hint of pink filled her cheeks. A sidelong glance told him Philip noticed, too, so he quickly finished his thoughts.

"Before I was interrupted, I was going to say that I think Hazel is lonely and I'd like to get her a dog to care for."

Josephine clapped her hands together. "Oh, that's a lovely idea."

"I thought maybe we might get a dog, too." He watched for Josephine's reaction and wasn't disappointed. Her eyes shone with excitement and she smiled with joy.

"That would be wonderful." She moved to pick up the pot of beans off the table and flinched. Josephine grabbed her right arm, gathering it protectively to her chest.

Thomas was on his feet and beside her in a flash. "Let me see your arm, Josephine." He touched her right shoulder gently, his other hand extended.

"There's nothing to see. I twisted it when I almost dropped the first piece of meat."

"Then let's see how badly it's twisted."

She gave him her hand and he gently raised it, carefully supporting her elbow. When it was just below shoulder height, she cried out. He felt along the muscles, gently moving and massaging as he went. He stretched her arm out straight, then applied a bit of pressure. At first she resisted, and then the stiffness eased and she relaxed. He lifted her arm again, and though it was sore, she could now raise it above her head.

"Tonight if you'll apply liniment to the upper arm, by morning it should be good as new."

Josephine rubbed where his hand had been. "Thanks, Thomas. I will do just that."

Thomas felt a cold gush of air as Philip opened the kitchen door. At Philip's and Josephine's exclamations, he turned to investigate. Big, puffy snowflakes drifted silently to the ground, rushing to cover every expanse of living and material things.

Philip groaned.

Thomas slapped him on the back. "Maybe it will stop before tomorrow." He grabbed his coat from the hook by the door.

Josephine looked at the two men in puzzlement. "What happens tomorrow? If you are worried about us going to town, we can do that when the weather clears."

Philip shook his head. "Woman, you were a Pony

Express rider. Didn't you have to ride in the cold and snow?"

She covered her mouth. "Oh, I'd forgotten that your run starts tomorrow, Philip." Josephine rubbed her arms as if chilled.

Thomas pushed Philip out into the fluffy snow. He turned and grinned at Josephine. "We'll hurry with the chores."

"I'll have hot coffee ready for you."

He nodded and then closed the door.

Thomas was glad to have Philip along with them as far as Dove Creek. The brothers parted ways there, and Philip headed out to the family farm, where he'd meet the Pony Express rider he'd relieve. Thomas and Josephine stopped in front of the sawmill.

The three of them all rode their own mounts. Thomas had wanted to take the buggy, but Josephine had insisted they ride. Now he was glad that she had. She seemed to love being on the back of the borrowed horse.

The snow had accumulated in several places along the road that led to town. With the horses, they'd made it just fine, but a wagon had the potential to get stuck in unseen potholes under the snow.

She now sat atop a pretty mustang, one of the Pony Express horses. The smile on her face spoke volumes of how much she'd missed riding. "I'd like to go to the general store while you order lumber, if that's all right with you."

"Of course. Tell me again what you'd like to make." Thomas leaned against the saddle horn and looked across at her. She was wearing her pants under her skirt and riding upright like a man in the saddle. Her cheeks were rosy from the cold and her copper curls wild from the wind.

"If you don't think it's too much, I'd like a bookshelf, a dresser, and a small table and chair." She tucked a wayward curl behind her ear.

"I don't see why you can't have that. Is there anything else you'd like us to make?"

Her eyes sparkled. "Not that I can think of at the moment." Josephine mimicked his stance and leaned on her saddle horn. "Is there anything you want from the general store?"

"Not that I can think of right offhand, but as soon as I finish my business here, I'll come over and see what might strike my fancy."

Her sweet laughter drew the attention of a couple of the men standing in the doorway of the sawmill. Thomas watched them smile appreciatively. "Well, you best be headed that way." He dropped down from his horse.

She nodded and turned her horse down Main Street. "I'll see you there."

Thomas walked toward the sawmill. The snow was about two inches deep on the hill where the mill sat. His gaze moved to the sky, where more snow clouds were gathering. He made the decision to hurry and order the wood and then head to the store.

"I hear you got married," Mr. English said as Thomas reached the door. Mr. English was an older gentleman who enjoyed hanging out at the sawmill and chatting with everyone.

Thomas nodded. "Sure did."

"Was that little redhead her?" a lanky young man asked.

Again Thomas nodded. "Yep." He stepped around the two men and continued until he found Mr. Ferguson, the owner of the mill.

"Those two giving you a hard time?"

Thomas laughed. "No, they're just curious."

"Don't matter how many times I tell them to leave folks alone, they just don't listen." He brushed sawdust off his leather apron and asked, "What can I do for you today, Thomas?"

"Josephine would like enough lumber to build a bookshelf, dresser, small table and a chair. I'd like to get it at a reasonable price." He grinned to take the sting out of his words.

Mr. Ferguson nodded. "Yep, and I'd like to make some money this winter." He slapped Thomas on the back. "Come on back here and I'll show you what I have in stock."

Together they walked to a large open room where lumber was stacked in all sizes. Thomas whistled. "You have been busy."

"Hafta stay busy to stay in business."

"I guess you do." Thomas walked among the stacks of lumber pointing at various pieces he thought would work for the furniture that Josephine had asked for. When he finished, he took the ticket Mr. Ferguson handed him and exchanged it for money.

"It might be a few days before I can get this out to your place. My son is making a delivery to your folks' place. I'm not sure if he's going to want to go back out into the weather for a while."

Thomas answered with a grin. "That's all right. Philip won't be back for a couple of days and he's the one building the things Josephine wants."

•

"That right?"

Thomas didn't like the way Mr. Ferguson asked the question. "Yes, sir. It is."

The older man chuckled under his breath.

"Care to share with me what you think is funny about that?" Thomas thought it funny because Josephine was going to work Philip hard when he got home, but he didn't see how the lumberman could know her intentions, and if he didn't know them, then what was he laughing about?

"I guess there isn't anything funny about it."

"Then why are you laughing?"

Mr. Ferguson laid a hand on his shoulder. "I am sure nothing is going on at your place when you are off riding the Pony Express, but I got a gander at your new wife and she's a pretty little thing."

Thomas left the mill mulling over Mr. Ferguson's words. He knew Philip and Josephine were not romantically inclined, but he didn't like that the townsfolk might start talking about his wife and brother. He shook his head. Well, this was a fine how-do-you-do.

His horse picked its way through the snow. Instead of guiding him to the general store, Thomas veered off to the bread store. He wasn't quite ready to see Josephine. What was he going to do? In two days Philip would be back, and the day after that, Thomas would be expected to ride out and leave them alone.

He tied the horse up in front of the bread store and walked the short distance up the wooden walkway. When he opened the door, the warm fragrance of fresh bread greeted him. Thomas walked to the main counter and shook the cowbell that was there.

Rosie Carter came from the back room. The moment

she saw him, her face lit up in a bright smile. "Well, Thomas Young, what brings you in here today?"

Thomas grinned. "The smell of fresh bread."

"I have plenty of that. Seems the snow has kept most of my regulars home today." She wiped flour on her apron. "What can I get you?"

He looked at the loaves of bread and knew he'd be taking two with him today. "I'll have a plain white bread and one of your cinnamon sweet loaves, too."

"How is married life treating you?" Rosie pulled the loaves down and began wrapping them in cheesecloth. "I'll put these in a flour sack for you, Thomas, but I'd like it back next time you come into town."

Did everyone know that he'd gotten married? It would seem so. "Married life is good, Rosie, and I'll be happy to bring the sack back in a few days."

She passed the sack across the counter and waited for him to pay. "That's good. I hear you up and married a redhead." Rosie fluffed her straight black hair.

"Can I ask you a question?" Thomas handed her the money for the bread.

Rosie leaned a hip against the counter. "Sure. But if I don't like it, I'm not obligated to answer." She grinned.

Thomas had wanted to ask what she thought about his dilemma with Philip and Josephine but quickly changed his mind. "Do you know anyone who has a dog or puppy they'd like to get rid of?"

She chuckled. "And here I thought it was a serious question." Rosie shook her head. "No, but there is a stray that's been hanging out behind the bank. Maybe you can see if she's the friendly type."

Thomas thanked her and took his bread. Did he want a stray for Hazel? He climbed back on his horse, tied the strings of the flour sack to the saddle horn and headed toward the bank. It wouldn't hurt to look at the mutt.

Once in front of the bank, he tied his reins to the hitching post and walked around to the alley. He heard the little dog before he saw her. Her teeth were bared and her ears laid back. Not very friendly.

She was white with reddish-brown fur around her ears and eyes. The same reddish-brown fur crossed her back and sides. Blackish-brown eyes stared at him. Daring Thomas to come closer, reminding him a little of how Josephine had first looked at him.

The sound of a soft whimper drew his attention behind her. A little black nose peeked around her. She had a puppy.

Thomas couldn't help but see that the bigger dog's ribs showed under her fur. He turned around and hurried back to the horse. Opening the flour sack, he pinched off a good portion of the white bread and returned to the dogs.

Thomas knelt a few feet away and held the bread out. "Come on, girl, it's fresh." He waved the bread.

Her nose twitched and she crept out a little farther.

He sat back on his heels and waited. The pup behind her inched out from her hiding place, as well. Thomas was thankful that the bread was warm, fresh and fragrant.

After several long moments the mama dog came forward. She watched him with leery eyes. "Come on, girl. I won't hurt you, and I can almost guarantee you a warm home with lots of food. Come on."

It took about thirty minutes before both dogs were close enough to eat the bread from his hand. Thomas knew dogs and this one didn't seem dangerous, just cold, hungry and wary of strangers. He continued to speak softly to them as they nibbled bread from his fingers. The mother ate daintily. The pup had no reservations about gulping down her portion of the bread.

Thomas inched his hand forward and rubbed the mama dog's long, fluffy ears. She looked up at him with big eyes. No longer did they hold fear. He gently picked up the puppy and rubbed her long ears, too.

Sure that Josephine was wondering where he was, Thomas risked picking up the mama dog, as well. She leaned into his body and trembled. He continued to talk gently as he walked back to the horse.

There was no way he could climb on his horse and hold the dogs. He sat the puppy down, untied the horse and tucked its reins in his back pocket. Then he scooped up the pup once more and started walking toward Main Street.

Josephine came out of the store as soon as she saw him. "What have you got there?" she asked, coming forward slowly and holding out her hand for the dogs to sniff.

"Do you think Hazel would like the mama dog? Or the pup?" he asked, handing her the pup.

She shrugged. "I don't know. We'll need to ask her." She rubbed the little dog's head and soft ears. The pup's tail wagged against her waist. "She is so sweet. Where did you get them?"

"They are strays, according to Rosie."

"Who's Rosie?" Josephine quit petting the pup.

Thomas laughed. "Rosie is the proud owner of the bread shop here in town." He liked the way Josephine's eyebrows had arched up when she'd asked about the other woman.

"Oh. So the dogs don't belong to her?" Josephine looked confused as she bowed her head and continued to pet the little dog in her arms.

"I don't believe so, but I do think she's been feeding them." He took the reins from his back pocket and tied the horse up by the watering trough.

"I don't know. They both seem awfully skinny to me." Josephine stroked the puppy's side. "Poor baby, you must be starving."

Thomas held the mama dog in the crook of his arm. "Did you find anything in the store you wanted?"

"Oh, yeah, I'll be right back." Josephine thrust the pup back into his arms and headed inside.

Within a few minutes she returned with a small paper bag. "I'm ready to go if you are." She looked up into the sky. "I think we are in for more snow today."

"I'm ready, too. Go ahead and get on your horse, and then I'll hand you the dogs while I get on mine."

Josephine did as he said. Within minutes they were riding out of town, each holding a dog.

Thomas couldn't help but wonder what the townspeople thought of them. And just to borrow trouble, he wondered if they were watching his living situation unfold and sharing their opinions with others. He still hadn't decided what to do about Philip and Josephine being at the cabin alone while he was gone. Should he really care what the townspeople thought? What would Josephine think if he brought the subject up with her? How did one bring up such a delicate subject with a lady?

Chapter Twelve

Snow drifted down steadily on them most of the way home. Josephine cut her eyes toward her new husband. He'd been very quiet most of the way home. Since Philip was gone, was Thomas worried about spending time alone with her?

As they came into the yard, Josephine recognized Hazel's wagon standing in front of the house. What was the older woman doing there? Was she all right? Hurt? Sick? Josephine slid from her horse and started to the house with the little puppy tucked under her coat.

Thomas called after her. "Josephine, wait up."

Worry ate at her as she paused for him to tie both of their horses to the porch rail.

The puppy squirmed against her ribs. It stuck its head out of her coat as if it sensed her unease. She rubbed the dog's small head.

Josephine frowned at Thomas. His fingers worked the string that held the flour sack to his horse. "Thomas, hurry."

He shook his head. "I don't know why you are in such a hurry."

"Something might be wrong with Hazel. That's why."

He finally got the sack untied and walked up to her. "I doubt that, but if so, we'll find out together and I'm going in first."

"Fine, just do it." Josephine gave him a little shove.

Thomas frowned at her over his shoulder. He kicked the snow from his boots and opened the door to the house.

Josephine looked around him.

Hazel sat with her bare feet propped up on the fireplace hearth. She'd been sleeping in Thomas's chair. "'Bout time you two got home." She yawned and stretched.

"See? I told you she just came for a visit." He set the mother dog down on the floor. She immediately shot off to Thomas and Philip's bedroom.

Josephine wanted to tell him that he'd said no such thing but decided now wasn't the time. She carried the puppy into the room and set it down. It followed its mother. Thomas handed Josephine the bread bag.

"Would you like for me to bring your bag in now or can it wait until I put the horses away?" he asked.

She'd forgotten all about her tea and sugar. "It can wait until you come back inside." Josephine turned to Hazel. "What brings you over?"

"Does a body need an excuse to come for a visit?" Hazel shot back.

Josephine grinned. She spotted the basket that Hazel stored the unfinished quilt in. "No, but I thought maybe you wanted to work on the quilt."

Hazel yawned again. "Not right now, but I would like to stay the night, if it won't be too much of an inconvenience." She followed Josephine into the kitchen and sat down at the table.

"Of course it won't be." Josephine turned to the coffeepot. Or would it? Where would Hazel sleep? She poured the hot liquid into three cups, then turned to set one in front of her guest. Sipping from her own cup, Josephine continued studying her problem. Perhaps she'd give the older woman her room tonight. Or Thomas could give Hazel his.

"Don't fret, Jo. I already sniffed out the sleeping arrangements." Hazel uncovered a plate in the center of the table and took out a molasses cookie. She munched it with relish. "I sure am glad you two are home. I'm as hungry as a polecat after hibernation."

Unsure what to say regarding Hazel's first statement, Josephine decided to address the second. "I hope you don't mind a sandwich and pickles."

"Not at all. And I don't suppose you'd mind heating up that jar of beans and ham to go with those sandwiches, would you?" Hazel motioned to the sidebar, where two jars of beans and ham stood.

"No, but you didn't have to go to all the trouble of bringing them over here." Josephine grinned, happy to see Thomas would get a hot meal, after all.

"Well, I suppose not. But I wanted to. You aren't going to deprive an old woman of doing the simple things that give her joy, are you?" She laid her cookie down and tried to look downtrodden.

Josephine laughed. "If you'll show me an old woman, I'll sure treat her nice." She walked over and picked up one of the jars. "Should I heat up one or two?"

"Let's open them both." Hazel went to the washbasin

and proceeded to cleanse her hands. "You ignored what I said a while ago."

Josephine pulled out a nice-sized pot to put the beans in. "No, I answered you."

"About the sleeping arrangements." Hazel dried her hands. "I thought we girls should have a talk before Thomas comes in."

For the first time, Josephine felt as if Hazel was butting in where she didn't belong. "Look, Hazel, Thomas and I agree on how things are."

Hazel nodded. "I'm not worried about you and Thomas so much as I am about you and Philip."

Josephine poured the beans into the pot. "What do you mean?"

"Well, I was thinking today about the last time Thomas rode for the Express." She pulled the flour sack open and took the bread out.

Instead of trying to figure out what Hazel was getting at, Josephine decided to just wait for her to spit it out. She handed Hazel a bread knife.

"You stayed with me."

Josephine nodded. "That's right."

"Philip stayed here."

"Yes?"

Hazel chuckled. "You really are young and thick-headed."

Josephine felt the insult down to her toes. She tightened her lips to keep angry words from spewing out of her mouth. Not only was Hazel insulting her, but she was doing it in Josephine's own kitchen.

"Look, you and Philip cannot stay in this house alone together. It might all be respectable, but that's not how the townspeople will see it should one of them decide to come out for a visit." She sliced the bread and placed it on a plate.

"I hadn't thought of that." Josephine sighed. "What are we going to do?"

"Well, I've been thinking on that, too."

Josephine stirred the beans. "What did you come up with?" She dreaded Hazel's answer. The older woman would probably suggest that she go to her house and wait for Thomas to return. Josephine did not want to do that. She wanted to make this cabin a home.

"If you don't mind, I'll come stay with you while Thomas is gone." Hazel grinned at Josephine. "I'm sure Philip won't mind going to my place and taking care of the chores there."

So that was her plan. Send Philip to her house. "So we'll do the chores here? What if a Pony Express rider comes through needing a change of horses?" Josephine tapped the spoon against the side of the pan, then looked back at Hazel.

"I figured Philip could take care of his morning chores here. He'll have to start a little earlier and then go to my house and do my morning chores. Then he'd be back here in time to take care of any riders that might come through."

Josephine liked this idea. Not only would Philip get another lesson in how he'd messed up things for her and Thomas, but also for himself and Hazel. "Then he would have to return to your place in the late afternoon to do chores at your place again, along with his chores here."

Hazel nodded. She clucked her tongue. "It's the only way to assure that you and he are never alone."

"I wonder what Thomas will think of this." Josephine inhaled the smell of ham and beans. Her stomach growled.

Clomping boots on the front porch told the women Thomas was heading into the house.

"We'll soon find out," Hazel answered.

He entered the house and called to Josephine. "Josephine, I went to the storehouse and got a hunk of ham for you to slice up for dinner."

She met him at the kitchen door to take the meat. Josephine tried to hide the grin on her face as she took the ham, but failed miserably. He held out the bag from the general store, as well.

His gaze studied her face. "You look as mischievous as an unbroken mustang horse. What have you two been up to?" Thomas asked, looking from her to Hazel.

While Josephine sliced the ham, Hazel filled Thomas in on their conversation. He tipped his chair back and listened. Josephine couldn't tell what her new husband was thinking.

"Well, that would take care of wagging tongues, I suppose."

Hazel nodded and then got up to help Josephine finish setting the table. "That's what I am hoping for."

She and Josephine sat down and bowed their heads. Thomas blessed the meal and then asked, "Who gets to tell Philip?"

Josephine grinned. "Well, you."

"That sounds about right," he muttered.

The pitter-patter of dog feet sounded loudly in the now-quiet room. He saw the mother and her pup coming to stand beside his chair. "Sorry, girl, you two have to wait for the scraps. We're not going to start feeding you from the table."

"What are you doing with two dogs, anyway?" Hazel blurted out.

Thomas frowned. "You didn't tell her?" he asked Josephine.

"She didn't give me a chance." She buttered a slice of bread and took a big bite.

"Tell me what?" Hazel demanded.

The urge to tease the old woman tore at him. "Aw, never mind. You don't want to know."

"Know what?"

Josephine tried to hide a grin behind her bread. Her pretty eyes sparkled at him as she enjoyed his teasing of Hazel. "It was probably a bad idea to start with."

"What was a bad idea?" Hazel looked like a hoot owl as her head swung back and forth between them. "One of you better get on with telling me."

Beautiful tinkling laughter spilled from Josephine. He couldn't control his own mirth any longer and felt a laugh build from his belly. At the growing frustration in Hazel's face, he finally said, "One of them is for you. You get first pick."

"Now, why in the world would you get me a dog?" Hazel stood up and walked toward the animals. The mama dog turned her head to the right and then to the left as she eyed Hazel. The puppy grabbed hold of the hem of her dress and began tugging and growling.

Thomas watched both Hazel and Josephine. Should he have offered his wife first pick? Josephine smiled as she watched Hazel coax the mama dog to her.

"We thought if you had a dog, you wouldn't get lonely."

"Who said I was lonely?" Hazel gently shoved the pup away, but she only came back again and again. The mama dog slowly inched her way to the older woman. "You sure are a pretty little thing." She slowly reached out and petted the dog's ears.

Thomas held his tongue and noticed that Josephine had the wisdom not to answer Hazel's question, either. His wife laughed when the puppy sank her teeth into Hazel's apron ties and pulled them free from the older woman's expanded waist.

Hazel ignored the pup and slowly inched her hands under the mama. "If it's all the same to you, I think Mama and I are more compatible. I'm not sure I could keep up with a puppy."

The mama dog allowed Hazel to cuddle her close. She closed her eyes and looked as if she enjoyed the scratches about her ears.

"I think she likes you, too." Thomas pushed away from the table and grinned at the two women.

Hazel smiled over the dog's head. "Of course she does. At my house, there are no rules. She can eat at the table if she wants to."

Thomas lost the smile on his face. He hoped Hazel was joking. If the weather wasn't so bad right now, neither of the dogs would be in the house, let alone eating at the table.

It was Hazel's turn to laugh. She pushed up from the floor, still holding the mama dog. "Does she have a name?"

"Nope, she was a stray. Thomas rescued her and the pup," Josephine said, carrying dishes to the washtub.

Hazel started to put the dog back down on the floor. "I'll clean the kitchen while you get acquainted with your new dog." Josephine motioned for Hazel to go into the sitting room.

Thomas saw the indecision on Hazel's face. It was clear she wanted to play with the dog but at the same time felt she should help with the cleanup. "Yes, go on. I'll help Josephine clean up the kitchen and we'll be right in."

Hazel looked at him speculatively. She nodded her head and chattered to the dog as she left the room. The puppy whined at Thomas's feet.

He reached down and picked her up. "Hungry again, aren't you?"

Josephine grabbed two small bowls. She filled one with water and placed scraps of meat and bread in the other. "There you go. That should keep her busy while I clean the kitchen." Josephine set the bowls by the back door.

Thomas couldn't believe how quickly she took care of the dog's needs and then continued on with her chores. "I'll help you." He set the pup down and walked to the basin to wash his hands.

"Here, why don't you take these scraps to Hazel for her dog?" She thrust a small cloth with ham and bread pieces at him.

Thomas took the food and frowned. Was Josephine trying to get rid of him? Or was she simply taking care of the animals?

Her gaze ran over his face. "It was really nice of you to get her a companion. And one for me, as well." Josephine turned back to the dirty dishes.

Thomas didn't know what to make of this new, shy woman. What had happened to the carefree laughter they'd shared earlier? Was she nervous about being alone with him in the kitchen? Or had she remembered he was a scarred man when she'd run her gaze over his face? Frustrated, he left the kitchen.

Chapter Thirteen

Thomas settled down on his makeshift bed in front of the fireplace, thoughts of the day running through his head. All in all, the day had gone well. That was, up until they decided Hazel should have his room and he should sleep here, on Philip's temporary corn-husk mattress.

He and Philip had brought it in from the barn when Josephine took Philip's room, and though Philip hadn't complained, Thomas knew now, as he shifted to get comfortable, that his brother must often get up more tired than when he went to bed. They'd have to fix this problem and soon.

Something else had been troubling him of late. The easy way Josephine asked him to pray, as if she had every confidence that he could get through to the Lord. Of course, she didn't know it had been a long time since he had done so and he planned to keep her from learning that sad fact. He closed his eyes and told the Lord he was sorry for his lack of communication with Him, that he planned to do better and his desire was to have a household of faith.

With the peace of the Lord, Thomas fell asleep, only to be awakened by something rubbing against the side of his face. He jumped and sat straight up. The sound of a smothered giggle had him turning to see who else was in the room with him.

Josephine sat beside him on the floor, her finger against her lips in silent entreaty. "Shhh. Hazel is still asleep."

Thomas felt his heart accelerate. She sat peering at him intently. Her shining, dark eyes full of intelligence and independence of spirit, her hair mussed from sleep. She took his breath away. Did she know how beautiful she was?

"I thought you were never going to wake up, sleepyhead. Has married life already made you lazy?"

Her infectious grin and teasing voice brought an immediate response. "Lazy? Woman, I feel like I just went to sleep."

"Shhh. Keep your voice down—you'll wake up Hazel."

He sat up and whispered, "What are you doing up so early? It's not fully daylight yet."

She held the pup out, both arms extended. "Little One here needs to go out."

At the last moment he tempered his laugh, but he wanted to guffaw. "Little One?" He quirked his eyebrows questioningly. "You named this poor pup Little One?"

She squeaked in self-defense, "Well, I couldn't think of anything else."

"Shhh. You'll wake up Hazel." He loved getting back at her. They both giggled like little kids, sharing the morning in perfect harmony. Happiness welled up in his heart. He was happy that they could be friends, even if they would never be true husband and wife. This was a pretty good way to start the day.

The puppy began twisting round and round, and Josephine's eyes grew big as saucers. "You better hurry, Thomas, or it's going to be too late."

He threw the quilt off and sprang to his feet, taking the puppy with him. He exited the back door onto the porch and set the puppy on the ground below the last step. The little dog immediately did her business and tried to leap onto the step. Thomas laughed, scooped her up and entered the house hopping. He'd rushed out without boots and now his socks were wet with snow and his feet were colder than a snowman's nose.

Josephine laughed quietly when the puppy ran into her lap, then laughed out loud, quickly covering her mouth with the back of her hand, when Thomas plopped down on the quilt. "Brrr. I about froze my toes off." He stripped off the wet socks and thrust his feet back under the quilt, pulling it up to his neck. "It's freezing outside. That's your puppy. Why was I the one who took it out?"

Josephine had placed her feet just under the edge of the quilt and his feet brushed against hers. His eyes widened as she immediately recoiled, but he motioned to her that he would move his feet to the far side and he raised the quilt in invitation. She slid her feet back under the quilt and he tucked the edges tighter.

She ignored his question about the puppy and asked a different one. "What are you going to do this last day before your Express ride tomorrow?"

"What do you mean?"

"Well, the day before I had to ride, I tried to do something special that I enjoyed or I planned something special for when I got to my next destination."

"Like what?" Thomas saw the puppy's eyes droop, then widen, and he smiled. At Josephine's questioning look, he nodded at the pup. She chuckled. She leaned over and nuzzled her face against its head and the puppy bit at her hair. Thomas asked again, "What do you mean about planning special things?"

"Well, the day before the trip, I'd spend the day with a good book or simply daydreaming. Or, if I didn't have time to relax before going, I'd ask the stationmaster what the next stop was like. If it had a restaurant, I'd plan on a big meal and a walk around town. If it wasn't a big town, I'd still get a meal and then take a walk in the woods or down by the stream or river. It broke the monotony of all those hours alone."

"Oh, well, usually I simply do chores and try to rest up before going." Thomas saw the first rays of daylight enter the window by the front door. Ordinarily he would have already been in the barn doing chores. Instead he lay propped on his elbow listening to his wife, a bevy of ideas flitting through his mind on planning a special day.

He heard a quickly smothered whine from the mother dog in his bedroom. He tapped Josephine's knee and motioned her to follow him, pulling her to her feet. He tiptoed to his bedroom door and quickly opened it. Hazel tumbled forward and only his quick thinking kept her from crashing into the hard wood floor. The dogs set to barking, Josephine giggled and Thomas straightened Hazel.

"What in blue blazes?" She placed both hands on her hips, her lips puckered with annoyance. If not for the faint tinge of pink creeping up her neck and into her cheeks, one might think she *hadn't* been listening at the door. Thomas decided to let her off the hook. After all, she was one of his favorite people.

"Sorry, Hazel. I thought I heard the dog wanting to go out, so I tried not to disturb you. Was just going to get the dog and let you rest."

She swept by them, the dog on her heels. She opened the door, the dog ran out and she shut the door with a bit more force than necessary.

Oh, no, Thomas thought. *I'm in the doghouse now.* He turned to Josephine. Teasing laughter filled her eyes. She knew it, too. He cocked one eyebrow, pointed at her, and she shook her head. She pointed back at him, then with both hands made a twisting motion as if breaking his neck.

His laugh was low and throaty. He sauntered to the kitchen, where Hazel loudly banged pots and pans.

"I'm so glad you're up, Hazel. Now maybe I can get a good breakfast instead of pancakes again."

The moment the words left his mouth, he wanted to call them back. He heard more than saw Josephine's quick intake of breath.

"Boy, you're in for a goose or a gander this morning, aren't you?" Hazel chuckled. "Gonna love watching you worm your way out of this one."

Revenge was such sweet contemplation. Thomas didn't like pancakes for breakfast? Oh, she'd teach him a thing or two. Josephine whirled around and all but ran for the bedroom. As she pushed the door closed, she glanced back at Thomas seated at the table. His arms were stretched out in front of him, hands clasped and his head down as if he were trying to pray his way out of the corner he'd backed himself into.

In her short time knowing him, Thomas had only shown kindness to everyone he met. Even with Hazel, he was considerate and tried not to upset her, and he always went to great lengths to make sure that she was cared for. So Josephine knew he had not meant to hurt her feelings over the pancakes, and though she needed him to know she didn't wear her feelings on her sleeve, her natural instinct urged her not to pass up a chance to tease him just a little. As she hurriedly dressed, she planned. And plotted. As she pushed her feet into her boots, she gleefully rubbed her hands together and had to stifle her giggles.

Assuming an expression of sadness, she opened the door, kept her head down and went to let Hazel's dog back in. Josephine stepped onto the porch to call the mama dog inside.

The dog bounded through the snow at the sound of the door opening. Josephine quickly gathered what she needed to get back at Thomas and then reentered the house, careful to keep her expression neutral. She walked up behind him and placed a hand on his back. His eyes swept over her face, eagerly assessing her mood.

His voice full of entreaty, he said, "I'm sorry, Josephine. I love your pancakes. I have no idea why I said that."

"Thomas Young, do you think I wear my feelings on my sleeve?" She let her hand sweep the back of his shirt where his hair met his collar. He accepted the touch, even seemed to lean into it. "Why, I'd never have made it as a Pony Express rider had I let little things such as that trouble me."

"But I am sorry." Thomas looked back at the table after a swift glance in Hazel's direction. "And I'm glad you're being so mature about it."

Josephine quickly pulled the neck of his shirt out. She dumped the handful of snow she'd been concealing behind her back down his shirt. Then squished it into his back.

He yelped and jumped from the chair, twisting and turning to get away from the cold spreading over his body.

"I didn't say anything about being mature." Josephine raised her voice to be heard. "Hazel, did you hear anything about maturity in my speech?"

"Not nary a word. No sirree, I sure didn't." Hazel bent double at the waist, laughing loudly.

When Thomas finally stopped dancing around, a puddle lay near his chair and water soaked the back of his shirt. He started toward Josephine, but Hazel stepped between them on her way to the table with a frying pan full of ham and eggs.

"Sit down, Thomas, and enjoy your breakfast. You've earned it." A trace of laughter made her voice sound a bit strangled.

Thomas took the seat directly across from Josephine. He waited for Hazel to take her seat, not once glancing in Josephine's direction. He prayed over breakfast, then filled his plate.

Josephine sat in the chair, her thin fingers tensed in her lap. Surely he wouldn't let a little thing like freezing snow down his back upset him. She stirred uneasily in the chair.

"Eat up there, girlie," Hazel prompted. "We're late getting started this morning and I, for one, want to catch up. We're burning daylight."

Josephine looked at her plate. She'd lost her appetite. The light seemed to have gone out of her day. There had to be great significance in that, but she could only wrap her mind around the fact that she had wrecked a wonderful, glorious morning with Thomas.

She glanced at Thomas again and froze. Her pulse skittered alarmingly. Thomas stared back at her, his eyes alight with merriment and a faint glint of something she couldn't identify but that gave her a warm feeling, nonetheless. Powerful relief filled her. She rested her chin on her hand, a smile tipping the corners of her mouth.

He wasn't angry. Hallelujah. He quirked his eyebrow questioningly. She shook her head, then picked up her fork.

"The barn dance is coming up, isn't it, Thomas?" Hazel drizzled honey over a biscuit that made Josephine's mouth water. Her appetite returned with a vicious roar.

"Shouldn't be too long now. I figure Ma is working up a storm getting everything ready."

"It's at your parents' farm?" Josephine felt the stirring of excitement. A get-together during the cold season when everyone had been snowed in for days was just the thing they needed.

"Yep. Been held there the last two years. But each year Ma tries to change things up. Let's hope we make it through this one without a fight." He and Hazel laughed together.

"What?" Josephine looked between the two of them, her interest piqued.

"Well, last year there was a little skirmish between two men fighting over the same lady. It's not like we have enough women to go around out here," Hazel said.

"Did anyone get hurt?"

"No." Hazel pointed a bony finger at Thomas. "You better thank the Lord you had this pretty woman hand delivered to your doorstep. The rest of the bachelors here would be trying to snatch her right out from under your nose if she wasn't already hitched."

Josephine watched Thomas closely.

He grinned. "Well, if she keeps stuffing my shirt with snow, I may just give her to them."

A smile touched her lips. Her new husband knew how to tease and that gave her a feeling of warmth that she didn't want to feel. Having a fun husband was one thing, but these warm feelings were another and Josephine vowed to keep them at bay.

Chapter Fourteen

Thomas slunk out of the saddle. Weariness poured through him as if he was a man who'd walked the desert without water. The only bright spot was that Josephine would be waiting for him when he arrived back at the house.

It was hard to believe they'd been married a month. Even so, they'd lost some of the playfulness of the first week. She'd become guarded and quiet. Thomas blamed this on the fact that he was gone more often than he should be.

He wondered what she'd think when he told her he'd resigned as a Pony Express rider. His back ached. Putting one foot in front of the other, he climbed the short stairs to the front door.

A small yelp announced his arrival. Thomas opened the door and was immediately attacked by the growing puppy. He bent down and rubbed her ears. "Hello, little girl. Thanks for this warm welcome." She licked at his gloves.

Philip sat before the fireplace with his Bible in his

lap. He looked up and grinned. "Welcome home. You look like how I normally feel after a hard ride."

"That could be because I feel like how you look after a hard ride." The two brothers smiled at each other. They had the same initial conversation after every ride. His gaze moved about the room looking for his wife and Hazel. Neither was present.

As if he could read Thomas's thoughts, Philip said, "She's over at Hazel's."

Thomas took off his gloves, hung his coat up and pulled his boots off by the door. Disappointment ate at him. A warm meal and Josephine's smiling face were the only two things he'd been looking forward to all day. "Did she leave me any grub?" he asked as he dropped into the rocking chair closest to the fire.

"Sure did. I'll get it for you." Philip put the Bible on a small side table and headed for the kitchen.

"I see we have a new table," Thomas called after his brother, admiring the sturdiness of the table that now held the Bible.

Harsh laughter came from the kitchen. "Yep, that wife of yours has been working me like a horse while you were gone."

Thomas chuckled. It was true. Over the past month, Philip had built a bookshelf, a table and chair for Josephine's room, a cabinet for her washbasin, a closet for her dresses and now a small end table in the sitting room. His gaze moved to the wood bin. It overflowed with wood and the basket of kindling was just as full.

"Ma wants to know if you are coming to the winter barn dance." Thomas took the bowl of soup and coffee mug from Philip. He set the cup on the floor beside his chair.

Philip sighed. "Yes, but I hope she's not matchmaking again this year."

Thomas bowed his head and said a silent word of thanks for the meal and then looked up at his brother. "Well, this year, thanks to you, I will be matchmaker free." The scent of creamy potato and sausage soup had him dipping his spoon in and sighing with contentment as the rich flavor coated his tongue.

Josephine was turning out to be quite the cook. Over the past few weeks she'd perfected several soups, casseroles and desserts. Thomas made a mental note to make her a box to put all the recipe cards in that she and Hazel had written up. At the moment, they sat on the counter with a pretty ribbon holding them together.

"I wish you wouldn't put your mug on the floor like that." Philip sat back down.

Thomas looked down. "Why not? That's how we used to do it before Josephine insisted we take all our meals at the table."

"Because if Josephine sees it, she will make me build another end table, like this one." Philip indicated the table by his chair.

"You do realize that she wants a new couch, don't you?"

Philip yelped. "What? She hasn't said a word to me about a couch. I'm not even sure I know how to build one." He ran his hand down his face.

Thomas laughed. "When you decide to quit the Pony Express, you could go into the furniture business. And you'll have Josephine to thank for all the experience you're getting now."

"That's not a bad thought." Philip sat forward in his chair. He gazed into the fire while Thomas ate.

Once he'd emptied his bowl, Thomas set it on the floor and picked up his coffee mug. "Philip, I sent a letter to St. Joseph today, resigning as a Pony Express rider. My last ride was tonight."

His brother turned to look at him in shock. "What will you do now?"

"I've told them I'd like to stay here and remain the relay station manager, just as I've always done." He watched as Philip's shoulders relaxed.

"Good. I'm not ready to stop riding just yet," Philip confessed. "And I wasn't looking forward to your leaving, either."

Thomas grinned. "Glad to hear that. But eventually Josephine and I will need to move to our own place." Where that would be, he wasn't sure yet.

"You have someplace in mind?"

"No, but I'm thinking I'd like to buy a ranch and maybe raise some cattle." Thomas picked up the empty bowl and carried it to the kitchen. When he returned, Philip was staring into the fire.

He spoke in a low voice. "Everything is changing."

Thomas sat back down in the chair, even though he'd rather go climb into his soft, warm bed. "I know. But I'm not leaving anytime soon. I haven't even talked to Josephine about it."

"I like her, but I wish I'd minded my own business." Philip's gaze met Thomas's. "I had no idea how much having a woman about would change everything."

Thomas smiled. "There have been good changes. We now eat regularly and what she cooks isn't burned, like it would be if we had to cook it. Our clothes get washed weekly. She makes sure to air out the mattresses." He looked around. "This house has never been cleaner."

Philip nodded. "I know, but I still wish I hadn't done this. You and I were close and now, well…I feel like I'm losing you."

"You can always come with us," Thomas offered.

"No, you now have a real family. Besides, chasing cows all day isn't the life I want." Philip grinned. "Can you just see me branding, feeding and moving cattle?"

Thomas laughed. "Naw, you would hate that."

"Well, I don't know about hate, but I do enjoy sleeping in a bed at night instead of under the stars."

"Who says I have to sleep in the cow pasture?" Thomas asked. Had Philip lost his mind or did he have no concept of what running a cattle ranch was like?

"Oh, I assumed you'd have to do a yearly cattle run and take them to market to sell. That would require several nights of sleeping under the stars. And when you brand the new calves, are you going to bring them all up to the house or do it in the pastures?"

Thomas shook his head. He was tired. He'd not thought of either of those events. What would Josephine think of his plans? Would she like living on a ranch where he'd be gone nights to take care of cattle? He stood.

"Headed to bed?"

"Yep. I'm beat." Thomas started to walk away. He stopped at the bedroom door. "Philip?"

Philip turned to face him.

"Don't say anything to Josephine about me not riding or about the cattle ranch. I'd like to break the news to her myself."

"Wouldn't dream of it."

Thomas ran his hand down the scar on his face.

"Thanks." He headed to bed. Again the questions plagued him as he undressed.

What if Josephine didn't want to live on a ranch? Would she leave him? He'd not seen hide nor hair of her uncle. Was it possible she'd lied to him? If so, what had she gained? A loveless marriage. She might be ready to move on.

He crawled between the sheets. His heart felt as heavy as his eyelids. Was it possible he'd lose Josephine? Thomas touched the scar once more. If only he wasn't scarred. Then maybe she'd fall in love with him.

Josephine fussed with some material. "This dress doesn't look right, Hazel. No matter how hard I try, I can't get the gathers right." She pushed the fabric away and rubbed her eyes.

"You're just tired, child. Why don't you put it away for tonight? It's about time we head over to your place, anyway." Hazel tucked the quilt square she'd been working on back into her sewing basket.

Maybe it was time to quit. Josephine folded her dress up and placed it in her sewing box. "I think I'll take it with me and work on it tomorrow. The dance is only two days away and I really want to wear this dress to it."

"I don't know what you are fussing about. It's almost done. I could finish it for you," Hazel offered. She walked to the door and pulled on her hat, gloves and coat.

Josephine followed and did the same. "No, I really want to do this one myself."

The mama dog, officially named Mama, looked up from her spot by the fireplace. She started to rise, but

Hazel stopped her by saying, "You stay here, girl. I'll be back shortly."

Josephine picked up her sewing box and followed Hazel out the door. Cold wind blew against her cheeks as they made their way to the barn. The setting sun winked over the mountain ridge.

Both their horses neighed as they walked inside the warmth of the barn. "We better hurry. I didn't realize it had gotten so late." Hazel saddled her horse and then waited for Josephine to finish saddling hers.

The two women left Hazel's small farm. Darkness descended around them. For the first time in a long time, Josephine wondered if her uncle would ever find her. She shivered.

Josephine's mustang raised her ears, alert to the night. A soft neigh sounded in front of them. The mustang responded. Josephine held her breath as she and Hazel pulled to a stop and waited to see who was approaching.

Philip pulled his horse to a halt. "I was beginning to worry about you two."

Both women set their horses into motion. "I'm sorry, Philip. It's my fault we're running late," Josephine said when they came even with him.

"That doesn't surprise me."

She ignored his sarcasm. "Is Thomas home yet?"

"Yep, he rode in over an hour ago. Looked worn-out, too."

Josephine wondered why her husband hadn't come to get them. Normally he did. Was he angry at her? Or had this ride been especially hard on him? "Is he all right?"

"He's fine, just tired. He went to bed about an hour ago."

Hazel spoke up. "I don't know how you young'uns can ride like that. I'd be plum tuckered out if I had to ride one day in the saddle like you boys do."

The little cabin came into sight. Josephine found herself wanting to check on Thomas. She knew that wasn't going to happen, because theirs wasn't a real marriage and he probably wouldn't appreciate her waking him up just to find out how his ride went and if he were all right. She looked over at Hazel. "Are you coming in for a cup of tea? I still have some left over."

"No, thanks, Jo. I want to get back to Mama. You know she gets nervous if I leave her alone for too long." Hazel was already turning her horse around.

Philip grinned. "I think I'll ride back with you. This fresh air is just what I need to clear my head."

"Of what? Cobwebs?" Josephine teased.

He glared at her. "Woman, if you were my wife, I'd…" Philip let the threat hang in the air between them.

Josephine laughed. "Yep, that's about all you'd do. Blow hot air and glare."

"Children, don't fight." Hazel laughed. "Phil, she's teasing you."

Josephine looked at her brother-in-law. Surely he hadn't thought she was serious. Had she been too hard on him lately? "I'm sorry, Philip. Hazel's right, I was only teasing."

He nodded. "Yeah, I know. We'd best get back to Mama, Hazel." Philip turned his horse toward Hazel's farm.

"Thanks for the sewing lesson, Hazel."

Hazel winked at her. "You're welcome. If you want help with that dress tomorrow, you know where I live."

She followed Philip into the darkness. Then called over her shoulder, "'Night."

Josephine watched them go. Maybe she had been too hard on Philip. She headed her horse toward the barn. Would she and Philip ever get over the fact that he was to blame for her being here? Thomas hadn't complained about being married to her, but he'd also not shown her that he'd like to make their marriage a real marriage. Not that she wanted him to, but still it might be nice to feel wanted.

She unsaddled the horse and sighed. This was her life now. Living with a husband who didn't love her and a brother-in-law she didn't trust.

Chapter Fifteen

Josephine woke with a headache the next morning. She'd worked on her dress until the wee hours of the morning and it finally looked right. Her gaze moved to where she'd hung it the night before. The pale blue shimmered in the morning sunlight.

Sunlight? She'd overslept. Josephine jumped from her bed and quickly dressed. The men would be starving. She glanced in the mirror and saw that her red curls were wild. In the past month her hair had grown and now touched her shoulders.

Grabbing a black ribbon, she pulled the messy mass into a ponytail and then practically ran from her bedroom. As soon as she opened the door, the smell of bacon and eggs filled her senses.

"Good morning, sunshine." Thomas stood at the stove dishing up eggs.

"Oh, Thomas, I'm so sorry. I overslept." Josephine looked around for Philip. "Where's that ornery brother of yours?"

Thomas laughed. "He's checking the henhouse for more eggs. They aren't laying as much as they used to.

But, then again, I guess chickens don't in the wintertime." He set the plate on the sideboard.

Her eyes widened. "He's doing my chores now?"

"Yep." Thomas carried a plate of bacon in one hand and a jar of jam in the other to the table.

Josephine groaned. "Oh, Thomas. I wish he wasn't doing that."

"Why not?" He placed a plate of eggs beside the bacon.

"I'm afraid I've been too hard on, Philip. He hates me." She sat down and dropped her head into her hands.

"What? I don't hate you," Philip said.

Thomas turned. "When did you come back in? And why did you come in the front door?"

Josephine ignored Thomas's questions. She looked at Philip. "Yes, you do."

"No, I don't. If anything, I love you."

This time it was Thomas who squeaked. "What?"

"Not love her, love her." He gave his brother an *Are you crazy?* look.

Both Thomas and Josephine frowned and said, "What?"

Philip laughed. He came into the room and sat down at the table. "I love her like a sister. Josephine, I need to apologize. I've been acting like a child. Thanks to you and Thomas, I now know what I want to do after the Pony Express."

Thomas set the coffeepot on the table with three cups. "And what's that?" He crossed his arms over his broad chest.

"Last night you mentioned I might enjoy making furniture and you were absolutely right. Even though I fussed at Josephine, the truth is I enjoy making things out of wood." He grinned at Josephine. "And to be honest, I think I can do an even better job than what I've done."

"That's wonderful, Philip." Josephine pushed the curls back that had escaped her sloppily pulled-up ponytail.

Thomas slapped his brother on the back. "Best news I've had all day. But are you planning on quitting the Pony Express?"

Philip shook his head. "Not for a while. I hope to make several pieces of nice furniture and then shop them around to see if they will sell." A sheepish grin crossed his face. "This could turn out to be like my idea of becoming a doctor. Short-lived. I might not be as good as I think."

Josephine took the plate Thomas handed her. "That's nonsense. I love the pieces you've made for us."

After the blessing was said, the conversation continued. Josephine listened to Philip and Thomas as they planned out Philip's future. She nibbled on a slice of extra-crispy bacon.

Not for the first time, the thought came to her that men had it much easier than women. If they wanted to do something, they just did it.

"Have you given any thought to how long it will take to actually get a business going?" Thomas asked.

Philip chuckled. "Surely not as long as it will a cattle ranch." He turned his attention to his breakfast.

What was this about a cattle ranch? Josephine's gaze met Thomas's across the table. He looked guilty of something, but what?

Philip glanced up. Mild shock filled his voice and he said, "You haven't told her yet?"

The sharp look from Thomas caused Philip to look away again. He muttered, "Sorry. I just thought…"

"It's obvious what you thought." Thomas clenched his teeth.

Josephine sat back and crossed her arms. Something was afoot here. Her husband looked both angry and guilty now. Philip also looked guilty. What could it be that Thomas had been hiding and Philip had been covering up for him? And why had she allowed herself to consider trusting Thomas?

Thomas felt her angry gaze upon him. All he'd asked of his brother was that he not tell Josephine his plans, to let him do it, and Philip couldn't even do that. He could understand her feelings of being left out and wanted to punch his brother like he had when they were kids.

Philip pushed his chair back, stuffed the rest of his bacon in his mouth and headed toward the door. "I'll go take care of the horses."

Thomas waited until the front door shut before looking back to Josephine. "Um, I was going to tell you this morning before my big-mouthed brother beat me to it."

"Tell me what?"

Was that anger or hurt in her voice? Thomas sighed. "I am no longer a Pony Express rider."

"All right." She crossed her arms over her chest and waited.

From the looks of things, she wasn't going to make this easy for him. He'd hoped to tell her his plans and hoped she'd be as excited as he was, but instead she looked across at him with speculation and mistrust.

"As Philip said, I'd like to start my own cattle ranch." Josephine reached for her necklace. He'd not seen her do that in quite a while. Now he understood that when she was distressed, the action seemed to offer some kind of comfort. "So we are moving?"

"Not for a while. I quit riding for the Pony Express, but I'm still the acting manager here at the relay station."

She took her plate to the hog bucket and raked her scraps inside. "I see."

Thomas pushed his chair back and followed her. He placed his hands on her shoulders. "Look, Josephine, I planned on telling you, but you slept in…"

She jerked away from him. "Oh, so now it's my fault you've been hiding things from me. You can't blame me, Thomas Young! This isn't a decision you just came up with this morning, is it?" She pushed the curls from her face and glared at him. Her brown eyes misted and her lashes moistened, but no tears fell from those beautiful eyes.

He reached for her and she stepped back.

"Thomas, I'm angry right now. So angry I'd appreciate it if you didn't touch me." With that Josephine spun on her heel and with a straight back marched to her room.

He flinched at the sound of wood banging into wood. Thomas felt rather than saw the new wall Josephine had just erected between them. His own anger began to simmer as he gathered the rest of the dishes and proceeded to pile them into the sink.

Perhaps he'd been foolish to quit riding for the Pony Express. He'd only done it so that he could spend more time with Josephine and make everyone's life more bearable. No, that wasn't entirely true. He'd also done it because he hated being away from home and with her arrival he'd been dreaming more and more about owning his own ranch.

Riding for the Pony Express was hard on a man's bones. He couldn't do that forever, but ranching, well, that was another thing altogether. It would be hard work, too, but it would be something that would establish him and Josephine. Who knew how long the Pony Express would run? Already the talk was that something called the telegraph would soon replace what they were working so hard to establish.

Thomas looked about. Josephine had turned the falling-down shack into a real home. He loved the simple womanly changes she'd made: curtains on the windows, pretty lace doilies that rested on various surfaces about the sitting room, even the fireplace bricks had been scrubbed clean of black soot and dirt from many years of use. He could only imagine what she could do in a real house.

His gaze moved to her bedroom door. Something shimmered in front of it. Thomas walked over and picked up the chain and locket. He started to knock on the door to return them to her, when he noticed the chain was broken. Thomas tucked it into his pocket to fix later. Right now, she was so angry, he didn't want to disturb her.

He returned to the job of cleaning the kitchen. Thomas poured fresh water into a pan and set it on the back of the stove to warm up so that he could do the breakfast dishes. Then he walked out to the well and pulled up fresh water, pouring it into the kitchen bucket that served as their drinking water.

"I'm sorry, Thomas."

Thomas turned at his brother's voice. He wanted

to blame Philip for his argument with Josephine but knew it was really his own fault. "It's not entirely your fault. I should have told her my dreams and plans long before now." He leaned against the well. "This being a husband is all new to me and I didn't think to tell her. I'm not used to sharing such stuff."

Philip nodded. "Yep, that's why I'm not the marrying kind. I have no desire to have to explain my every action to a woman."

Was that why Josephine was so angry? She expected him to tell her every little decision he made? Could he do such a thing? Did he even want to? Thomas was pretty sure he didn't.

"What are you doing out here, anyway? Shouldn't you be in there trying to make up to her?" Philip eyed the water bucket with interest.

"Nope, she's pretty angry. I think I'll let her stew for a bit before I try to reason with her again." Thomas picked up the freshly filled bucket and headed back to the kitchen door.

Philip frowned. "See, I'm not ready to have a wife. I'd go in there, tell her what's what, and then she'd just have to live with it."

Thomas laughed. "Yeah, and she'd shred you to bits with that sharp tongue of hers." He opened the door and stepped back inside the warm kitchen.

"No, she wouldn't. A woman needs to know her place," Philip said as he followed him back inside.

Thomas shook his head. "Philip, God never meant for us to tell a woman where her place is. He took the rib from our sides as a representation of where she belongs. Beside us, not behind and not under our feet."

The rude noise coming from Philip had Thomas

turning to face his brother. Thomas shook his head and told him, "You are right. You're nowhere near ready to get married. I suggest you read the Good Book before you ever propose to a woman. Because, brother, you need the help."

"You're just soft," Philip answered. He spun and headed out the back door. It, too, slammed on its hinges. At the rate his brother and wife were going, he'd be replacing the doors in no time.

Was he soft? No, Thomas didn't think so. He respected women and wished Philip felt the same way. The female race may not have treated either of them right, but God wouldn't want them to judge every woman by the actions of others. His hand moved to the scar on his face and Thomas frowned.

He sat down at the table and waited for the water to heat so that he could do the dishes. He dug into his pocket and pulled out Josephine's locket. Carefully he laid it down and studied the chain. The clasp had simply come lose from one of the links, a simple enough fix. He picked up the locket.

It was heavier than he expected. Thomas turned it over in his hand, admiring the delicate etching of leaves and flowers on its face. The clasp was different than others he'd seen, as well. It was fastened tight. He doubted Josephine had ever opened it.

What could be in there? Curiosity got the better of him and Thomas pried it open. He gasped as the contents were revealed. He quickly shut it back up tight and fixed the chain. Then he placed the necklace on the table at Josephine's spot.

Did Josephine have any idea that her necklace contained a gold nugget? His wife was rich. If she knew about the gold, would she have come out here to marry him? Thomas doubted it. She'd arrived scared and worn-out from riding the Pony Express. But, then again, maybe she was using him and Philip to hide her gold from her uncle. But why continue to stay with him now? So many questions rushed through his mind. Thomas didn't know what to think. His gaze moved to the necklace. Thomas wished with all his heart that he hadn't pried it open.

Chapter Sixteen

Josephine pressed her ear tighter against the bedroom door. Now that Philip had left, she could hear Thomas moving about the kitchen. It sounded like he was doing dishes.

He'd told Philip that women belonged at the side of a man, but he'd not allowed her into that position. She reminded herself that theirs was a marriage of convenience. In all reality, with that arrangement, she didn't belong beside Thomas. Or did she?

It was all so confusing. They'd never really talked about this aspect of their marriage. Oh, sure, they'd had fun and laughed a lot like friends, but not as life partners, not as husband and wife.

Josephine walked back to the chair that now sat by her bedroom window. Her fingers itched to pick up the Bible that lay on the table. What would the book say about her circumstances now? Did the Lord approve of her and Thomas's arrangement? Or had they muddied the waters of marriage in God's eyes? She both wanted to know and didn't want to know.

If the Bible said they should have a real marriage,

Josephine wasn't sure she could do that. She didn't trust Thomas. Couldn't trust him. And so far, he hadn't done anything to earn her trust.

She pushed up out of the chair and decided it would be best to face the man in the kitchen. Even though the tears she'd shed earlier were already dry, Josephine wiped at her face. She pulled the ribbon from her hair and ran a brush through the tangled curls. Once they were tamed, Josephine opened the door to her bedroom and faced her husband.

Thomas sat at the table, cradling a coffee mug in his hands. His green eyes met hers. His light brown hair was ruffled, as if he'd been raking his fingers through it over and over again.

She walked to the stove and found that beside the coffeepot was a pot of tea waiting for her. He'd thought about her needs once more. Why couldn't he have just told her what his plans were? Why had he hidden them from her? Josephine poured herself a cup of tea and added a generous amount of sugar to it. Only after she'd taken a sip of the sweet brew was she able to turn back around and face him.

"If I could go back in time, I would tell you about the Pony Express and the cattle ranch before Philip did," Thomas said in a still, firm voice. "But I can't. All I can do is say I'm sorry. I should have told you sooner."

Josephine nodded. "I know and I'm sorry, too. For a moment this morning, I forgot this wasn't a real marriage and you don't have to tell me all your plans." She set her cup down. Her necklace lay on the table. Josephine picked it up with a frown.

Her hand went to her neck. When had she lost her mother's locket?

"The chain broke. I found it and fixed it for you," Thomas said. He sipped at his coffee. His green eyes studied her as she put it back on.

"Thank you. I didn't even know I'd lost it." Josephine went to her dry larder and scooped out enough dry beans for several meals. She carried the bowl of beans to the table and carefully poured them out. Then she sat down and began sorting them, looking for rocks and small chunks of dirt. Josephine kept her eyes lowered on the job at hand.

"What are your dreams, Josephine?"

His question caught her off guard. "I guess I don't really have one anymore." She shrugged her shoulders.

Thomas pulled a pile of beans in front of him and also started sorting. "What did it used to be?" he asked.

"Well, when Ma was still alive, I wanted to learn doctoring, like her. But when she died, that dream died, too." Josephine looked down at the beans. "Now that I think about it, I only wanted to learn doctoring stuff so that I could be with her. So I guess that was my dream, to be close to my mother."

He pushed the clean pile to her and pulled more of the others to himself. "Josephine, I'd be honored if you would share my dream with me. And if you should ever think of something you want to do, I'd be pleased to be a part of that, too."

Josephine smiled at him. He was trying, and for that she was grateful. "Thank you. I've never lived on a cattle ranch, but if it will make you happy, I'm willing to try."

"I've been saving the money I've earned riding for the Pony Express. I'm not sure when I'll have enough saved to actually buy the land and cattle we'll need to get it started." Thomas finished the last bit of beans he'd pulled toward him and pushed the clean pile back to her, then scooped up the rocks and tiny dirt clods into his hand.

She watched as he walked to the back door and tossed the debris away. When he returned to the table, she asked, "Why did you stop riding? With the money the Pony Express pays, you could afford to get your ranch much quicker."

"I wanted to be closer to you." His green eyes bored into hers. "I thought if I stayed home, we could have a more natural life."

Josephine felt her heart do a flip. "You stopped riding because of me?"

He nodded. "I didn't like leaving you here for days at a time and I'm still making money being the relay station manager." Thomas chuckled. "And I am tired of the harshness of the ride."

She understood the latter part of his statement. Riding for hours on end at a grueling rate, through all types of weather and dangers, had grown old for her real fast. She was more than happy to leave the Pony Express trail behind. But did he really mean it when he'd said he quit because of her? He missed her? Could it be true?

Thomas stood again. "There's a rider coming through here in a little bit. I best get out there and get his mount ready for him." He walked to the door and pulled his coat from its hook. "You need any help with preparations for the Christmas dance?"

"Not unless you can sew." She smiled up at him, then it dawned on her. "I'm so sorry, Thomas. I should have asked you and Philip if you needed something sewed or repaired. Maybe a shirt washed?"

"No, I reckon not. I took mine out of storage and hung it out to air. Should be right as rain if I haven't gained a few pounds from all the good cooking you do."

"Thomas!" she scolded. "You bring those clothes to me and we'll get them washed and spruced up. We can't have you smelling all stale and hackneyed."

He stepped into his bedroom and gathered the items from nails along the wall. She took them from him and gave him a backward glance over her shoulder. "I may even have a surprise for you to wear."

"Well, I will treasure that surprise for certain."

"How do you know? It could be something feminine or an equally detestable color of fabric." Josephine found teasing him to be so easy, especially if it made him smile as he did now.

"Then I'll explain that my new wife made it for me and not one person will fault me." He turned to the door. "Of course, they will wonder what kind of wife would embarrass her husband so."

He burst out laughing as he turned back in time to see her place a hand on her hip, sputtering and indignant. "Why, Thomas Young. As if I could ever make something ugly."

As he left the warmth of the house, Josephine felt a chill run through her body. She pondered the past hour or so with Thomas. Was it possible he had begun to have feelings for her? Or was he simply stating that he felt that now that he was married, his place was to stay close to home? Josephine laid the clothes on the table and carried the beans to the stove. Now she wished she'd asked him what he meant by saying he didn't like leaving her for days at a time. Would she ever be able to ask him what he meant? Or had she missed her opportunity?

* * *

Thomas raised his chin high, fiddling with the bow tie's unfamiliar tightness. He cleaned up pretty well, if he did say so himself. An excitement had permeated their cabin these past few days as they'd worked together, doing chores ahead of time and washing and ironing clothes that hadn't been worn since the last barn dance. He knew it was the same way at Ma's, too.

He'd been at the past two Christmas dances, and the hard work had paid off, but Ma had driven them like an army sergeant. At least this year he and Philip had gotten out of the flurry of all that preparation.

He wondered what Josephine would say about his clean-shaven face. On a whim, he'd decided to show her what his respectable self looked like and he'd shaved all but his mustache. He ran a hand over the smoothness. He'd take some teasing from Philip, for sure, but it would be worth it if his Josephine liked it.

It wasn't lost on him that the scar could be seen a bit clearer, nor was he unaware that Josephine's opinion had come to mean a lot to him. But far from worrying him, this made him happy.

Somewhere along the line, his defenses had begun to subside. Their marriage had an indefinable feeling of rightness, even though it still served as a marriage of convenience. And though it bothered him that she might be concealing the fact that she carried a gold nugget around her neck, he found he enjoyed her easy nature and teasing ways.

A short rap sounded on the door and Philip entered, then whistled loudly. "Someone outdid themselves," he called over his shoulder. "Josephine, come see."

She rounded the door frame. "Oh, Thomas! You're so

handsome, you take my breath away." She crossed the room and stood before him, her eyes studying his face.

"You like it?" His voice seemed to come from a long way off. He cleared his throat. He turned his head side to side so that she could see his clean-shaven face.

"It's different, but I love it." She took his face in her hands and caressed the smoothness of his cheeks and underneath his chin.

He caught her hands between his and held them out to her sides. "And look at you! How lovely. Why, you're actually glowing." He spun her around, loving her giggle. "You'll be the belle of the ball this evening."

"Don't be silly, Thomas. I can't hold a candle to the pretty girls that will show up." Her hand moved to her mass of curls.

"In my eyes, you'll be the only one I see." Where had the confession come from? He searched her face to see what kind of reaction such bold words would have.

She leaned lightly into him, tilting her face toward him. He felt as if his breath were suddenly cut off and not by the bow tie. Was she leaning in for a kiss? Or was she simply going to tease him once more before dancing away?

"What's going on in here?" Hazel stepped into the room. "We're going to be late."

Josephine immediately pulled away from him. Frustration welled up in Thomas. Would he never be alone with his wife? Did he really want to be?

"Well, now, Hazel, you interrupted a syrupy little scene where the two lovebirds were gushing over how beautiful they are to each other. It was pert near nauseating." Philip laughed. "Thank the Lord you came in when you did." His teasing caused stains of scarlet to appear on Josephine's cheeks.

Thomas was having none of it. He tucked her hand into his elbow and walked with her to his door. "There was a time when a man's bedroom was his sanctuary. Uninvited guests could be tossed out on their ear."

Philip roared with laughter and Hazel chuckled. "That's rich, brother, since Josephine and Hazel are the uninvited guests. It's my room, too."

"And as I've already pointed out," Hazel said, "that situation needs to be resolved."

"And you've also pointed out that we're going to be late, so let's get into the wagon. Let's get going." Thomas noted Josephine's silence, but the eyes she turned up to him were openly amused. Then her eyes rounded and she pulled away from him.

"Thomas, I almost forgot your gift. Philip, will you carry these things to the wagon, then help Hazel in, while I show Thomas what I made him especially for tonight?"

"Hmm, Hazel, let's go. I think we've just been dismissed."

Thomas felt a grin pull at the corners of his mouth. His little wife knew how to clear a room if she wanted to. He found her actions almost as pleasing as the idea of a gift. As the door closed behind the other two, Josephine went to the hearth and lifted a small package off the mantel. She handed it to him, then clenched both hands in front of her. When he kept staring at her, she gestured for him to open it.

"This is lovely." Inside lay a silken piece of fabric, almost the same color of the blue shirt he wore. As he lifted it out of the package, he tossed the wrapping on the chair behind them. The softness of the fabric against his palm felt amazing.

"It's a scarf, Thomas." She took it from him and, standing on tiptoe, placed it around his neck. Her hair touched his cheek and her breath against his ear sent a tingle of happiness down his spine. She crossed the ends over each other under his chin, then patted his chest. Her eyes glowed with pride at her accomplishment. "Oh, it looks so good on you, Thomas. The color is perfect."

He studied what he could see of the scarf and noticed a green thread mingled with the blue, a contrast that would allow him to wear it with several different colors. But none could compare with the glow and color in the brown eyes staring up at him. "Yes, the color is perfect, and so are the hands that made it." He took her hands and placed a kiss in each palm. Then he pulled her into a close hug. They remained like that, each lost in their own thoughts and feelings, till a shrill whistle rent the air. Thomas gathered her close under one arm and led them to the wagon.

This promised to be the perfect evening.

Chapter Seventeen

Josephine's mouth dropped open in awe and a soft gasp escaped her. The Young family's new barn was a delight to behold. Tiny lanterns were strung from the rafters, adding a golden glow to the freshly cut logs and wood floor. Sprigs of mistletoe and holly were placed high and in bunches along the walls. Knitted socks striped like candy canes hung behind the woodstove and the crisp greenery scents stated Christmas loud and clear. Pine cones filled a huge basket and red bows decorated the sides of the basket.

And if that weren't enough, the smell of cinnamon and pumpkin bread wafted through the air, drawing them toward tables set near the woodstove. But the center of attention could only be the huge Christmas tree reaching almost to the eaves. It held decorations of every kind, type and make. There were wooden ornaments, cloth ones and paper chains. Josephine had never seen anything like it.

"Looks like a good thing we didn't get the stalls made and the tack room finished. This open floor is perfect for a barn dance." Thomas addressed Philip but included Josephine in the conversation, making her feel that she belonged.

Philip placed the basket of food Josephine had prepared on the table with the other bowls. She began removing the dishes she'd brought, Hazel doing the same. Thomas helped her place the deer stew with the meat and the sweet-potato pie with the vegetables. Philip lent the women a hand, but they were still close enough to talk undisturbed.

"I didn't know you were supposed to be working on this barn," Josephine said. "I've had you making furniture every free minute you had. I fear your ma might be a tad upset with me."

"No, no, it's not like that. We helped get it under roof last year when the barn burned down, but Seth didn't want the inside built with green logs. If you look closely, you'll see the logs are cut and drying but being used as seats around the dance floor." Philip pointed them out to her and she breathed a sigh of relief.

Then they heard Seth clear his throat and begin welcoming everyone to the dance. Rebecca stood by his side, beautiful in a new white dress that looked straight out of the pages of a magazine. She stared at her husband as if he was the best thing since warm buttered popcorn. Josephine felt a tiny bit of envy. What would it be like to know that kind of love?

Everyone bowed their head for prayer, and then the fiddler started a round of "My Bonny Lass." Before long they lined up to do a Virginia reel and Josephine whirled and glided till she felt completely out of breath and begged to sit a few songs out. Thomas teased her, but his mother came to her rescue.

"Josephine, will you come to the house with me?

I need to fetch more bread and check on my stew. I kept it cooking on the house stove so others could heat things up in here."

Josephine started when Rebecca hooked their arms together and enjoyed a sense of belonging she hadn't felt in a long time as Rebecca greeted others, instructing them where to place certain items. She felt like a real daughter-in-law, though there was nothing further from the truth.

Outside the barn, the winter air cooled her flushed cheeks and she shivered, thankful for the warmth of their close bodies. They entered the house and Josephine stopped in her tracks.

Then she said the first thing that entered her mind. "You certainly go overboard for Christmas." She immediately regretted the words and tried to explain. "I don't mean in a bad way. Just that there are lots of decorations here and in the barn. They're so beautiful."

Rebecca didn't seem in the least offended. "Let me explain." She headed straight to the stove while Josephine took in the tree, not quite as tall as the one in the barn and decorated in angels made from hankies and paper—there were even knitted ones—as well as crosses and tiny handmade paper Bibles. It was the cutest thing she'd ever seen and so unique.

Then her eyes caught the mantel. Five white china plates, painted with the manger scene and a yellow star, were propped in a groove carved in the wood. A strand of holly with red berries twined between the plates, making the art stand out even more. On the hearth were wooden replicas of Mary, Joseph and Baby Jesus. Josephine reverently touched the pieces, her heart in her throat.

"When I was a kid in the orphanage, there was no celebration of Christmas at all," Rebecca said. "And if the headmistress caught us with candy canes or even a red bow, she would discipline us. In school we made paper chains to put all over the room and were given an orange to eat, but absolutely not at the orphanage."

She paused as if in deep thought, then shook her head slightly and continued. "My faith grew so strong during that time. It's actually the only thing I had to rely on. It kept me sane and I repeatedly asked if I could read the Christmas story from the Bible to the other kids, but was never allowed to. I so enjoyed the passage from chapter two in the book of Luke, and I made cloth dolls with the manger scene occupants to secretly entertain the younger children. But the headmistress found them and punished me without supper that night. I made my mind up then and there that when I became an adult, I would celebrate the birth of our Savior more than any other holiday that we might observe."

She lifted the stew from the stove and set it on the table. "But then life happened and I forgot it. Then, one night, I told John all the things I missed as a child and how much I'd especially missed Christmas. From then on, every Christmas, the decorations became more meaningful and more…well, just lots more." She laughed and Josephine could see why all the Pony Express boys loved her so much. Rebecca nodded at a linen-covered platter. "Will you bring the bread, Josie?"

Josephine stared at her a brief moment and then hurried to do as Rebecca asked. Only her uncle and Mr. Grossman had ever called her Josie. But instead of saying it with mockery, there was a warmth in Rebecca's tone.

Josephine was of a mind that you only gave nicknames to the people dear to your heart. Could that be why Rebecca had called her Josie? She felt a warm glow flow through her. She exhaled a long sigh of contentment. Tonight there were no shadows across her heart.

When they reentered the barn, she noticed Thomas seemed agitated as he spoke to Hazel. Hazel nodded toward where she and Rebecca stood by the door waiting for a pathway to the tables. Immediately his frown cleared and a smile as intimate as a kiss crossed his lips. He made his way toward them, weaving through the bodies that seemed to have tripled since their trip to the house.

She watched him, impressed with the presence he commanded and happily flattered with the eager affection he seemed not to care that anyone saw. His hands closed over hers where they held the platter. He leaned in close, his mouth near her ear.

"I missed you."

The intensity in his lowered voice and the shared private moment gave her a pulse-pounding confidence. She smiled into his eyes, placed a hand on his chest and spoke in a voice she hardly recognized. "Likewise." Josephine knew it was true. She had missed him in the short time they were apart.

"Yes?"

"Oh, yes. Definitely." In the background the fiddle music had become sweeter and someone began playing a soft medley on the harmonica.

"Then may I have this dance, Mrs. Young?"

She eagerly passed the plate of bread to the nearest person, not even sure who it was, and placed her hand in that of her husband. They danced in front of the tall

Christmas tree. Josephine knew this would become a night she'd never forget, no matter the circumstances ahead.

Several days later, Josephine paced the sitting room. Darkness filled the windows as the clock on the fireplace mantel ticked the hours away. Where was Thomas? He had gone to town to pick up supplies for the Pony Express and had said he'd be home by dark. It was almost midnight.

She heard the sound of a horse arriving in the front yard. Josephine hurried to the front door and pulled it open. It would be either Philip, who had been gone hunting all day, or Thomas. She held the lantern up over her head and waited for the rider to come into view.

A man entered the lamplight and called out at the same time. "Josephine Dooly, is that you?"

Her heart rate sped up and Josephine almost stepped back through the doorway and slammed the door. He'd found her. She swallowed the lump in her throat and answered, "Yes, Uncle. It is me."

He rode his horse up to the porch and slid out of the saddle. Tying the reins to the railings, he said, "I'm so glad I found you. It is freezing out here." His boots pounded in the night air as he climbed the stairs a short distance from her.

Josephine's heart raced in her chest with such force she was sure her uncle would see it under her dress. "Come in." Was that her voice? Why was she inviting him inside?

When he passed her, Josephine thought she smelled liquor on his breath. She followed him inside and shut the door. "What do you want, Uncle?"

He turned. "Is that any way to treat your guardian?" His black eyebrows rose in question.

He'd definitely been drinking. Josephine had known this day was coming. She knew he'd find her, but she'd hoped that Thomas would be home when he did. "You aren't my guardian any longer. I got married." Her voice shook, but she raised her chin and stared him straight in the eyes.

"Married, huh?"

"Yes, sir."

"How long?" He rubbed his chin.

Josephine leaned against the wooden door. "Long enough."

His gaze dropped to her stomach. "I see."

She hadn't intended for him to assume that she was carrying a child, but, since he had, Josephine decided not to correct him. It might just keep him from pressing her to leave. "I am a married woman now, so you can't marry me off to Mr. Grossman."

Her uncle dropped into the rocker closer to the fireplace. "What am I going to do now?" he moaned. "If only I had the gold your father found all those years ago."

Josephine straightened from the door and shook her head. "What gold?"

He ignored her question. His gray eyes looked up at her. "Where is this husband of yours?"

It never occurred to her to lie to him, but it was obvious from his expression that that was exactly what he thought she was doing now. "He went to town to get supplies for the Pony Express." She walked to the stove and poured a cup of coffee. "And I don't know what gold you are talking about."

"The gold your father found that helped him and your mother get rich."

He'd had too much to drink if he thought her parents were rich. She'd never heard of her father finding gold. Josephine carried the hot coffee back to her uncle. "Here, drink this. It will warm you up." *And hopefully sober you up, too*, she thought. Josephine crossed her arms over her chest.

He took the drink. "Thank you."

"Uncle, I think you are mistaken. My parents never told me of any gold. Papa worked hard at the factory to make his living." She sank down into Thomas's favorite rocker.

He laughed. "But how did he come to own the factory, if he didn't have money?"

Josephine shook her head. "He worked hard, and when the old owner died, he willed the factory to Papa. Remember?" The more he talked, the more she was sure her uncle was sick or drunk. Her parents' home was nice, but they were far from truly wealthy.

He studied her face. "Perhaps you are right. But, Josie girl, Mr. Grossman isn't a man to be trifled with. I'm sure we can get you out of this marriage." He stood.

"I don't want out of my marriage." She stepped away from him. "For the first time in a long time, I'm happy." Josephine realized what she was saying was the truth. She was happy with her life here at the Pony Express relay station.

He frowned. "Josie girl, you would be so much better off with Mr. Grossman. He has money, a fine house and lots of wealthy friends."

She shook her head. "I'm not leaving my husband, Uncle."

"Then you have condemned me to death." He sat his cup on the side table and dropped his head into his hands.

Josephine watched his shoulders shake. She didn't want harm to come to her uncle. Yes, he'd treated her badly and attempted to sell her to cover his debts, but at the end of the day, he was still her family. Her only family. "Uncle, I have a little money put away. You can have it."

He looked up at her between his fingers. "How much?"

Josephine walked into the kitchen and pulled out a jar where she'd put her household money and the money she'd made while working as a Pony Express rider. She couldn't give him the household money, at least, not until she spoke to Thomas about it, but she could give him her wages. Carefully, Josephine separated the two. She tucked the remainder of the money back into the jar and then returned to her uncle.

His gaze met hers as he took the cash. "Thank you, child. This will keep him at bay for a while. I'll figure out how to get the rest." He tucked the bills into his shirt pocket and smiled at her.

"I'm glad I could help." She wanted to send him on his way, but it was cold outside and the snow-covered roads were hazardous to travel at night. Where was Thomas? Her gaze moved to the door. Surely he or Philip would return soon.

"Would it be all right with your husband if I camped out here by the fireplace tonight?" he asked, pulling Josephine from her thoughts.

She wanted to tell him no, that he couldn't stay, but instead nodded. "I'm sure Thomas won't mind." Josephine went into her bedroom and got a quilt and blanket for him to use.

He quickly spread the blanket out and used it as a bed, then took his boots off. "You have a really nice place here, Josephine. Your ma and pa would have been proud to see where you live today."

Was he being sincere or sarcastic? That was the problem. Josephine had never been able to read her uncle. She simply rubbed her arms. It wasn't cold in the room, but having him under her roof left Josephine feeling odd and unhappy.

"Well, if you are comfortable here, I believe I'll retire to my room." Then she thought about the poor horse tied to the front porch. "Uncle, aren't you going to take the horse out to the barn? I'm sure Thomas wouldn't mind if you put him in a stall out there."

"Naw, he'll be fine for the night. I plan on leaving before the sun rises. The weather won't hurt him any." He turned his back on her and faced the fireplace.

Josephine didn't like it. Horses deserved better treatment. The temptation to go out and take care of the horse pulled at her. What would Thomas think when he came home and discovered a strange horse at the porch and a stranger sleeping in his house?

She made the decision to stay up and wait for him to come home. Her uncle's soft snores filled the sitting room. Good, maybe now he'd sleep off the strong drink he'd enjoyed earlier. Josephine walked to her room and quietly shut the door.

The bed looked inviting. Josephine pushed the thought aside and walked to her table and chair. She'd sit down and read the Bible until Thomas came home.

A few hours later her neck and back ached. Josephine

raised her head from the table where she'd fallen asleep. Wind whipped about the window. Snow and sleet pelted the walls of her bedroom. The sound shot pain through her already aching head.

Josephine stood and stretched her back. Then she remembered her uncle in the sitting room. He'd said he wanted to get an early start. She could just imagine his anger at her for sleeping late. She walked to the door and quietly pulled it open.

His bedding lay near the fireplace, folded neatly, but he was nowhere to be seen. Josephine hurried to the front door and pulled it open. Cold air rushed past her and snow swirled about her feet. The horse was gone. She sighed in relief and closed the door. He'd taken the money and left. For that she was grateful. Until she noticed that her money jar was empty and the door to Thomas and Philip's room stood open.

Chapter Eighteen

Thomas had begun to think that Josephine had made up the story of her uncle and his plans to marry her off. Now he wished she had. "So he took all our money?"

Josephine nodded. "I'm so sorry. I never dreamed he'd steal it from me." Tears marred her face.

"It's all right, Josephine. At least he's gone now. We'll start saving again." He thought about the gold nugget that hung from her neck but just as easily shoved the thought aside. It was hers, not his or Philip's.

"But what about your ranch?"

Thomas pulled her to him and wrapped her in a tight hug. "If it's God's will, He'll supply a way for us to get the ranch."

Philip grunted. "Yeah, he took my saddle money, too."

Josephine pulled out of Thomas's embrace. "Saddle money?"

"I've been saving for a new saddle." Philip tossed kindling into the fireplace. "It's my own fault. I felt the Lord urging me to come home last night, but I thought I might get another big buck."

"Oh, Philip. I am so sorry." Her brown eyes filled with sorrow. "I shouldn't have trusted him."

Thomas patted her shoulder. "I'm just glad he didn't hurt you."

"Yeah, me, too." Philip stood. "Josephine, do you think he'll come back?"

She shook her head. "No. He got what he wanted." Her hand moved to the necklace resting on her chest. "More than likely, my uncle will look for the closest card game. He always thinks he'll make enough money to pay off the men he already owes."

The snowstorm beat against the cabin walls. Had Josephine's uncle gotten caught in the snowstorm? Was he somewhere freezing to death? Thomas prayed not; he wouldn't wish that type of death on any man. He didn't think Josephine had thought of that possibility yet. Hopefully, she wouldn't.

"If you two don't mind, I'd like to go lie down for a little while." Josephine turned toward her bedroom. "I didn't sleep well last night and my head is achy today."

Thomas prayed she wasn't coming down with a cold. "No, go ahead."

Philip sent her a smile. "It's a good day to rest. With this weather, I doubt we'll be doing much more than that ourselves."

"Thank you." She shut her door.

Thomas walked over to where Philip stood. "Poor dear. She's been through a lot."

Philip sat down in one of the rockers. "It would seem so." He waited a few moments, then lowered his voice and asked, "How long should I wait before I go out looking for him?"

The fire crackled at their feet. "You thinking he got caught in this storm, too?"

"He's a townie. Probably only has a light coat on." Philip shook his head. "I'll go look for him. If Josephine is correct, he's headed back to Dove Creek."

Thomas stood. "I'll go."

"No, you should stay here with her. Don't tell her that I've gone looking for her uncle. There's no need to worry her." Philip pulled his boots back on.

"Thanks for taking her feelings into consideration."

Philip sat up, then stood. "That's what family does." He pulled his coat from the nail by the door. "I wouldn't be a good husband, but I'm not a bad brother-in-law." He grinned as he put on his gloves.

"You are that. Don't stay out too long. If you can't find him within the hour, come home."

"Will do." Philip pulled the door open and disappeared in a cloud of swirling snow.

Thomas sat back down in his chair. He reached over and picked up his Bible. Worrying about Philip and Josephine's uncle would accomplish nothing. Reading God's Word would soothe his troubled mind and educate him at the same time.

Forty-five minutes later, Philip returned. He came in the door looking as if he'd walked instead of riding his horse through the snow. Thomas didn't need his brother to tell him he'd found Josephine's uncle dead.

"Where did you find him?" Thomas poured Philip a hot cup of coffee and carried it to him.

Philip took the mug and sipped from it. He leaned back his head and closed his eyes. "He was half in and half out of the river." He opened his eyes, sighed and took another sip of his hot coffee.

Thomas swallowed. "Where is he now?"

"I put his horse in the lean-to with mine and covered his body with snow behind the barn." Philip yawned.

"Thank you. Now go get some rest. I'll tell Josephine when she gets up from her nap." Thomas ran a hand over his face.

Philip finished the coffee and stood once more. "He was clutching his shirt pocket when I found him." Philip pulled a wad of money from his front pants pocket. "This is what was inside."

Thomas took the money and sighed. How would Josephine take this news? He wasn't looking forward to being the one to tell her that her uncle had died. But it was his responsibility as her husband to break it to her gently. How did one go about doing that?

Josephine still couldn't believe that her uncle had frozen to death. She had cried tears for him and wished that he hadn't left when he had, but in her mind the loving uncle she knew as a child had long been dead. She sighed. Now it was time to decide what to do with his body.

Thomas touched her shoulder. "Josephine, Philip and I will take care of your uncle."

"The ground is frozen, Thomas." Her voice sounded small in her own ears.

He knelt down beside her chair and took her cold hands into his warmer ones. "Yes, but a while back Philip and I discovered a small cave. We can move him there. It will make a good grave site. Don't you think so, Philip?" Thomas rubbed his thumb across the back of her hand.

Philip stood by the window looking out at the falling

snow. Her brother-in-law seemed lost in the storm outside. He'd already helped so much; she couldn't bring herself to ask him to do more.

"That it would." He turned to face them. "I'm so sorry, Josephine. If I hadn't written to you, this would never have happened."

Josephine stood.

Thomas released her hands.

She walked over to Philip. "This wasn't your fault, Philip. My uncle allowed his gambling to direct his actions. You are not to blame. Not in my eyes and not in God's." Josephine hugged him about the waist.

He enfolded her in his arms for a quick hug. "Thank you." Philip released her and stepped back. "I should be comforting you, not the other way around."

Thomas walked over to them. "We comfort each other in times like these. That makes us a strong family unit. We may not be wealthy in money or material things, but we're rich beyond measure in the important things that count."

"Ma says that all the time." Philip's grin somehow lightened the atmosphere in the room and Thomas swept a hand through his sandy-brown hair as if relieved there would be no more serious sadness for the day.

Thomas reached for his coat, his green eyes alight with warmth. "Let's get our evening chores out of the way. The temperature seems to be falling faster than night."

Philip nodded and then hurriedly tucked into his coat, gloves and scarf. He opened the door and left the two of them alone. Thomas turned to Josephine. His soft eyes looked deeply into hers. "Are you all right?"

"I am. It's sad that he is gone, but it's also a relief.

I know that sounds horrible, but it's how I feel." Josephine offered him a wobbly smile.

He walked over to her and hugged her close. "Well, if things should change and you need someone to talk to, I'm here for you." Thomas tilted her face up so that he was looking into her eyes.

His sincerity touched her heart. She nodded. "You will be the first to know." Josephine stepped out of his grasp. "You better get going. Philip will have both your chores finished and I won't have time to get my surprise done."

He grinned, brushed the side of her face with the back of his hand and opened the door. Cold air rushed into the room, causing Josephine to shiver. "After all this, you have a surprise for us?"

"Yep, I think it's something you both will enjoy."

As the door closed behind him, Josephine went into action. She mixed a cake batter Hazel had just given her the recipe for and put it in the side oven of the cookstove. So far they'd had pies and fritters, but not once a cake, especially a chocolate one. She fried ham slices and made biscuits, but the secret she'd mentioned to Thomas was the two ears of popping corn Hazel had shared with her.

Hazel had told her that popping corn had been scarce since the drought from this past year's growing season. The general store had gotten in an order and Hazel had been fortunate enough to be there when it arrived and had purchased several ears.

The men returned right as she took the cake from the oven; the smell filled the house with mouthwatering goodness. Both of them crowded round, oohing and ahhing, until she made them leave the kitchen.

She sat the cake in her room to cool so she could frost it, another treat they would share, and then she called them to the table for ham, biscuits and coffee. When Thomas finished, he reached for the jar of apple butter, but Josephine lightly smacked his hand.

"Don't you dare spoil dessert. Have you already forgotten that beautiful cake?"

"I'm pretty sure I have room for an apple butter biscuit and cake." He reached again and she moved the jar closer to her.

"But you might not have room for my surprise."

Thomas and Philip both froze. "You mean the cake is not the surprise?" Philip all but licked his lips, his face brightened at the suggestion.

"The cake is only half." Josephine laughed. "You both look like kids on the night before Christmas."

They finished their meal, laughing and teasing, and Josephine felt her smile broaden with approval when Thomas patted his stomach and exhaled a long sigh of contentment. She washed up the dishes, and then when the men settled into chairs in front of the fireplace, she put oil and butter in her biggest cast-iron pot. She took the kernels from the two ears of corn, which she'd stripped from the cobs earlier, and as quietly as possible poured them into the kettle.

Every evening they sat together and Thomas or Philip read from the Bible, but this evening she had a new book for them to enjoy. She went to fetch it from her bedroom and on the way back placed the pot on the stove. Josephine handed the book to Thomas.

"What's this?" Thomas turned the book to read the cover. "*A Christmas Carol* by Charles Dickens." He glanced at Philip. "Isn't this the story Rebecca reads just about every Christmas?"

Philip nodded. "I think it is. You're right, Josephine. This is a special treat."

And at just that moment, the first kernel popped and both men jumped. "What was that?" Philip asked.

More popping sounded from the kitchen area. The smell of butter and popcorn filled the air. She waited to see which of the men would learn her secret first.

"Popcorn!" Thomas raised his eyebrow at Josephine. "That's the surprise?" At her nod, a grin the size of Texas split his face. "We haven't had popcorn since this time last year. Where did you get it?"

"An order came in at the general store last week and Hazel was there. She bought several ears and shared them with us."

Josephine hurried to shake the pot, not wanting the popcorn to stick or burn, and the sound drowned out conversation for a few minutes, but she noticed that both the men were up and had big bowls ready for their share of the treat. She almost laughed out loud. "And where is my bowl?"

"This is our bowl," Thomas replied, to her interested amazement. "That's the fun of having popcorn. Sharing it."

A new and unexpected warmth surged through her. She poured the popcorn into each bowl and still had leftovers in the pot. Josephine sprinkled a bit of salt over both servings and they took their seats again in the sitting room.

Philip tossed a few kernels into the air and caught them with his mouth. He grinned at Josephine, who quickly did the same, proving to him that girls could do that, too. She shot a grin back at him.

"Marley was dead." Thomas's voice as he began reading was strong and assertive, making the story come alive. He managed to grab handfuls of popcorn from their shared bowl as he read.

His munching and reading at the same time didn't take away from the story. Instead it seemed to bring them closer together as they enjoyed the evening and the book.

Josephine fought back the sadness her uncle's death brought. She'd lost her uncle, but she'd gained a family she'd only dreamed about since the death of her mother. Something that Josephine needed.

She looked to her husband, who continued to read and munch on the popcorn treat. Pulling her focus back to the story, Josephine felt her hand touch Thomas's as they both reached for popcorn at the same time. It felt right and natural, but would it last?

With the passing of her uncle, she couldn't help but think about her father. He'd deserted her when she needed him most. Would Thomas do the same? Josephine didn't know. And that scared her almost as much as the emotions that Thomas's touch brought to her.

Chapter Nineteen

Two days later, Thomas came through the back door. "I've been thinking. How would you like to go out in a little bit and we'll get a Christmas tree?"

Josephine set her pan of fresh bread on the sideboard with the two loaves she'd made earlier. Having a Christmas tree in the house was new to the area and she was thrilled to get to be a part of it. "I would love that. Give me a few minutes to put on a warmer dress." She pulled her apron off and hung it by the stove.

He turned to leave. "I'll go tell Philip you agreed."

"Is he going with us?" Why was she feeling disappointed that it wasn't going to be just the two of them?

Thomas shook his head. "No, he'll need to stick around here. We're expecting a rider this morning."

Joy hit her and she had to quickly turn so that he couldn't see the pleasure those words gave her. "I'll get ready."

He chuckled. "I'll finish my chores and speak to Philip." The door clicked shut behind him.

Happiness at the sound of his pleasure caused her to pause. Was she falling in love with her husband?

Or had that already happened? Josephine pushed the foolish thoughts away. She didn't want to love him, because with love came trust.

She walked to her bedroom. A couple of months ago she'd felt truly alone in the world. Today, even though she'd recently lost a family member, she felt the warmth of loved ones. Not romantic love—but the kind that said, *we care, we're here for you.*

Josephine exchanged her day dress to a heavier dress and put on thicker socks. She felt the surge of excitement at the thought of going out to cut down a Christmas tree. Her mind began to work on how to decorate for the holiday. Rebecca's house had been beautiful with all her many decorations. Some her family had made; others were store-bought.

At the winter dance, she'd enjoyed Rebecca's story about the Christmas decorations and the tree. Josephine had hoped Thomas would want to do the same in their home but hadn't asked. Then her uncle had arrived and, until today, she'd forgotten all about the tree.

She came out of her bedroom and wondered how long Thomas would be gone. Her gaze moved about the sitting room. Should they get a grand tree like the one at Rebecca's? Or a smaller one to sit on a table? She'd wait and ask Thomas, although a small tree would be easier to cut down and for her to decorate.

The fireplace mantel could use some little decorations, too. Josephine walked back into her room and pulled out the various colors of yarn she'd been using to make both Thomas and Philip scarves for Christmas, green, blue, yellow, brown and black. In the bottom of the bag, she found the red yarn.

Josephine carried everything to the bed and sat down

on the edge. She dropped the balls of yarn on the quilt cover. When the black one rolled off the bed, Little One grabbed the ball and took off running. Josephine laughed and let the puppy go. Little One would enjoy the yarn and wouldn't be whining to get on the bed.

Using all but the black, Josephine pulled them together and placed a knot at one end. Then she began to twist the various colors into a braided rope. It would look beautiful hanging over the mantel.

As her fingers worked, she thought about Thomas's green-and-yellow shirt. It was almost complete. Her gaze moved to the blue-and-brown material that rested on the bed. She'd have to get busy on Philip's shirt soon. The scarves were going to match them perfectly.

Placing the gifts around the base of the tree was going to be so much fun. She thought of her friend Hazel, whom she knew was also making gifts for Thomas and Philip. Maybe if they got a small tree, they could get one for Hazel, too.

The older woman was such a good friend to her. A tree with ready-made decorations might make a nice gift for Hazel. She'd also have a place to put her gifts while they all anticipated Christmas Day, which was only two weeks away.

Thomas's voice boomed through the kitchen and into her bedroom. "Josephine! Are you ready?"

She quickly laid down the long braided garland and hurried into the sitting room. "I'm sorry. I got busy making decorations for the fireplace mantel. Let me slip into my coat."

"We're not in that big of a hurry. Take your time. Don't forget your gloves and scarf, too. It's really cold out there."

Thomas shut the door behind him. He picked up Little One and untangled the yarn around her little feet.

After wrapping her scarf around her neck, Josephine looked to her husband. "Ready?"

He set the puppy back down and set the yarn on the table. "I thought it might be good to hitch the sled to the horse and take it instead of walking. There is no telling how high the drifts are out in the woods."

Josephine clapped her hands. "A sleigh ride." She hurried out into the cold air and breathed in deeply. Her breath came out in a white cloud. "Brrr, it is cold out here."

Thomas laughed. "I told you so. Are you sure you want to venture out today? It might warm up tomorrow."

Her gaze moved to the sleigh. It was painted red. The horse shook its head and the sound of bells filled the cold air. Josephine smiled. Did Thomas realize how romantic this all was? Or did he simply see it as a trip in the woods to cut down a tree?

"Oh, no, there is no way we are waiting until tomorrow. I'm ready now." To prove it she hurried to the sled but then stopped. "Well, almost. Hold on a moment."

Thomas followed her back inside. "What are you doing?"

"I'm getting some things we might need." She poured hot coffee into two jars and wrapped them each in a towel. After setting them on the table, she hurried to the bedroom and pulled two heavy blankets out of the trunk Philip had made for her.

She carried them back to Thomas. "See? These will keep us warm." She handed him the blankets and then went for the jars.

His green eyes shone. "You really are amazing."

Josephine wasn't sure what he meant by that but returned his smile. "Why, thank you. I think you're pretty amazing, too." She tucked one of the jars under her arm and opened the door once more.

Thomas pushed the puppy back inside with his foot, shut the door and hurried to help her climb aboard the sleigh. His green eyes met hers and sent her heart into a tailspin. She laughed and settled on the sled.

Josephine tucked the coffee against her side and reached for the blankets. She wrapped one about her legs and then waited for Thomas to climb aboard. As soon as he was seated and had the reins in his hands, she tucked the other blanket around his legs.

They waved goodbye to Philip, who stood in front of the barn watching them. Thomas laughed and yelled to him, "There is fresh coffee on the stove."

Philip called after them. "Have fun."

Josephine planned on having fun. For the first time in a long time, she felt free of worry. Her uncle could no longer hurt her and her husband had her heart aflutter with just one look. What could be better?

Thomas guided the horse behind the house and along the small path that Hazel took to her house. He had already scouted out the perfect tree for their small house and hoped that Josephine liked it as much as he did. Snow began to drift lazily around them as they rode.

"Oh, Thomas, it's beautiful." Josephine stuck her tongue out and caught a snowflake. She giggled and looked up at him.

A hint of the fragrant lavender water she enjoyed drifted under his nose on the breeze that carried the snowflakes. "Yes, it is." He wasn't talking about the snow but about his lovely wife. Her pretty red curls hung to her shoulders, her beautiful brown eyes sparkled with happiness and her sweet pink lips begged to be kissed.

He looked away. Her strength after losing her uncle, and now her excitement over Christmas, had him admiring her far more than he should. "I hope you like the tree I have picked out."

"I'm sure I will." She seemed to take in their surroundings all at once. "It's been a long time since I've been out in the snow. I can't get over how everything is glistening."

He smiled. "It's pretty if you aren't trying to get the mail through."

"You don't miss it, do you?" she asked.

Thomas shrugged. "Sometimes I do. It was exciting being a part of something so big. What about you?"

"I miss the freedom of the open trail. But I don't miss the constant cold, the worry of the Indians chasing me as I hurried through their lands, and I really don't miss the outlaws that tried to steal the mochila." She grinned at him.

He pulled the horse to a stop at the edge of a grove of trees. "This is it. We'll have to walk the rest of the way. The trees are too close together for the horse and sled." Thomas jumped from the sleigh. He helped Josephine down and reached for the ax under the seat. "Hopefully the snow won't be too deep."

"We're not that far from Hazel's, are we?"

Thomas started walking toward the tree line. "No, she's just over that little hill." He pointed to his right.

"Do you think we can get her a tree, too?"

He felt her hand slip into his left one. Thomas

glanced in her direction and realized that she was struggling to get through the deepening snow. "Sure, if you think she'd like one."

"Well, I thought maybe we could get a small one and then make a few decorations for it tonight. It will be fun to take it to her tomorrow." She panted, trying to keep up with him. "Kind of an early Christmas present."

Thomas slowed down. "That is a very sweet thing to do. I'm sure she'll love having a tree of her own." He stopped walking and turned to face her.

Her cheeks were a pretty pink. Her lips were red. He couldn't stop himself. Bowing slightly, Thomas gently brushed his lips across her cool ones. He watched her eyes widen and then her lashes drift down. Thomas pulled her tighter into his arms and kissed her again.

When he released her, Josephine asked, "What was that for?"

He rested his forehead against hers. "Because you are so sweet and, well, I just wanted to kiss you."

"Oh, all right." She giggled and reached up to touch his face.

Thomas felt her gloved fingers trace the scar that marred his cheek. The reminder pulled him back to his senses. He stepped away from her and cleared his throat. "It might be easier for you if you follow me and walk in my boot prints."

Why had he allowed himself to think the scar wouldn't matter? It seemed every time they were close, she touched the hated scar. Why? And did it matter? Was she simply touching him?

Thomas tried reasoning with himself. Hadn't she responded just a little bit to the kiss? Could she respond if she absolutely hated his face? He'd thought his heart might burst out of his chest as their lips met, and when she closed her eyes as if savoring the experience, he'd felt on top of the world.

But when she traced the scar, years of mocking and bullying came crashing back, vicious taunts and rhymes that belittled. No one had ever loved him but his brothers and sister and Ma, and everyone knew Ma had a heart for strays that no one else wanted.

Had Josephine learned to care about him like Ma? Or maybe like a wife? He pushed the thoughts away. What had he been thinking? She couldn't possibly be feeling for him what he was beginning to feel for her. He should never have kissed her. Thomas berated himself over and over again as he led her to the special tree. How could he expect her to love his scarred face when he didn't?

Chapter Twenty

Josephine felt the cold begin to seep into her bones as they rode back to the house with two small trees. The joy of their outing had ended after their shared kiss. How much more obvious could Thomas make it that he regretted kissing her? He'd turned into a silent man who just seemed to want to get back to the house and away from her.

She swallowed the hurt welling up inside. Why had he kissed her? And why had he regretted doing so? Men were so complicated.

Thomas helped her down and quickly turned away to get the trees from the sled. Josephine continued to the front porch. In her arms she carried the blankets and now-empty jars. Philip bounded across the yard and helped her open the door.

One look at her sad face and he asked, "What happened?"

Josephine shrugged. "We got two trees."

"And that's bad?"

She opened the door and the puppy bounded off the porch. Josephine watched her go to Thomas. She looked at Philip. "I didn't think so, but you'll have to ask your brother."

Philip shook his head. "All right, go on inside. I'll take care of Little One."

"What?" Josephine stared at him in shock.

"Little One." Philip looked at her as if she'd grown two heads. "What did you think I said?"

Josephine shook her head. "I thought you called her Mistletoe. That's the name of my horse. Well, she used to be my horse until my uncle sold her."

Philip chuckled lightly. "Did one of the trees hit you on the head? Little One and Mistletoe don't even sound the same. You act like you're in a trance."

Weariness rested on Josephine's shoulders. She didn't bother explaining. "No, I'm okay. Thank you for taking care of the puppy." She walked into the warm house and shut the door.

Pulling her coat off, Josephine realized that she'd almost trusted Thomas today with her heart. Their shared kiss and his reaction to it was her wake-up call. Men couldn't be trusted, not with anything—especially a woman's heart.

Thomas saw the determination in Philip's steps as he walked toward him.

"What happened? When you two left, you both looked happy. You come back and she's looking like she lost her best friend and you have that persimmon face again." Philip grabbed one end of the Christmas tree that Thomas was tugging on. Thomas grunted as it came off the sleigh.

Thomas led the way to the porch. "Stay out of it, little brother."

"Oh, now I'm little brother?" Philip set his end down.

Thomas stood the tree up on its stump and rested it against the doorjamb. "Would you rather I call you nosy brother?"

Philip chuckled. "No, little brother works, but I still want to know what happened."

"Let's just say I forgot myself and leave it at that." Thomas walked back to the horse and sleigh. He tugged on the other tree.

Together they carried it to the porch. As soon as it was on the porch, Thomas walked to the horse's head and led it to the barn. He was very aware of Philip's constant staring at his face.

"You kissed her," Philip blurted in triumph.

Thomas stopped and glared. "Now, why would you say that?" he demanded, a little more tellingly than he'd intended.

"Because you both have that *Now what?* look about you."

Thomas began walking again. "Oh, really?"

"Yep. Did she not enjoy your kisses, big brother?"

Thomas knew goading when he heard it. He ignored the question and stopped the horse at the side of the barn. As he unhitched the wagon, his thoughts went back to that moment in the snow, with Josephine in his arms and his lips on hers. Had she enjoyed his kiss? She'd kissed him back, so he'd assumed she did.

"I think you are your own worst enemy." Philip leaned against the barn wall.

Thomas finished with the horse and led it inside the warm barn. "You're probably right," he admitted.

"We used to talk about girls and the way they acted

around us," Philip said, following him to a stall, where Thomas released the little mare.

"You mean we used to talk about how they treated me," he answered bitterly. His memories of those talks hadn't faded. Philip had always stood up for him when the girls had called him ugly or Scar Face.

Philip nodded. "Yep. Did Josephine say something about the scar?"

"Nope."

A frown marred Philip's otherwise handsome face. "Then what did she do?"

He swallowed. "If you must know, she touched it."

Philip barked. "That's it? She's touched your face before. Remember? Before the dance, Josephine touched your face and told you how pretty you are."

Thomas shook his head. "This was different." How could he explain his feelings to his brother when he didn't really understand them himself?

Hardness entered Philip's voice. "What did she say?" All teasing had been tossed to the side. Anger that Josephine had hurt his brother in some way filled Philip's face.

"Nothing," Thomas admitted.

His brother frowned. "I'm confused. Did she not say anything? Or do you not want to tell me what she did say?"

"Philip, it really is none of your business."

He nodded. "I see. She didn't say anything. You let the words of the past spoil your day together." Philip sighed. "Thomas, you have to forget those girls and their cruel words. I've seen the way Josephine looks at you. She doesn't see the scar."

Thomas curled his hands into fists. "What does she see, Philip? You know my wife so well, tell me."

Philip took a step toward Thomas. "I'm not the enemy here, Thomas. But I won't let you hurt her and push her away because of some cruel words spoken to you when you were twelve."

He felt the fight leave him. Philip was right. He needed to forget the past. But how did one do that? How do you simply forget the cruel words that have haunted you for years? Thomas didn't know how and he didn't know if he'd ever be able to trust that Josephine didn't see the ugliness of his face.

"Let's head to the house. I'm cold and hungry." Philip slapped him on the back. "Whatever you did or didn't do, I'm sure Josephine will forgive you."

Thomas nodded. "Yeah, I'm hungry, too." He felt as if his boots weighed a ton. When they got to the porch, he said, "Help me get this tree in the house."

Philip willingly did so. They stomped their feet as they came through the door.

Josephine came from the kitchen. "I thought we might set it beside the window." She pointed to the area she meant.

Thomas watched her walk back into the kitchen. He'd hurt her with his silence today. He knew it but didn't know how to fix it. He'd start by setting the tree up for her. Maybe that would bring back some of the joy he'd snuffed out.

The smell of frying ham pulled him to the kitchen. "Something smells good in here," he said.

"I hope you don't mind, but I thought I'd make some flapjacks and ham for dinner." She kept her back to him.

Thomas walked to the counter and leaned a hip against it. "I'm sorry, Josephine. Will you forgive me?"

She looked up at him. Her eyelashes looked moist. "For what? Being quiet?"

He took a deep breath. "That and spoiling our outing."

Josephine nodded. "All right, I'll forgive you, but will you tell me what I did wrong?"

He busied himself pouring coffee into three mugs. "It wasn't you. It was me."

She turned the ham over in the skillet. "I understand that part. What I don't understand is what I said that caused you to draw away from me." The hurt in her voice pulled at him.

Thomas ran a hand over the scarred side of his face. "I've had this scar all my life."

A frown tugged at her eyebrows, but Josephine didn't interrupt. She focused on the meat.

"When I was younger and living at the orphanage, the girls there would taunt me. Tell me I was ugly, call me names." He swallowed the hurt. "Today, when you traced the scar, all I could hear were their voices. I felt that hurt again, and instead of seeing it as a thing of the past, I pulled away from you. I'm sorry."

Josephine removed the skillet from the top of the stove and put it on a hot plate. She walked over to him. "Thomas, that's horrible. Have you not looked in a mirror?"

He tried to smile. "I avoid mirrors."

"Well, you shouldn't. The scar is simply a fine white line on your face. It's not ugly and it certainly doesn't take away from your handsome features." She returned to the stove and her skillet of ham. "I forgive you."

Thomas nodded. "Thank you."

"Go ahead and give Philip that cup of coffee before it gets cold," she ordered with a soft smile.

He looked at her face. She smiled, but her eyes still held distrust. His scar was on the surface for the world to see, but Josephine's ran deeper and he'd hurt her today.

Thomas nodded and carried the cup to Philip. It would take time, but he hoped to regain her trust. As for her love, Thomas had a feeling they both had a way to go before they were ready for such strong emotions.

After dinner, Josephine spent the next few hours working on Christmas decorations. Thomas had created a stand to keep the tree from falling over. She and Philip had strung berries while Thomas read to them out of the Bible.

They worked as a team, but her mind didn't stay focused on what they were doing. She kept thinking about the girls who had hurt Thomas as a child. Why would they be so cruel? Her heart went out to the young man of the past. Would he be able to overcome those hurts? She prayed that with the Christmas holiday coming up, he'd be able to forget past hurts and move on into their future. Maybe it was time she did the same.

Philip held up a slice of dried orange that he'd pushed a wire through and bent into a hanger. He asked, "What do you think of this?"

She smiled at him. "I like it. We also have lemon slices you can do that to." Josephine walked to the kitchen, where she kept the tin with her dried fruit. She carried it back to him. "On Christmas Day, we can take some of it off and make spiced tea with it."

He took the tin. "Like the kind Ma had at the dance?"

Josephine smiled. "Maybe. I have a recipe from Hazel. It might or might not be the same." Her gaze moved to her now-silent husband.

Thomas sat reading the Bible quietly to himself. Earlier, he'd read the story of Mary and the angel who came to tell her that she'd have the baby Jesus. Josephine watched as his eyes scanned the pages of the Bible.

Philip nodded. "I think that would be a right nice Christmas treat." He focused on pushing the wire through the fruit without tearing it up. "What time are you going to take Hazel her tree tomorrow?"

"I'm not sure yet. I guess that is up to Thomas."

Hearing his name, he looked up. "What's up to me?"

Philip grinned. "What time are you taking Hazel her tree tomorrow?"

"Oh, we can go after the morning chores are done."

Josephine picked up another berry to string for the tree's garland. Would they have enough decorations for both trees? She looked at the small pile they'd completed so far. They had small paper chains, yarn rope that could be used as garland, dried fruit on hooks and tapered candles.

Philip yawned as only a man can do. He laid the last piece of dried lemon down with the others and announced, "I'm heading to bed. Tomorrow afternoon I'll be leaving for my ride."

"Already?" Josephine was amazed at how quickly the days passed.

He grinned. "Yep, time flies. It seems like only yesterday that I was coming home."

She chuckled. "I suppose so. It takes several days just

to recover, and then it seems as if you're right back on the horse and the trail again."

Thomas laid the Bible down in his lap. "I still can't believe that just a couple of short months ago you were working as a Pony Express rider." He smiled at her, causing her heart to turn over.

Josephine ran her hands through her hair. "I can't believe how fast my hair is growing. I'm not sure I could do it again without chopping off these red curls."

"Don't you dare. Your curls are beautiful."

Both Josephine and Philip looked at Thomas. The force of his voice caused them both to stare at him. She watched the red flush start at his neck and move into his face.

"Thank you, Thomas." She grinned at his embarrassment.

Philip grunted. "I'm going to bed. You two are about to get mushy again."

She felt the heat rise in her own cheeks. "I think I'll turn in, too." They hadn't kissed, hugged or even touched each other since they'd gone out to get the tree. Josephine didn't want to admit she was nervous about spending alone time with Thomas. She set her berry garland to the side and stood.

Thomas stood, also. "Good night, Josephine."

A smile touched her lips. She knew he was trying to renew the comfort with each other they'd lost earlier. "Good night, Thomas." Josephine walked to her bedroom.

She closed the door and leaned against the cool wood. Would they ever feel comfortable around each other again? She knew it wasn't Thomas's earlier behavior that had them feeling ill at ease with each other but the kiss they'd shared. When would they be able to enjoy each other's company again without it feeling strange? Without her longing for what she couldn't have?

Chapter Twenty-One

Just as Josephine had hoped, Hazel was thrilled at receiving a Christmas tree and decorations. She had fussed as Thomas put it up for her and then oohed and aahed over the homemade decorations.

"These are exquisite, Jo. I love them," Hazel said, dangling an orange slice over a low-hanging branch.

Josephine laughed. "I'm glad you like them. Philip made most of those." She picked up a string of dried berries and handed it to Hazel. "I can't wait for you to come over and see the house. We've decorated the tree and the fireplace mantel and even hung a sprig of mistletoe over the back door."

Hazel laughed. "Trying to get that man of yours to kiss you, are you?" She finished hanging the berry garland and then reached for another piece of dried fruit.

Heat filled Josephine's cheeks. "No. It was Philip's idea."

"Uh-huh."

Josephine tried to convince her. "It's true. You can ask him next time you see him."

"Which won't be for a few days. Isn't he supposed

to be riding out today?" Hazel stepped back to admire her tree. She'd had them place it in the corner of the room close to her rocking chair.

"Yes, but he'll be home in time for Christmas." Josephine straightened the string of berries, then stepped back to enjoy the tree, too. "You will be coming over for Christmas Eve dinner, won't you?"

Hazel gave an unladylike snort and said, "Wouldn't miss it."

Josephine chuckled. "Good. It wouldn't seem right without you." She hugged Hazel. "I'm so glad you are a part of my life now."

"So am I."

Thomas reentered the house. "I milked that stubborn cow of yours, Hazel." He held up a bucket of milk. "Can't believe she's still giving this much."

The two women parted. "She's a keeper," Hazel answered with a grin.

Josephine wished their cow would give as much milk. Most days they got only half a gallon in the morning, and if they were lucky, another half in the evening.

"Do you need more milk, Josephine?" Hazel walked to the milk pail.

"With these two men, I can always use extra milk, if you don't need it," Josephine answered. Philip loved drinking milk and could drink a gallon a day. "And I'll be making a couple of desserts in the next few days."

Hazel poured the thick white milk into jars for Josephine.

Thomas came farther into the kitchen. "Josephine, would you mind visiting with Hazel for a little longer? I'd like to ride with Philip as far as Dove Creek. I can come back and get you this evening."

"If it's all right with Hazel, it's all right with me," Josephine answered, happy to have time to talk to her friend about the strange feelings Thomas's touch and look created in her.

Hazel waved her hand. "Of course it's all right with me."

Thomas grinned. "Good. I'll be back shortly." And then he was gone.

Josephine stared at the closed door. She sighed.

Hazel chuckled. "You got it bad, Jo."

"What? What do I have bad?"

The older woman shook her head. "You don't know?"

Was she sick? Had Hazel seen something in her that she hadn't been aware of? Josephine touched her hand to her forehead.

"You don't have that kind of fever, child." Hazel shook her head. "I forget how young you are."

Josephine frowned. "Then what do I have?"

"You've fallen under the spell of the love bug." Hazel laughed.

Embarrassed, Josephine ducked her head. "No, I don't think I have."

"Humph. If you aren't in love, I'll eat that row of dried berries you strung on that tree." Hazel walked back to the sitting room and sat down on the sofa.

Had she fallen in love with Thomas? No. This wasn't love. She admired him and was thankful he was a kind man. But Josephine Dooly Young was not in love with her husband. She shook her head.

"Oh, so when your hands accidentally touch, you don't feel a small spark of electricity? Hearing his deep laughter doesn't thrill you to your toes? And I'd wager that when he kisses you, you aren't thinking about chores." Hazel picked up her knitting and began to work the wooden needles through the yarn.

Josephine felt heat rise in her cheeks. Wasn't this what she wanted to talk to Hazel about? She groaned. "Oh, Hazel, what am I going to do?"

Hazel looked up at her with a frown. "Now, what kind of silly question is that? You're going to tell him how you feel."

Josephine rolled her mother's locket in her hand. "No, I'm not."

"Why in the blue blazes not?" Hazel laid her needles to the side.

"Because I can't be in love with him." She played with the locket's clasp.

Hazel frowned. "Is there something you aren't telling me? Because I can't think of one good reason why you can't love your husband."

Josephine took a deep breath and released it slowly. "Hazel, I don't trust him. It's not his fault. I don't believe I can ever trust any man."

Hazel jumped to her feet. "That is one of the stupidest things I believe I've ever heard."

Had Hazel just called her stupid? Josephine swallowed the lump in her throat.

"Thomas Young has been nothing but kind to you. Even Phillip has changed and has been a wonderful brother-in-law. How can you not trust him?" Hazel paced in front of the sofa. Mama dog paced with her.

"I know, Hazel, but a part of me doesn't feel like I can trust him." Josephine stood up, too.

This was a bad idea. She should have known Hazel would defend Thomas and Philip. After all, Hazel had been their friend long before she was hers. Josephine walked to the door and pulled on her coat.

Puzzled by Josephine's actions, Hazel asked, "Where are you going?"

"I'm going home. I shouldn't have told you that I don't trust Thomas." She pulled her scarf around her neck and her gloves onto her hands.

Hazel shook her head. "Jo, you don't need to go home."

She looked to the old woman. Concern reflected in Hazel's eyes. "I do. I'm going to go home and pray about my feelings. As you pointed out, I have no reason to distrust my husband." Josephine pulled the door open. Cold air lifted the edges of her scarf. Before Hazel could protest further, Josephine closed the door behind her.

It didn't take long to saddle the horse and start for home. Thankfully the route to Hazel's house was stomped down well. Thomas and Philip made daily visits to Hazel's to make sure she was safe and had worn the snow down on the path. By the time she got home, her nose and cheeks were frozen.

Josephine made quick work of settling the horse in the barn and hurried to the warmth of the house. The puppy rushed outside and did her business while Josephine took off her coat, gloves and scarf. As soon as the puppy was back inside, Josephine walked to the kitchen, where she poured water into a pan to heat, thinking spiced tea would settle her emotions.

Hazel had meant well, but her words and insinuation that Josephine was stupid cut deep. Little One danced around her feet as she poured hot water over the tea leaves and lemon slices.

While it steeped, Josephine went to her bedroom

and pulled out Thomas's Christmas gift. The shirt was almost complete; all she needed to do was sew on the buttons.

Josephine carried it to the small chair and table that sat by the window. She was sure Thomas would take his horse straight to the barn, giving her plenty of time to put his gift away before he could see it.

While she sewed, Josephine prayed. She asked God to help her overcome this fear of trusting. Thomas was a good man and he deserved a wife who would stand by him and trust that what he said and did was true. She asked the Lord to make her that wife.

When the last button was sewed into place, Josephine stood and stretched. She'd almost forgotten her tea and went into the kitchen to pour it into a cup. Her mother had always preferred her tea hot, but Josephine liked it warm. She scooped up a small spoonful of sugar and stirred it into the cup. Taking the tea into the sitting room, Josephine sat down and picked up the Charles Dickens book.

Little One followed her into the sitting room, where she flopped down on her rug by the fireplace. "This is a luxury, Little One. Most women don't have time to sit and sip tea while reading a good book in front of the fire."

"I'll say."

Josephine jumped at the unfamiliar voice. Little One barked with excitement. Josephine turned around and saw that a big man stood in her kitchen doorway.

Her heart skipped a beat as she recognized Mr. Grossman. Her brain screamed that he wasn't supposed to be there. He must have come through the back door. She scooped up the puppy. "What are you doing here?"

He ignored her question. "Aren't you going to invite me to sit down?"

"No, I'm not. I want you out of my house and I want you gone now." Josephine tightened her grip on the yelping pup. "Hush, Little One."

He shook his head. "Now, that is no way to speak to your husband, Josie." His large body caused the rocker to creak as he sat down.

"Mr. Grossman…"

"Call me, Stan. We are married, after all." He picked up her discarded teacup and took a sip. Immediately he spat the tea back into the cup. "Josie, don't you have something stronger than this? I'm chilled to the bone. Be a good girl and go get it for me."

Heat rose in her chest. Who did he think he was? This wasn't his home and he had no right to boss her around. She put the puppy back down on the floor. "Mr. Grossman, we are not getting married and I am not going to get you anything to drink."

For a man of his size, he moved quickly. His hand clutched her arm and he yanked her toward him. "I didn't say we were getting married. I said we are already married. Now do as I say."

Josephine tried to pull away from him. "No! I am already married. I can't and won't marry you." Pain shot up her arm where his fingers dug deeper into her flesh. She couldn't understand what made the man delusional enough to think she was married to him.

His hot breath fanned her face as he snarled. "If you are married, where's your man?"

She swallowed. Josephine wanted to lie to him, say that Thomas was in the barn, but knew it was wrong.

Plus, he'd catch her in the lie. "He's gone to town but will be back soon."

He released her arm. "I don't think so."

Josephine rubbed where his beefy hand had been. She took a step back. Maybe if she stalled him, Thomas would return and make him leave.

"If you aren't lying, then when did you get married to this man who isn't home at this time of night?" he asked, sitting back down and extending his hands to the fire.

"In October."

His laugh sounded triumphant. "Then your marriage isn't legal."

Confused by his confident-sounding tone, Josephine argued. "Yes, it is. We got married in front of a judge."

"You were married to me in September."

Had he gone mad? There was no way they could have been married in September. She'd been working for the Pony Express in September. Josephine decided to keep him talking and sat down on the rocker opposite him. "I don't understand. What do you mean?"

"We were married by proxy. Your uncle made sure that you belonged to me." He looked at Little One. The puppy had returned to her rug but continued to snarl at him.

"Proxy?" Was that possible? Could her uncle do that?

He looked at her and frowned. "Josie, I still don't have my drink."

She stood. "All I have is coffee, tea or milk." With distaste she looked at her cup. "Obviously you didn't like the tea. Would you prefer a cup of coffee or do you want me to warm up some milk?"

Through clenched teeth he growled. "I want whiskey."

Josephine tried not to let her irritation show in her voice. "Mr. Grossman, we don't keep spirits in the house."

"Aw, Josie, even I know country folk keep a bottle around for medical purposes." He glared at her. "Now get it."

She walked to the kitchen. How was she going to convince him that they really didn't have any form of liquor in the place? Trying not to panic, Josephine said, "You didn't tell me what you meant by proxy." Just stall him, Thomas would be home soon.

"Proxy is when two people get married but one of them isn't there. Your uncle was more than happy to stand in your place and sign the marriage license for you," he answered.

Josephine poured coffee into a big tin mug. She carried it back to the sitting room and handed it to him. Was a proxy marriage legal? Was it possible she could be married to two men at once? The thought of being married to the gambler turned her stomach. He didn't look as fat as she remembered, but he still smelled worse than rotten eggs.

His booming voice pulled her back to the present. "This isn't whiskey!"

Keeping her voice calm, Josephine answered, "No, sir, it isn't. We don't have anything stronger than coffee."

He threw the cup against the fireplace. Coffee sloshed onto the little dog, who yelped in fright and pain. "If you don't have it here, we'll go into town and get it!"

He grabbed her by the arm and proceeded to drag her through the kitchen. The big man shoved whatever was in his path to the side. Her pretty side table hit the floor with a crash.

Going through the kitchen, Josephine grabbed at the chairs to keep from being pulled out into the snow. "I am already married. I'm not going with you!" she screamed, even as the cold air wrapped around her.

"You are going with me. I bought you and married you, and now we are going home," he ground through clenched teeth.

"Why? Why do you want to be married to me so badly?" Josephine grabbed the back porch handrail and hung on for dear life. She ignored the sharp coldness of the ice that had frozen to the wooden bars.

He stopped and looked at her. "For the money, of course."

"What money?"

He slapped her hard across the face. Pain shot through her lip as she felt the flesh split. Cruel laughter burst from his throat. "I guess I should tell you everything, now that we're married and there's nothing you can do about it."

Josephine sighed as he released her arm once more. She touched her mouth and pulled away cold fingers stained by red blood. "Let's go inside. It's cold out here." If she could get closer to the door, she'd lock him out.

As if he knew her thoughts, he grabbed her arm again and jerked her down onto the step. "No, Josie, what I have to say won't take long." He pulled his coat tighter around his thick waist and continued. "Did you know that your pa found gold in California in the early fifties?"

She shook her head. Why hadn't she run when she had the chance? Miserable, Josephine wrapped her arms around her waist and prayed Thomas would get home soon.

He laughed. "Nope, from the look on your face I'd say you didn't."

His grip tightened on her arm. She felt his beefy fingers press against the bone. Josephine clenched her teeth together willing herself not to cry out.

"Well, he did. It just so happens that he and I use the same bank. And the banker there is free with his information."

She tried to put space between them by leaning toward the porch rail. The cold seeped through her dress, but she ignored it. Josephine had to keep him talking. "Uncle said something about this when he was here. I thought he was lying."

"Not this time. Your pa put a lot of gold in that bank. Only, his will says that no one can touch it except you, and only then on your twenty-first birthday." He frowned. "That's in a couple of years, so we'll have to wait to collect it. But until then, we are happily married."

Josephine didn't correct him about her age; she was already twenty-one. Instead she tried to keep him talking. "That can't be right. My parents would have told me." She paused as if seriously considering his words.

"Oh, it's right. I pretended not to believe the banker and got him to prove it by showing me your family's bankbook." His gaze moved off into the distance as if remembering that day.

Josephine shook her head. "If Papa had been rich, I don't think he would have left me in Uncle's care." Even in her own ears, her voice sounded small and childlike.

He shook his head. "Didn't your uncle tell you? Your pa is dead."

Stricken, Josephine whispered, "How can you know that?"

He leaned down until their noses almost touched. "Because I killed him and dumped his body in the St. Joe River." Cruel laughter filled the air. "Isn't that funny? Your uncle thought so. Your papa is in a river named after a saint."

Josephine recoiled from him, pulling free. She tried to run, but her feet tangled in her skirt.

His hand shot out and once more he was dragging her to his horse. "Come on! I've waited seven years to finally marry you and take what is rightfully mine."

Josephine dug her heels into the snow. She hit him with her fist. Tears streamed down her face. She wouldn't go with him. She wouldn't.

Chapter Twenty-Two

Thomas didn't know what drove the urgency within him to get home, but something screamed at him that if he didn't hurry he would be too late. He pushed the horse as hard and fast as the snow would allow. Before the horse came to a complete stop, he jumped off and ran up the steps to Hazel's house.

Hazel opened the door at his rapid knocking. "Sakes alive. What set your tail on fire?" she asked.

"Where's Josephine?" Thomas panted. His body fought for breath.

A sad expression crossed the old woman's face. "She insisted on going home about two hours ago."

He didn't stay to hear more. Thomas mounted the horse and turned it toward home. *Lord, please let her be all right.* The silent prayer repeated itself over and over within his mind.

After a short while, Thomas entered the yard and dismounted beside the front porch. He could hear Josephine's screams long before he saw her. His boots slipped and slid as he raced to the side of the house.

A big man was trying to push her onto his horse. She kicked and screamed. He wasn't close enough to stop the man, and Thomas watched in horror as the man raised his fist and punched Josephine in the face several times. She fell like a sack of seed at his feet.

A curse filled the air. "Get up."

Rage boiled within him. Thomas continued at a dead run. He lowered his head and rammed into the oversize man's body. His fists worked while his mind shouted that Josephine was hurt.

The two men rolled in the snow. Thomas felt his body being hit again and again, and he kept fighting. Even as his fists flew, his mind questioned the other man's motives.

Why was he trying to steal Josephine away? Who was he and what had possessed him to hit her? Who did he think he was? No man should ever strike a woman. Especially his woman.

Thomas was vaguely aware of Hazel running to Josephine's side. The fight continued and Thomas sensed that the big man was about done for. He felt his own body giving out as he punched the older man repeatedly.

At last the man crumpled at Thomas's feet. Blood, both his and the stranger's, marred the white snow. Thomas looked to where Hazel cradled Josephine in her lap.

Tears poured down the old woman's face.

"Is she…?" He couldn't bring himself to finish the question.

Hazel looked up at him. "She's not dead."

Thomas bent down and scooped his wife off Hazel's lap. "Let's get her inside." He cuddled Josephine close. She had no coat on and her body was cold to the touch.

"I shouldn't have let her come home alone," Hazel said as she held the kitchen door open for Thomas.

He carried Josephine to her bedroom and gently laid her down on the bed. "Don't blame yourself, Hazel." Thomas gasped. Josephine's left eye was swollen, a tiny stream of blood seeped from her nose and her jaw was turning black before his eyes. A split in her lip also bled freely.

"Let me see." Hazel pushed him to the side. "She needs a doctor."

Thomas nodded. He gently brushed red curls away from her forehead. "I'll go get him." Unable to tear his gaze from Josephine's bruised and battered face, Thomas wasn't sure he could bring himself to leave her side.

Hazel patted his arm. "I'll take care of her. You have to take care of that man out there and get her a doctor."

He nodded, bent over and gently kissed Josephine on the temple. "I'll be back with Doctor Bridges as quick as I can."

"And the man?"

"I'm tempted to let him freeze out there," Thomas ground between his clenched teeth.

Hazel nodded her understanding. "Yeah, but while you're gone, he could wake up. I'd rather you take him to the sheriff so he'll be punished for what he's done to our Jo."

Thomas nodded. "Take care of her, Hazel. I can't lose her now."

Josephine groaned but didn't awaken.

"I will. You just hurry. I don't know if she's hurt anywhere besides her face or not." The urgency in Hazel's voice had Thomas leaving the room.

With the strength of ten men, Thomas shoved the big man onto his horse on his belly and tied his hands and feet together under the horse's belly. He worked fast and prayed hard. Then he mounted up and rode as fast as the horses could go.

His first stop in town was Doctor Bridges's office. Thomas explained as best as he could that Josephine had been beaten up by the big man on the horse. When the doctor promised to leave immediately, Thomas nodded and took the stranger to the sheriff's office, where he untied the man's hands and feet and allowed him to fall to the hard, cold ground.

The sheriff stepped out on the porch. "Whatcha got there, Thomas?"

"A woman hitter."

The sheriff's spurs jingled as he walked across the boardwalk. "Who's the woman?"

Thomas raised his head. "My wife."

"Is he dead?"

"Not yet."

The sheriff nodded. "How's your wife?"

"When I left her with Hazel, she didn't look so good." Experience told Thomas to be patient. The sheriff wasn't a fast-talking man and often was even slower in his actions.

The sheriff walked around the big man. "Don't recognize him, but you didn't exactly leave me much of his face to recognize." He looked up at Thomas. "You know him?"

"Nope. First time I saw him he was hitting my wife." He ground his teeth. The last thing Thomas wanted to do was stand in the street and discuss the man who'd hurt Josephine. But he knew it had to be done so that the man would be put in jail where he belonged.

"Does Josephine know him?" The sheriff motioned for his deputy to come on out to the road with them.

Thomas shook his head. "I don't know. All I know, Sheriff, is that I rode with Philip into town. He was heading out to the folks' to start his Pony Express run, and I came to get Josephine a gift for Christmas. When I got back to the house, this skunk was trying to force her onto his horse, and when she fought him, he hit her square in the face with his fist and knocked her out cold on the ground."

The sheriff and the deputy lifted the man by his boots and shoulders, then proceeded to carry him to the jailhouse. "You didn't ask her if she knew him?" the sheriff puffed as he walked past.

"Josephine's not in a condition to talk. Last I saw her, she was unconscious." Thomas hurried around them and held the door open.

Thomas saw that a cell was already open and waiting for its next guest. He gleaned some satisfaction when the two lawmen dumped the man onto the cold wood floor.

"I suppose you want to get home, then?"

Finally. "Yes, sir, I do."

The sheriff nodded. "Then head on out. When Josephine is feeling up to it, I'll need her to stop in and let me know who this polecat is. He'll sit here until I talk to her."

Thomas hurried to the door. "I'll make sure to tell her."

He was back in the saddle and pushing the horse hard to return to the house, but his horse wasn't a Pony

Express horse and he just wasn't as young as he used to be. The old gelding wasn't up to running at breakneck speeds all the time, especially in cold weather. Thomas slowed down to an easy gallop. "I'm sorry, boy." He patted the horse's neck.

Thomas told himself to take it easy on the horse. Josephine was in good hands. She was with Hazel and hopefully by now the doctor was there and had her patched up.

He'd known for a while now that he loved his wife. She was kind, considerate and resourceful. It felt good to admit it, and if the Lord permitted him to live long enough, she would know the full force of his love once this had all blown over.

His hand moved to the scar on his face. And for all intents and purposes Josephine didn't seem to mind that he was a scarred man. Thomas fought down the doubts in his heart. He'd been pushing feelings of love away because he feared Josephine would reject him. Over the years he'd allowed the scar to make him the man he thought he was.

No more.

Today he'd almost lost her. Who knew, he still could. Her pale, battered face came to mind. He shook the image away and focused on what had happened.

He had no idea what the stranger wanted with his wife. What made the big man think he could just come and take her away? A shudder shook him. He might have succeeded, if Thomas hadn't arrived in time.

The thought tore his heart. She would have been gone without ever knowing that he loved her. Once more Thomas urged the horse to run faster. He would tell Josephine he loved her. She might reject him and break his heart. If so, Thomas would learn to live with that. He loved her and his love didn't depend on her loving him back.

Josephine awoke with a start. Where was she? She jerked upward and immediately cried out in pain.

Hazel's soft voice and hand on her shoulder broke through the agony. "Easy does it. You've got a couple of broken ribs."

Comforted to know Hazel was there, Josephine slowly laid back down. "Is my head broken, too?" She couldn't decide which to hold, her head or her sides. Just speaking sent sharp pain through her temple.

"Naw. Doctor Bridges said your head is too hard for that." The old woman chuckled. "And, thank the Lord, he says you'll live."

Josephine looked about the room and realized that she could see out of only one eye. Memories of Mr. Grossman hitting her repeatedly in the face came crashing back upon her. "Where is he?" She hated the sound of fear in her voice.

"That man who did this to you?" Hazel wiped a cool cloth across Josephine's forehead.

She nodded and a new pain made its way down her back. Would she ever stop hurting? A groan tore through her throat.

"Thomas took him to town to the sheriff. He can't hurt you anymore." Hazel moved to the small table beside the window. She poured some type of liquid into a large spoon and came back.

So Thomas had returned. Josephine tried to sit up,

but the pain in her ribs and head forced her back down to the sheets with a cry.

But the pain couldn't stop her silent questions. What if Mr. Grossman told Thomas they were no longer married? Would he be pleased? That thought caused her heart to hurt.

"Jo, stop moving. The doctor says you need to lie still and rest." Hazel held the spoon out to her. "Here, take this. The doctor said it will help you sleep."

How many more times would Hazel say the doctor said? Josephine dismissed the silly question. If whatever Hazel held in that spoon would stop the pain, she'd take it. Josephine lifted her head from the pillow and allowed Hazel to pour the sweet liquid down her throat.

The brightness of the room hurt Josephine's head. She shut her eyes in the hopes of blocking out the pain. "Did Mr. Grossman say anything?"

"Not that I'm aware of, but when I got here, that husband of yours wasn't giving the big man time to say anything."

"What do you mean?" Josephine yawned and her ribs protested the action.

Hazel chuckled. "I've never seen our Thomas so full of rage. He didn't stop until your Mr. Grossman hit the ground for the last time and didn't get up. Then he carried you in here and took that no-good son of a skunk to town."

"He did?" Did that mean Mr. Grossman hadn't had time to tell Thomas anything?

"He sure did." Hazel paused. "I'll be right back. I'm going to pull one of those rockers in here so I can sit with you a spell."

So he'd been angry at Mr. Grossman. Had it been

because of her? Or had the big man said something offensive before Hazel arrived? Had he told Thomas that they weren't really married? The sound of the chair being dragged into the bedroom sent fresh reels of pain through Josephine's head.

Then she heard Hazel drop into the chair with a big sigh. "You know, I've never seen your husband more worried over anybody. That man loves you."

Josephine wanted to believe that Thomas loved her. She felt the effects of the medicine slowly relaxing her body and mind. Still, she couldn't push back all the memories that Mr. Grossman's visit had imprinted on her thoughts.

Her father was dead, murdered. She was married to the madman who had killed her father. And Josephine had money in the bank back home. Sleep claimed her senses and Josephine welcomed its interruption of her memories.

Josephine didn't know how long she slept. It could have been hours or minutes, but the sound of her husband's whispering voice filled her ears. "How's she doing?"

She tried to open her eyes, tell him she was fine, but Josephine found she could do neither. Maybe she was still dreaming. Or maybe the medicine just had her body so relaxed it refused to obey her mind.

"The medicine that Doctor Bridges left put her back to sleep a few minutes ago," Hazel answered.

"I thought he'd still be here when I got back. What did he say?"

"The Johnson kid came by and got him. Mrs. Johnson is having the baby, so he left pretty quickly."

Josephine felt a calloused hand touch her cheek.

Then she heard Thomas's voice close to her ear. "What did he say about Josephine?"

"She has a couple of cracked ribs, but as far as he could tell, no other broken bones. He wrapped her ribs before he left and gave me that brown jar of medicine to help her relax." The chair rocked. "If you don't need me, I think I'll head back to the house and milk the cow."

"Thank you for coming by when you did," Thomas said. He paused. "By the way, why did you come over?"

Hazel's voice wavered. "I just wanted to see Josephine."

Inwardly Josephine sighed. Her mind became fuzzy, but she pulled herself from its warm cocoon when she heard Thomas ask, "Did she know who that man was?"

"She called him Mr. Grossman. What did the sheriff have to say?"

Thomas exhaled loudly. "He wants her to come to his office when she's feeling better."

Her mind worked. Had Mr. Grossman claimed her as his wife? What had the man told them? Troubled, Josephine drifted back into the deep warmth of sleep.

Chapter Twenty-Three

Josephine woke up with Thomas sitting in a rocker beside the bed. For the past two days, he'd stayed by her side. His soft snores filled the room.

She eased out from under the bedding, careful not to wake him. Josephine took small steps and inched toward the kitchen. Each step felt excruciating, but she needed a drink. Her mouth felt stuffed with cotton. And she was tired of lying about.

When she got to the table, Josephine eased into a chair. Weariness rested on her shoulders like a heavy blanket. Thanks to the medicine the doctor had left, she'd slept away the past couple of days, waking only long enough to eat and assure both Hazel and Thomas that she was feeling much better.

Thomas hadn't asked her many questions, but he'd cared for her as if she were made of fine china. Every so often it appeared he wanted to say something, but then he'd shut his mouth and simply smile at her.

Josephine looked toward the stove, where the coffeepot sat. If only she had the strength to walk over and pour herself a cup. She sighed.

"What are you doing out of bed?"

She turned to find Thomas leaning against the doorjamb. "I was thirsty." Josephine grinned but winced at the pain in her lip.

His light brown hair was tousled from sleep. Green eyes studied her. He stood in stocking feet. "You should have woken me. I would have gotten you some water." Thomas yawned as he walked to the bucket.

Josephine pushed away from the table. "I'll get it. You are exhausted, too."

"Stay put. I'm already here." He looked down at the water. "I think I'd like something stronger. How about I make a fresh pot of coffee?"

She smiled. "That sounds wonderful, but can I have a little water while I wait for the coffee to brew?"

He got her the water and then began to make the coffee. Once he had it on the stove heating, Thomas came back to the table and sat down. "I'm glad to see you felt like getting up. How are the ribs?"

"Sore, but I'll be all right." Josephine combed her fingers through her tangled hair. She must look a sight. Split lip, black eye and swollen jaw.

"Good." He leaned back in his chair. "Feel like talking about what happened? You don't have to, if it's too painful."

"No, I need to tell you. I'm not sure how you are going to feel about me when I'm done, but I have to tell you." She sighed. *Lord, please let him understand.*

Thomas reached across the table and took her hand in his. "Whatever happened, we are in this together." His thumb rubbed the back of her hand in soothing circles.

Josephine swallowed. "I'm not sure how much of what Mr. Grossman said is true. Maybe none of it. It just seems like a nightmare now." She ran her tongue over the split in her lip.

"Well, then, maybe you don't have to tell me at all."

"No, I have to tell you." Hot tears filled her eyes. "He said that my uncle made sure we were married in September by having a proxy wedding." Her lips trembled.

"How can that be? And what does it mean for our wedding?" His thumb stopped moving.

"Well, if he's telling the truth, I guess it means I am legally married to him and illegally married to you." She pulled her hand away from his.

"I see."

She took a deep breath. "There's more."

Thomas looked into her troubled eyes. "What?"

Josephine shut her eyes tightly. "He bragged that he murdered my father and dumped his body in the St. Joe River." The hot tears eased between her eyelashes.

His hand pulled hers back into his grasp. "Josephine, I am so sorry. Why would he kill your pa?"

She opened her eyes and the tears spilled down her cheeks. "Papa found gold in California, and according to Mr. Grossman they banked at the same bank. He talked the banker into letting him see our family accounts, and he found out that if anything happened to my parents, I am to receive the money."

Thomas stood and walked to her side of the table. He bent down beside her chair and gathered her into his arms. "I'm so sorry."

Josephine allowed him to hold her close while she cried tears of sorrow for all that had been lost to her. After several long minutes she pulled away. "He may have been lying about the money."

He sighed. "I don't think so."

"What makes you say that?" She took a sip of her water and tried to dry her face with her dressing gown.

"Josephine, have you ever looked in your mother's locket?"

She shook her head. "No. I tried once, but it was too stiff to open."

"May I try?" he asked, sliding into the chair beside her.

This turn of events confused her, but she nodded. "I'm not sure I can take it off by myself."

"You don't have to take it off." He reached for the chain about her neck and pulled the locket from under her nightgown.

"Just hold your hand out under it."

She did as he said and watched in fascination as he unlatched the locket. He tilted the opening toward her outstretched hand. Josephine gasped as a heavy stone fell into it. "It's a rock."

"It's a gold nugget," Thomas answered.

Josephine looked up into his green eyes. He didn't seem surprised. "You knew about it?"

"Yes."

"How did you know?" She turned the golden-tinged rock over in her hand. What Mr. Grossman had said was true?

"Remember the other day when the chain broke?" At her nod, he continued. "I opened the locket then."

"Why didn't you say something?" Josephine studied his face. Both her uncle and Mr. Grossman would have stolen it. With shaky fingers she replaced the nugget into its place in the locket, but no matter how hard she tried the clasp wouldn't close.

Thomas shrugged. "There wasn't anything to say."

He gently removed her hands from the locket and firmly closed the clasp. Then Thomas studied her face and said, "If Grossman told the truth about the money, then he's probably telling the truth about your marriage to him."

Josephine sighed. "Yes." She stared at him. What was he thinking? He'd proven that he could be trusted not to steal from her, he'd said they were in this together—but if they weren't legally married, where did that leave them?

He'd come so close to telling her that he loved her. Now Thomas watched her face. If she was legally married to Grossman, then he didn't feel he had the right to confess his love. It would only confuse her more and make their separation harder.

If she wasn't his wife, she might never be. That thought tore at his heart.

Thomas stood. "I'll see if the coffee is ready."

She pushed her chair back. "My head is hurting. Do you mind if I go back to my room? I may have overdone it a little."

"Of course not. I'll get your medicine."

Josephine held up her hand. "No, I don't want to take it anymore. It makes me sleep too much."

Thomas wondered if she feared he'd try to steal the gold from her locket. He watched as she shuffled slowly to the bedroom. "Josephine, I will never take what is yours."

Her hand went to the necklace. She clasped the locket and offered a lopsided smile. "I know. Thank you." Trust seemed to shine from her brown eyes. Then she shut the bedroom door.

Thomas had never seen that emotion in her eyes before. Just when she'd learned to trust him and he'd decided he loved her, they discovered that they weren't legally married. Life wasn't fair.

The door to the cabin opened and Philip came in shaking snow from his hat and coat. Thomas welcomed the sight of his brother. "You're back early."

Philip laughed. "Hello to you, too."

Thomas grinned. "I'm sorry, we didn't expect you until tomorrow."

"Yeah, I know. Heard you had some trouble out this way, so I came on home instead of staying at the home station. Is Josephine all right?"

Thomas poured coffee into two mugs and motioned for Philip to join him at the table. "She's recovering."

Philip sat down with a sigh. "I'm glad to hear that. She needs to go into town and set that Grossman straight." He took a sip and wrinkled his nose. "You never were any good at making coffee."

Thomas ignored the jab at his coffee-making skills and asked, "What's he saying?"

"Oh, just that you two aren't married. That he's married to her and he wants her out of this house now. As soon as he gets out of jail, he's taking her home." Philip's serious gaze met Thomas's. "You gonna let him do that?"

"Nope. Soon as the sheriff learns that Grossman killed Josephine's pa, he'll never get out of jail."

Philip whistled low. "What about his accusations that you two aren't married?"

Thomas sighed. "I'm not sure what will happen with that."

A cocky grin came across Philip's face. "Well, if he

hangs for murder, he won't be married to her anymore and you two will still be married."

Leave it to Philip to think like that. "Philip, I don't think that's how it works." Thomas shook his head.

"Probably not." He took another drink of his coffee and then sat the cup down. "I'm going to bed." Philip stood and clapped Thomas on the shoulder. "I'm glad you are all right, too."

"Thanks." He watched his brother head to the bedroom. Thomas took their cups to the washtub and set them inside. Then he headed out to the barn to do his chores.

He didn't want to lose Josephine. No matter what the outcome was, Thomas knew he wanted Josephine to be his wife and just prayed she'd want him to be her husband.

Chapter Twenty-Four

What would Thomas think when he found out she'd sent a letter to the bank in St. Joseph? She had to find out if what Mr. Grossman had said was true or not. If she was wealthy, then they'd be able to start the ranch that Thomas wanted. Wouldn't that make him happy? She wasn't sure.

She heard the front door shut, indicating that Doctor Bridges had left. Josephine pulled her housecoat about her body and walked into the sitting room. Thomas turned from the door. "The doctor says you are doing very well."

"Yes, that's what he told me, too." She eased into one of the rocking chairs.

He joined her. "Do you think you'll feel like going into town tomorrow?"

Josephine looked at him. "If I need to, I suppose I can."

"The sheriff has requested that you come as soon as you feel up to it. There is still the matter of what to do with Mr. Grossman." He leaned his arms on his knees and studied her bruised face.

Josephine sighed. She didn't want to face her attacker and her father's killer but knew it had to be done. "I suppose I'll feel up to it."

He frowned. "If you don't, we can put the trip off. I don't want you to go if you aren't feeling up to it." Concern laced his green eyes.

Josephine offered him a weak smile. "I'll be fine. I just dread the jostling my poor ribs are going to take in the wagon." She didn't bother telling him that she didn't want anyone to see her bruised and battered face.

"Philip got in last night. He's still sleeping. If you don't mind, I'd like to go over to Hazel's and see how she's doing." Thomas stood and stretched.

The muscles along his shoulders and ribs drew her attention as they flexed beneath his white shirt. "No, I'll be fine. Doctor Bridges said I need to start moving around more now, anyway."

He stopped stretching and looked at her. "What are you going to do?" Worry filled his voice.

What did he think she was going to do? "Oh, just make some tea and maybe work on a dress for Joy's doll. I thought that might make a good Christmas present for her."

He tilted his head to the side. "You aren't going outside, are you?"

"Why would I go outside?" she snapped. Josephine couldn't stop the irritation that his questions were evoking. "I'm not stupid, Thomas."

Thomas looked as if she'd just slapped him. "I didn't say you were. I… Oh, forget it. I'm going to go do my chores and then head to Hazel's. If you need anything, wake Philip." He slammed his hat on his head, grabbed his coat and left.

Josephine sighed. She'd let her nervousness about going to town make her quick-tempered with Thomas. He didn't deserve that. As much as she hated apologizing, she knew that was exactly what she'd do when he came back inside.

While the hot water was heating for her tea, Josephine went to her room and found the doll dress she'd been working on. If Mr. Grossman hadn't attacked her, she would have made Joy a matching dress, but as it was, Josephine was behind on her Christmas gifts. She made her tea and then walked to the sitting room to work on the dress.

She'd just gotten settled when Hazel came through the front door. Cold air entered ahead of her, but thankfully it wasn't snowing. She hoped it would hold off until they returned from town tomorrow. "Hello, Hazel."

"Oh, good, you're up." The older woman took off her many layers of warm clothing and hung them up by the door. She carried her sewing basket with her to the other rocker. "I was hoping you'd feel up to visiting today."

"The doctor was here a little while ago and said I could move around a bit more."

"That's what Tom said. Although he seemed a little out of sorts when he said it."

"I'm sure he did. We had a little spat." Josephine focused on the light blue fabric with little white flowers that was in her lap.

"What did he do?" Hazel asked, setting the rocker into motion.

Josephine laughed. "What makes you think it was Thomas that started the argument?"

Hazel dug in her bag. "It is always the man's fault."

Josephine sobered. "Not this time. It was mine. I

snapped at him for no good reason." She wished she could take back what she'd said but feared the damage had already been done.

"Aw, Thomas doesn't stay angry long. Just ask that brother of his." Hazel pulled out a sampler and began stitching on it.

They worked in comfortable silence for a few moments. Josephine spoke first. "He wants me to go into town tomorrow and face Mr. Grossman." Her voice sounded small.

Hazel grunted. "I suppose you have to, if you want him to pay for all he's done."

"Yes, but I'm not looking forward to the trip. My ribs hurt just moving and I haven't tried putting my dress on by myself, either. You've had to help me change my nightgown." She licked her still-sore lip. "I just don't know if I can do it."

Hazel looked up. "Put on a dress? Or face that villain?"

Josephine waited several moments before answering. "Both."

"I'll be happy to help you dress in the morning and I could ride along to town with you, if that would help." Hazel set the rocker back in motion.

Josephine twisted on the hard seat. Why hadn't she asked Philip to make her a settee? The hard wooden chairs were not comfortable when you were already battered and bruised. "I'll take the help with the dress, but you don't have to go into town."

"I know I don't have to go, but if you want me to, I'll be happy to do so." Hazel pushed the needle through the cloth.

Josephine took a sip of her tea. "Hazel, would you

like a cup of tea or coffee?" Where were her manners? That should have been the first thing she'd offered.

"Not right now. I'm just happy to sit here and rest my bones."

They continued working.

Hazel broke the silence. "Have you given any more thought to what you are going to do about your marriage?"

"Oh, I've thought about it but have no idea what to do. Thomas and I were married and I have the paper to prove it." Josephine laid her needlework down. "I just don't know if that paper is worth anything now."

Hazel stared into the fire. "I've never heard of anything like this ever happening before." She made a tsking sound. "Maybe you and Tom can ask the sheriff about that, too." Her eyes met Josephine's.

"Hazel, would you like to stay the night? I think I would like for you to go to town with us tomorrow." Josephine felt as if she needed her friend. The thought of going without Hazel didn't appeal at all. Thomas would be with her, but she didn't know how he felt about any of it and, if the truth be told, she was afraid to ask him.

Thomas entered the house. What kind of mood would Josephine be in? He understood that she'd been through a lot and that her waspish attitude earlier was a result of the events unfolding in her life. His anger at her words had already evaporated like water off a duck's back.

Hazel stood in the kitchen. From the smell, she was cooking up venison steaks. Josephine stood by the fireplace. His gaze ran over her face, searching for clues to her temper.

She tried to smile but winced instead. "It's safe. I promise not to bite your head off."

He pulled off his coat and gloves and moved to stand by the fireplace with her. Thomas lowered his voice. "I'm sorry for whatever it was that I said earlier." Maybe if he apologized, she'd forget that he'd left the house in a huff.

"Oh, Thomas, it was my fault. I shouldn't have snapped at you. I'm the one who is sorry." She reached out and touched his arm.

He laid his hand over hers. "Are you feeling better now?"

"A little. I've asked Hazel to spend the night and to go with us tomorrow." She removed her hand from his arm and returned to staring into the crackling fire.

Why had she invited Hazel to spend the night and to go with them? Thomas wished he could read women's minds. It would make his life a lot easier.

"I hope you don't mind my intrusion," Hazel said as she dished up the meat. "Josephine needs a little help getting dressed in the morning and I wanted to do a little last-minute Christmas shopping." She set a plate of biscuits on the table with the meat.

Why hadn't he realized Josephine would need help getting dressed? Her ribs had to be smarting from simple movements. Getting into a dress and buttoning up shoes would be almost impossible for her. "Hazel, I don't know how to thank you for all your help."

Philip stuck his head out of the bedroom door. "Are those steaks I smell?" His blond hair stood on end.

Hazel laughed. "Yep. Leave it to your stomach to rouse you."

He yawned. "Well, all this loud talk of going to town tomorrow didn't help, either."

Josephine covered her mouth. Her eyes danced with merriment. Even with a black eye, split lip and swollen face, she had to be the most beautiful woman in the world.

Thomas smiled. "You coming to town, too?" he asked Philip.

"Do we have a rider coming in tomorrow?"

"Nope."

Philip headed to the table. "Then I'll stay home and catch up on sleep."

Josephine lowered her hand from her cracked lip. "But if there was a rider coming, you'd have to stay here. Why did you ask, if you were planning to stay either way?" she asked, following him.

Thomas stepped around her and pulled the chair out for her. It was a good question. He waited to see what his brother would say.

"I just woke up."

Hazel laughed. "Yeah, he's always a little addled when he first wakes."

"Thank you for fixing dinner, Hazel. It looks and smells wonderful," Josephine complimented her.

Thomas said a quick prayer and they all dug in. To show their appreciation for Hazel's cooking, Thomas and Philip tore into the deer steaks as if it were their last meal. Josephine nibbled at the bread and picked at her vegetables.

Thomas wiped his mouth off. "You know, Josephine, if you aren't feeling well, we can put off our trip to town for a couple of days."

Hazel nodded her agreement.

Josephine shook her head. "I might as well get it over with."

"In that case," Hazel said, pushing her chair back. "Phil, would you mind riding back to my place with me? I've got a small chore for you to do, if you don't mind."

Philip shoved bread into his mouth and wiped his mouth. He stood, swallowed and said, "I'll be ready to go in about ten minutes."

"Good." She took her apron off. "Josephine, leave these dishes be. I'll do them when I get back." She hung her apron on the hook by the stove and then returned to the table with the coffeepot. Filling Thomas's cup, she grinned. "As for you, young man, be nice to our Jo, she's had a tough time of it."

Thomas chuckled. "Yes, ma'am." He pushed his chair back, picked up his plate and dumped the scraps into the bucket, then turned back around. "Josephine, how would you like to take a walk out to the barn with me?"

She looked up from her plate. A pink tinge filled her cheeks. "Why?"

"I just thought you'd like a little fresh air. You haven't been out of the house for a few days." He wiped his hands on the tea towel.

Josephine looked down at her dressing gown. "I don't know. I'd have to get dressed."

"Nonsense. Just throw your coat on and borrow a pair of old boots from Thomas. Girl, you need the air," Hazel said, replacing the coffeepot. She glanced at Philip's bedroom door, and as if she'd made a decision, Hazel began clearing the table.

Thomas waited to see what Josephine would say about going out. She'd dropped her gaze once more to the table. If only he could get her out of the house, it might make her feel better.

Her pretty brown eyes looked up at him. "Do you have another pair of boots?"

He nodded. "I use them in the summer when we have a pig. I'll go get them." Thomas realized she might think he was calling her a pig and turned back around.

Hazel and Josephine were looking at each other. Josephine was trying to cover the cut on her lip. But her shoulders shook with merriment.

"I wasn't saying you are a pig," he gasped.

Philip chose that moment to come out of the bedroom. "Who are you calling a pig?" He grinned, aware of his brother's discomfort.

"No one." Thomas pushed past him. The sound of laughter filled the house. He glanced out the bedroom door and saw that Josephine was laughing, too.

Good. He was thankful to see that she could still laugh, regardless of what had happened to her over the past week. He found his mud boots and carried them back into the living room.

With her hair in disarray and her brown eyes shining with laughter, Josephine was the prettiest woman he'd ever seen. Could he give her up now? Now that she knew about her gold and the fact that the men who had threatened her were gone, would she no longer need him in her life? His heart ached at the thought that she might leave him. What would he do then?

Chapter Twenty-Five

The trip to town had been more excruciating than Josephine anticipated. She should have known it would be too much for her. The night before she'd not even been able to walk the complete distance to the barn before she'd worn herself out.

And even though Hazel had tightly bound her ribs, they felt as if they were coming through her skin. She'd not let on for fear that Thomas would turn the wagon around. The sooner she faced her attacker, the sooner she and Thomas could get on with their lives.

He stopped the wagon in front of the sheriff's office. Josephine sighed with relief. The jolting had stopped and the pain began to subside, slightly. She watched as Hazel climbed down from the wagon with ease. Oh, to feel that good again.

"I'm going to go visit Mrs. Ring's shop." Hazel turned and looked up at Josephine. "Will you be all right?"

The desire to beg to go with Hazel pulled strongly. Josephine would rather do anything than go inside the sheriff's office. Instead she answered, "I'll be fine. Thomas will be with me."

He piped up. "The whole time."

Josephine braced herself as she climbed from the wagon. Clammy sweat broke out all over her body. She bit her lip to keep from crying out. When her feet touched the ground, she leaned heavily against Thomas.

He rubbed her arms. "I'm sorry, Josephine. We should have waited."

"No, I wanted to get it over with and we are." She forced herself to stand upright again. "I'm ready."

Thomas tucked her hand into the crook of his arm. "Lean on me. If nothing else, it will do the sheriff good to see your pain."

Josephine tried to ignore the people who walked around them. She could feel their curious gazes upon her face. Now she understood how Thomas felt about the scar that marred his face. Only, in her case the bruises were still fresh and colorful.

When Thomas opened the door to the jailhouse, she gratefully stepped inside. It took all she could do to remain standing.

The sheriff came around his desk and quickly turned a chair for her to drop down into. "You must be Mrs. Young," he said, looking to Thomas for confirmation.

"Yes, sir, I am." Josephine also looked to Thomas, who simply nodded.

The sheriff moved back to his chair behind the desk. Josephine took a moment to glance around. They were in a small room with the desk on one side and a wood-stove on the other. A door led out of the room on her left. She assumed that was where Mr. Grossman was being held.

"Mrs. Young, can you tell me what happened out at your place the other night?"

She nodded. "I was having tea when Mr. Grossman came through my kitchen and into the sitting room. He told me he'd come to take me back to St. Joseph. When I told him I wasn't going, he insisted." Josephine ducked her head to hide her bruised face.

Thomas laid his hand on her shoulder. The gentle contact was what Josephine needed to raise her head. She looked to the sheriff.

He leaned forward. "Did he say or do anything else?"

"Yes, he said two things that greatly disturbed me. He told me he murdered my father and dumped his body in the St. Joe River in St. Joseph." Her voice caught in her throat. Tears burned the backs of her eyes and her breathing quickened. So far Josephine had fought that grief; she told herself to fight just a little longer.

He finished writing down what Josephine assumed was what she'd just said. "I know this is hard for you, Mrs. Young…"

"Please, call me Josephine." She took the handkerchief that Thomas handed to her and wiped the moisture from her eyelashes. *Don't cry, don't cry*, she silently ordered herself.

"And the other thing?"

Josephine looked up at Thomas. He gently squeezed her shoulder again and nodded his encouragement. She took a deep breath and turned her attention back to the sheriff. "He said that he and I were married by proxy back in September."

The sheriff sat back in his chair. "Were you?" His eyes studied her face intently.

"If we were, it was not with my consent. I signed on

with the Pony Express as a rider in September to keep from having to marry him. He said that my uncle stood in for me." How she hated that. Had her uncle feared the man so badly that he would sell her like that? And why hadn't he told her?

Thomas held his breath as he watched the sheriff's face. What was he thinking? His eyes and face gave away nothing of his thoughts.

"Well, I can help you in both of those cases. I'll send word to St. Joseph to search the river for your father's remains and hang on to Grossman until I hear one way or the other. As far as your marriage to Grossman is concerned, all you have to do is have a judge annul the marriage, and then you can legally marry Thomas here." He folded his hands behind his head and smiled as if he'd solved all their problems.

"Is that all?" Thomas asked, not bothering to keep the annoyance from his question.

"Afraid so." The sheriff stood. "Thank you for coming in, Josephine. I'll let you know what I hear from the authorities in St. Joseph as soon as I hear."

Josephine stood. "I don't have to see him?"

"Not unless you want to."

She shook her head. Relief filled her voice. "No. I hope to never see him again."

Thomas shook the sheriff's hand. "Thank you." He meant it.

He put his hat back on and opened the door for Josephine to exit. Once outside, Thomas wasn't sure what to do. The sheriff hadn't come right out and said it, but he and Josephine weren't married. She couldn't be married to two men at once, and since her marriage to him came after her marriage to Grossman… He let the thought hang in his mind.

"Do you think we could go to the general store?"

Thomas met her gaze. "Sure."

A sad little smile pulled at the corner of her lips. "Good."

He fell into step with her as she took small steps down the boardwalk. Thomas wanted to talk about their visit to the jail, but he was afraid to. What were they going to do about their marriage?

"Thomas?"

"Hmm?"

She inhaled and then winced. "Do you think I should move to Hazel's? I mean, we aren't married."

Thomas didn't want her to move out. She'd turned their run-down house into a comfortable home. He would miss her sweet smiles and teasing ways. But, for the sake of appearances, she should move out. "Probably, but people are going to talk now, anyway."

"Yes, but as Ma always said, there is no need to add fuel to the fire."

Her voice sounded sad and Thomas wondered if she felt the way he did. Miserable. If only there was some way to fix the problem today. "Josephine, did Grossman say he had proof that you were married to him?"

She stopped in front of the general store. "He said my uncle signed a marriage license."

"Did he show it to you?" Thomas opened the door for her.

Josephine frowned. "No, why?"

Thomas laughed. "He might be lying. If he doesn't have the paper, he has no proof you are married to him. Wait here, I'll be right back." He didn't give her time to respond. Thomas hurried back down the boardwalk until he got to the sheriff's office.

The big man looked up when he came through the door. "Have you had a chance to talk to Mr. Grossman yet, about Josephine's statement?"

He nodded. "Yep, says she's lying. He never said he killed her pa."

Thomas growled low in his throat. One thing he knew about Josephine was that she wasn't a liar. "What about the marriage?"

"Says they are married."

"Does he have proof?"

The sheriff turned his head sideways. "Didn't think to ask him."

Thomas lowered his voice. "Josephine just said that he told her that her uncle signed a marriage license. I'm not even sure the state of Missouri issues licenses."

"I don't know, either."

A thought began to form in Thomas's mind. "What if he's lying and he doesn't know for a fact that they do or don't issue them?"

"If I tell him they don't, then he might confess he's lying."

Thomas nodded. "It's a possibility."

"You stay out here and stay quiet." The sheriff walked to the door and opened it. He left it cracked.

Thomas eased up to it to listen.

"Hey, Grossman, I was just thinking. Did you say you have a marriage license to prove you are Josephine's husband?"

"Sure did."

"Where is it?"

"In St. Louis."

Confidence oozed from the sheriff's voice. "That's not very likely."

The sound of springs protesting could be heard. "What makes you say that?" Grossman asked. Thomas heard the uneasiness in his voice.

"Well, first off, if you had one, you would have brought it to persuade Josephine to go with you. Instead of using your fists. And second, they don't issue marriage licenses in the state of Missouri."

Grossman cursed. "That was a dirty trick. You knew all along we weren't married. What game are you playing, sheriff?"

Thomas's heart soared. He released the air in his lungs that he'd been unaware he'd been holding in.

The sheriff laughed. "Well, I got to thinking, if you would lie about the marriage, you probably lied when you said you didn't tell Josephine that you'd murdered her pa."

Another ugly curse filled the air.

"I believe you did kill him."

"You have no proof!"

"You're right, but I soon will, and when I get it, I have no doubt that the judge will hang your sorry hide."

Silence filled the jail. Thomas could imagine the look on the big man's face as he realized he'd soon be hanging from the tree closest to town. Thomas stepped back when he heard the sheriff's footsteps on the other side of the door.

The sheriff closed the door. "You heard?"

Thomas couldn't keep from smiling. "Every sweet word." He grasped the sheriff's hand and gave it a good hard shake. "Thank you."

He practically ran back to the general store. Thomas couldn't wait to tell Josephine that they were still married. That Grossman had lied. They could celebrate by having dinner at the new restaurant that had opened up on Maple Street.

Josephine and Hazel stood looking at the spices when he entered the store. Thomas hurried to their side. "Oh, good, Hazel, I'm glad you're still here."

His gaze moved to Josephine. Her pale face and trembling lips told him she wasn't feeling well. The stress of the day had been too much. "I was wondering if you two would like to spend the night in town, to celebrate."

Hazel's worried gaze met his eyes. "I think that's an excellent idea. Don't you, Jo?"

She nodded. "I wouldn't mind. I'm a little tired." Her pretty brown eyes met his. "What are we celebrating?"

He grinned broadly at both the women. "Grossman just confessed that he lied about being married to you."

Josephine smiled. "That's wonderful news, Thomas."

Hazel clapped her hands. "I knew it. That old skunk couldn't be telling the truth."

Thomas nodded. "Do you feel up to eating before we head over to the boardinghouse?"

Josephine looked as if a strong wind would knock her over. "Maybe food is what I need. Let's eat first."

"Good. After we eat, I'll get you two settled at the boardinghouse, and then I'll take the horse and wagon to the livery." He started to walk to the door.

When he got to it, Thomas turned around to see that Josephine was taking very small steps and leaning heavily on Hazel. If only he could endure the pain for her. Thomas wanted to ease all her aches and pains, both the ones that were physical and those that he knew were emotional.

Chapter Twenty-Six

Pain shot through her body with each step. Josephine held back tears. Then, as if in a dream, her legs seemed to give out. Thomas's face blurred right before the room went black.

When she woke, Doctor Bridges was standing over her. "There you are." He gently helped her into a sitting position.

Josephine grabbed her side and groaned. "What happened?"

"You, my dear, fainted and scared your family." He pressed a spoon to her lips. "That husband of yours practically ran you to my office."

She opened her mouth and took the bittersweet medicine. "I hate that stuff."

"I know, but it will help you rest and give those ribs some time to heal." He screwed the lid back on the dark bottle.

Josephine frowned. "Why are they hurting so bad? I was doing so much better."

"Well, I think one of them might be broken. Earlier I believed it was cracked, but after the ride into town,

I'm not so sure that was the case." He helped her stand. "Come along. Hazel and your husband are about to wear out my carpet with their pacing."

She took small steps but managed to get to the door that Doctor Bridges now held open for her. Josephine smiled as Thomas hurried to her side. She remembered they were still husband and wife. Her heart soared at the news.

"How are you feeling?" He brushed a curl from her forehead. "I am so sorry, Josephine. I should never have talked you into coming to town."

"I'm fine, Thomas. I just overdid it. You can't blame yourself. I wanted to come." She wanted to hug him for being so kind. "If we are going to eat, we better hurry. The doctor made me take the sleepy medicine."

Hazel laughed. "Well, thank the Lord you are feeling good enough to eat."

"You'll need to keep those ribs bandaged up tight for a while, Josephine." The doctor handed Thomas the dark brown bottle of liquid medicine. "Make sure she takes a teaspoon every six hours until it's all gone."

Thomas agreed. "I will, Doc. What do we owe you?"

The doctor looked to Hazel. "How about Sunday dinner?"

Hazel grinned. "Fried chicken sound good to you?"

"Sure does."

Josephine yawned. "I'll make a pie."

They left the doctor's office. "Josephine, how would you like to eat in your room at the boardinghouse? I could go get our meal and bring it back," Thomas suggested.

"I don't want to put anyone out," she protested after another big yawn.

Hazel frowned. "The restaurant is one and a half blocks away. The boardinghouse is across the street. I think it would be best if we go get two rooms and meet you back here."

"Sounds good. I'll be right back." Thomas turned to walk to the restaurant.

Josephine took slow, small steps as they walked to the boardinghouse. She could already feel the medicine working. The pain had begun to ease and she felt sleepy.

They arrived in front of the boardinghouse. It was a tall house that looked to have plenty of room for two more women and a man. At least, Josephine hoped so.

"You seem to be walking a little better," Hazel said. She opened the door and waited for Josephine to pass.

"I'm not hurting as bad, but I feel kind of funny. We should probably hurry up and get our rooms."

Hazel nodded. While Hazel talked to the owner, Josephine looked about. The house wasn't very old. New wood lined the walls and the staircase looked sturdy. The smell of fresh lemon-scented furniture polish filled the air.

"Ready?"

She turned at the sound of Hazel's voice and walked over to her. "Thank you for taking care of me," Josephine replied. A smile touched her lips. Hazel was such a good friend; Josephine felt as if the other woman cared for her as well as her own mother.

Half an hour later, after finding out which two rooms he and the women were staying in, Thomas carried three plates up the stairs. Hopefully Josephine would still be awake enough to eat. He knocked on the door to let Hazel know he was there.

She answered with a smile. "I'm glad you're here."

Thomas frowned. "Is everything all right?"

Hazel nodded. "Yes, but your stubborn wife has been fighting the effects of the medicine. She doesn't want to go to sleep without you in the room."

He wasn't sure if he should feel happy or concerned. Thomas continued on into the room. Josephine sat on the edge of the bed. She motioned for him to come sit beside her. Thomas handed Hazel the plates.

"I missed you," Josephine said, smiling at him like a child.

He smiled back. "Does your lip hurt?" he asked.

"Nope. Nothing hurts." She leaned against his side. "I'm glad you are back."

Hazel handed her a plate. "Here, eat this, and then you need to lie down." She shared a grin with Thomas.

Josephine's behavior was that of a happy drunk. The medicine Doctor Bridges had given her seemed to have a different effect than the drug he'd given her in the past. "Did you hear the good news? We're still married," she said.

Thomas looked to Hazel, who simply smiled and shrugged her shoulders.

"I did hear. That's wonderful."

"Yep. I don't have to move in with Hazel now."

Hazel huffed. "Eat your dinner," she called from where she sat at the only table in the room.

Josephine looked down at her plate and curled her nose at the sight of the roast beef and potatoes. "Yuck! Didn't they have pie?"

He laughed. "Yes, but you can't have any until you eat your dinner."

She nodded and ate, and leaned against Thomas

until her eyelids drifted shut. Hazel took her plate while Thomas gently laid her back onto the bed.

Hazel and Thomas quickly ate their meals. "I'll keep an eye on her if you have any last-minute Christmas shopping to do," Thomas offered.

"I'm done." Hazel smacked her lips as apple pie syrup coated them. "This is the best pie I've had in a long time."

Thomas looked to Josephine. Her face had relaxed with sleep, making her appear sweet and vulnerable. "Yeah, I hate that she fell asleep before she got to sample it."

"We'll save her piece. She can have it for breakfast."

He finished his pie and sighed. "I need to take the horse and wagon to the livery. Do you think we should go home tomorrow or stay an extra day?" Again his gaze moved to Josephine.

"Go home. We can give her some more medicine and make her a pallet in the back of the wagon. We both need to be getting back to our places."

"Then I'll only pay for tonight's boarding." He continued studying Josephine's face. The bruises were now black and green with a hint of yellow. She'd been through so much he hated causing her more pain.

"You love her," Hazel said.

Thomas nodded. "I do."

"Are you going to tell her?"

"Someday." He grinned. "But I want to wait until she's feeling better."

Hazel made a huffing noise. "If you tell her now, she'll feel better."

He frowned. "You don't know that. It may make her

uncomfortable. And if she chooses to leave, I want her feeling her best."

"You saw how she was acting tonight."

Thomas laughed. "That was medicine talk and behavior."

Hazel studied his face. "You know what I think?" She didn't give him time to answer. "I think you are putting it off because you are afraid she'll hurt you."

Was she right? Thomas looked toward his sleeping wife. What would it hurt if he waited? It wasn't like they weren't already married.

Hazel reached across the table and took his hand in hers. "Would it make it easier if I told you I think she feels the same way about you?"

Thomas searched the old woman's eyes. "Did she tell you that?"

She shook her head. "No, but didn't you see how she leaned on you tonight. Josephine told you that she missed you."

He gently pulled his hand out from under hers. "Missing me and loving me are entirely two different things." Thomas stood. "I'll go take care of the horse."

Over the next few days, Thomas had plenty of time to think about his relationship with Josephine. She was doing light chores and cooking their meals again.

He still hadn't told her he loved her. It seemed that either Hazel or Philip were always with them. Not wanting them to see if she rejected him, Thomas had held his tongue and tried not to show his emotions.

Philip pulled him from his thoughts. He sniffed the air and announced, "I love Christmas Eve dinner almost as much as Christmas Day."

Thomas chuckled. "Good thing Ma isn't here. She'd think you didn't like her Christmas Day dinner."

Hazel carried the sliced ham to the table. "You two could help us."

"I'll be happy to help you eat it." Philip pushed out of the rocking chair. "But first I have to go get something out of the barn." He looked at Thomas. "I need your help."

Thomas grinned. "Sure." He stood and followed Philip to the door, where they both donned coats, gloves and hats.

Philip raised his voice so that Josephine could hear him in the kitchen. "Josephine, will you watch for us out the window, and when we get to the door, open it?"

She came into the room. Her hair hung about her shoulders in waves of coppery red. "All right."

Hazel frowned. "What are you two up to?"

"It's a surprise." Philip grinned from ear to ear.

Then Thomas understood what they were about to do. He nodded. "Yep, a surprise."

"Well, hurry up. Dinner's about ready." Hazel shooed them out the door.

Thomas hurried after his brother. Thankfully the night wasn't as cold as it had been and it wasn't snowing. They hurried into the warmth of the barn. "Which should we give first?"

Philip opened the last stall and waited for Thomas to join him. "Why don't I give her my gift first? That way she'll be happy with it. And then you can give her yours, because we both know she will love yours best."

Thomas couldn't hold back his smile. "She will love mine best, won't she?" He bent down and picked up his end of the covered settee.

Philip grunted as he did the same at his end. "She's going to love getting that horse back. I'm still surprised you were able to get her."

"Me, too. I'm just glad Grossman brought the little horse for her to ride back on."

Philip grunted. "How did you know it was hers?"

"She described her to me weeks ago." They worked their way out into the center aisle of the barn. "I'm just glad that Grossman refused to pay for Josephine's mare's board. The livery owner sold her quickly. If we hadn't decided to stay overnight in Dove Creek, I would have never known she was there."

Philip nodded. "Do you think you can talk and walk faster at the same time? This end is heavy."

Thomas laughed. "Well, next time you'll choose lighter wood for this size of furniture."

"True." Philip huffed.

When they got to the door, Josephine opened it. She gasped as they hurried inside. "That's huge."

They carried it the rest of the way into the room and carefully set it down. Philip smiled. "It's for you."

Josephine smiled, her brown eyes bright with excitement. "Can I pull the cover off now?"

Philip nodded. "Merry Christmas."

She pulled the sheet off and gasped again. "Oh, Philip, it's beautiful."

"I'm glad you like it."

Josephine touched the smooth wood. "Oh, I do. Thank you." She hurried to her brother-in-law and gave him a big hug.

Thomas watched as Philip awkwardly patted her back and murmured, "You're welcome."

When Josephine pulled away, Philip blurted out, "Thomas has a gift for you, too."

She turned to look at him, her big eyes curious. "You do?"

Hazel asked, "Can it wait until after supper?"

Thomas watched as disappointment filled Josephine's face. He looked to Hazel and saw a twinkle in her eyes. She was teasing Josephine. He grinned. "I suppose so. What do you think, Philip?"

"I say we make her wait," he teased.

Josephine grinned. "Oh, so that's how it is." She pushed her hair away from her face. "Then I'll just enjoy my new couch."

Hazel had slipped into Thomas and Philip's bedroom. "Not without these you won't." She carried out a long cushion for the seat and several fluffy pillows for the back. "Merry Christmas, Josephine."

"Here, Hazel, let me help you with those." Philip took the biggest from her and put it on the seat of the settee.

Josephine oohed and aahed. "Oh, Hazel, they are so pretty." She ran her hands over the fabric. "I love these light brown colors." She quickly hugged Hazel.

What would her reaction be when she saw her horse, Mistletoe? Thomas wondered. Would he get a hug, also? Unable to wait to find out, he nodded to Philip and slipped out the front door.

He hurried to the barn, where he'd housed Mistletoe, the little black mare with the star on her nose. She bobbed her head in greeting. Thomas tied the big red bow Hazel had made around her head. He stepped back and looked at what he'd done. Laughter poured from his throat as he realized she looked like she had a toothache.

Thomas left the bow in place and led the horse from

the barn. He tied her reins to the porch rail and slipped back inside the house.

Josephine looked up as soon as he entered. Her gaze moved to his empty hands, then traveled up to his face. "I thought you had a Christmas gift for me." Disappointment filled her voice.

"I'm sorry—mine's too big to bring inside. Do you mind slipping on your coat and stepping out onto the porch?"

She eyed him as if unsure, then looked to Hazel, who nodded her encouragement. "Give me just a moment." She set Little One down on the floor and went into her room.

Thomas felt like a schoolboy with a crush on his teacher. He rocked from foot to foot. What was taking her so long? He stared at her door.

Philip chuckled. "I do believe the lady is deliberately making you wait."

Josephine chose that moment to reenter the room. She had put on her cloak and gloves. "I'm ready."

When she got to the door, Thomas smiled. "Philip, you open the door." He put his hands over Josephine's eyes. "No peeking until I tell you."

"How is she going to peek? Your big ole paws are over her eyes," Hazel barked behind him.

He ignored the older woman and nodded to Philip. Cold air rushed inside. Thomas gently urged Josephine forward. When they got to the entryway, he removed his hands. "Merry Christmas, Josephine."

She whispered, "Mistletoe?"

The horse bobbed her head and neighed.

Josephine rushed off the porch and threw her arms

around the horse. Tears streamed down her face as she hugged the little mare close.

Mistletoe seemed to lean into her embrace.

"I never thought I'd see you again." She petted the animal's head, ears and neck, then ran her hands down her back, side and legs. "It really is you."

"I take it you like her?"

Josephine turned to face Thomas. Tears streaming down her face, she said, "I love her." Then she walked up the porch steps, stopped in front of him and took his face in her hands.

He felt her gentle tug as she raised up on tiptoes and kissed him soundly. She leaned her forehead against his and whispered, "Thank you so much." Her salty tears touched his lips and Thomas pulled her close and held her tight.

"I'm starving." Philip slipped past them.

Thomas buried his face in Josephine's hair and inhaled her sweet scent. The air stirred about them as Hazel followed Philip. Josephine pulled away from him and smiled.

"Thank you. That is the best Christmas present anyone has ever given to me." She ran her gloved hand down his scarred face. Love shone from her eyes. "I love you, Thomas Young."

Uncertainty filled him. Did she really love him? Or was she just overcome with joy at having her horse back that she claimed to love him? Thomas didn't want to say he loved her back until he was sure what she was feeling was for him and not just the horse. He hugged her close once more and said, "We better get in there before Philip eats all the ham."

She looked down and nodded. "I'll put Mistletoe

away." Josephine hurried off the porch and untied the horse.

Thomas started to follow her to the barn, but she waved him back. Fresh tears poured down her face. "Go eat. I'll be in shortly."

Had he broken her heart by not saying he loved her? Or was she just happy to have her horse back? Thomas wished he could go back in time and tell her he loved her, too, but it was too late. He'd missed his opportunity and might never get it back.

Chapter Twenty-Seven

Josephine couldn't believe it was Christmas Day. She smiled as they pulled up in front of the Young family home. Mistletoe brought up the rear. She'd insisted they bring the little mare. Even if she couldn't ride her yet, Josephine didn't want to leave her at the relay station.

Her gaze cut to Thomas. He was deep in conversation with Philip, who rode beside them. She'd confessed her love for him and he'd treated her as if it wasn't important. It was then that Josephine realized he didn't feel the same for her.

She didn't know where they would go from here. Maybe, with time, her husband would grow to love her. Until then, she'd love him from afar. What more could she do?

Benjamin and Joy came running out of the house to meet them. Thomas stopped the wagon and jumped down to greet his brother and sister. He tousled Benjamin's hair and swooped Joy up into his arms. "Merry Christmas!" His voice echoed about the yard with merriment.

"Guess what, Thomas!" Joy practically bounced in his arms.

He grinned at her. "What?"

"Ma got me a new doll. And it has real hair, too." She scooted out of his arms.

Thomas gently placed his little sister on the ground. "Where is this new doll?"

"Inside. Ma says she isn't allowed outside." Joy grinned. "I'll show her to you. Come on." She tugged at his hand.

"Not yet, we have to help Josephine inside." He lowered his voice to a loud whisper. "She's still sore from her accident."

Josephine stood to climb down from the wagon. She loved that Thomas doted on her. In his own way, she supposed he loved her. Maybe not as a husband should, but he'd proven she could trust him and to her that was almost as good. Almost.

"Here, let me help you down. Those ribs are still on the mend." Thomas reached up and gently eased her to the ground.

Josephine smiled her thanks and motioned for him to get the gifts she'd brought with them out of the back of the wagon.

"You brought us gifts?" Benjamin asked.

His question caught Joy's attention. "For me, too?" she asked.

"For everyone," Josephine answered. She couldn't contain her joy. The only thing that would make Christmas better was if she and Thomas were truly husband and wife. If he had said he loved her, too. She forced the thoughts away. Josephine told herself to stop dwelling on the impossible. "Why don't you two help Thomas carry the packages inside?"

The front door opened again and this time Clayton came out. He held out his elbow for Josephine to take and grinned down at her. "How was your trip out here?"

Josephine thought of all the bumps that the wagon wheels had found and how each one had set her ribs to throbbing. "It wasn't as bad as it could have been," she answered, not wanting to complain.

Thomas laughed behind her. "One of the things I love about this woman is her attempts to make everything positive." He juggled several larger packages while his little brother and sister carried smaller ones.

Clayton helped her up the steps and then held the door for all of them to enter. "Josephine, Ma said to go into the sitting room. She wants to bring you a special treat."

"All right." What did Rebecca have in store for her? Was it a Christmas present? Josephine smiled as she eased into one of Rebecca's overstuffed chairs.

Rebecca and the kids made Josephine feel as if she was a part of their family.

Josephine took a deep breath, trying to still her heart. Thomas had just said one of the things he loved about her was her positive attitude. She smiled, not exactly what every girl wanted to hear, but she'd take it.

What would he think of her Christmas gift to him? Would he understand that giving him her bank account numbers proved that she trusted him? That she wanted to build a ranch with him? And someday, the Lord willing, start a family on that ranch?

Joy came running into the room. The little girl had changed into a pretty pink dress and her hair was pulled up on the sides with a white ribbon. "I got to put on my new Christmas dress," she announced with excitement.

"You look beautiful," Josephine said, smiling at the little girl.

Seth and Rebecca entered a moment later. Rebecca gently scolded, "Joy, how have I told you little girls enter a room?"

Joy bowed her head. "Like a princess, not a horse."

"That's right." Rebecca's lips twitched as if she were trying not to smile. She turned to Josephine. "This surprise is from Philip." Rebecca turned to face the door.

Philip entered first, followed by a stranger Josephine had never met. Then Thomas entered the room. Josephine stood nervously. The last time Philip had surprised her, she'd been presented as Thomas's mail-order bride. A bride Thomas had no idea was coming.

Thomas came to stand beside her. He turned to face the stranger and Philip. The rest of Thomas's family entered the room.

She looked first at Thomas, who simply smiled nervously at her, and then to Philip, who looked equally nervous. "What's going on?"

Philip took both her hands in his. "Josephine, I am the one who sent for you back in August. I'm the reason you married Thomas." He paused. His blue gaze met hers.

"I know that," Josephine finally said to break the silence in the room. "So what are you up to today?" She dreaded his answer. Had he bought her a one-way ticket home?

He looked to Thomas. "I got to thinking, and the last couple of weeks have been very rough on you. First your uncle, then Mr. Grossman attacked you, and then you had to tell the sheriff that Mr. Grossman killed your pa. You also thought that you were married to two men." Philip looked around the room as if unsure what to say next.

"Yes, all of that is true." Josephine tugged on his hands to get his attention. "But what does that have to do with now?"

Philip looked to the stranger. "Well, I thought it would be nice for you to have a real wedding as my Christmas gift to you."

"What?" Both Josephine and Thomas blurted out at the same time.

Josephine looked to Thomas. "You didn't know about this?"

He shook his head. And glared at his brother. "No, it's all a surprise to me, too."

Seth stepped forward. "Thomas, would you like to step into the kitchen and discuss this with Josephine?" He frowned at Philip. "I thought you said Thomas knew about your surprise."

"No, I said he was all right with me inviting Reverend Michaels to spend Christmas Day with us." Philip grinned sheepishly.

Thomas took her hands from Philip and answered Seth. "Yes, I would like to speak with my... Josephine."

She'd noticed that he'd stopped short of calling her his wife. Josephine whispered, "I'd like to talk to you, too."

He looked to his family. "If you will excuse us..." Then he gently led her from the room and the many eyes of his family.

Once in the kitchen Thomas turned to her. "I'm sorry. I didn't know Philip was going to have the reverend perform a wedding today. I simply thought he was being kind by inviting the traveling preacher to spend the holiday with our family."

Josephine believed him. Thomas hadn't lied to her yet and she didn't think he'd start today. "What are you going to do?"

"What I should have done when I first met you." Thomas knelt down on one knee in front of her. "Josephine, I love you. I have for a long time, but because of the scar on my face, because of the trouble with your uncle and Mr. Grossman, I didn't know when to tell you. And then last night I was taken by surprise that you loved me, too. I hope I didn't miss my opportunity to make this a real marriage. Will you marry me again?"

She looked down at him. "You love me?" Josephine fought the hot moisture that threatened to tumble from her eyes.

"With all my heart."

Josephine reached down and touched the fine scar on his face. She bent down and pressed a kiss against his cheek. "I love you, too. I can't imagine not being married to you."

He stood and carefully gathered her into his arms. "I feel the same way. I love you so much that it scares me." Thomas pressed his face into her mass of curls.

She pulled away enough to look into his face. "I've felt the same. You are the first man that I could trust and truly love."

Thomas bent his head and kissed her. His warm lips captured hers and all his love flowed into her being. This was what it felt like to be loved and to love. He pulled away slowly and smiled. "We have a minister who is willing to marry us and a family waiting to hear if we are going to get married a second time."

Josephine hesitated. "Before we go back in there, I have something else to tell you."

His frown told her that she'd given him cause for worry. "All right."

"Remember when I told you Mr. Grossman said my parents were wealthy?" At his nod, she continued. "Well, when Doctor Bridges came back to check on me, I asked him to send a letter to the bank back home. I also asked him not to tell anyone that he was doing it."

"I see. Have you heard back from the bank?" He played with a wayward curl on the side of her face.

Josephine nodded. "Yes. Two days ago he came out with a new letter."

His hand fell back to his side. "Are you going to tell me what it said?"

"Yes. I'm not only rich, I'm very rich. It seems my pa didn't just find a few nuggets, he hit a gold vein. I'm not sure what that means other than I'm rich." She held her breath waiting to see what he'd say.

"I'm happy for you, Josephine."

She pulled a small package from the pocket of her dress. "You don't look happy. Maybe a present will cheer you up."

Thomas looked at her like she were a demented squirrel. "You want me to open a gift now?"

"Why not?"

Thomas grinned. He took the small package and pulled the red ribbon from around the green cloth that held his present. It opened to reveal an envelope. Thomas laid the ribbon on the counter and opened the envelope.

Josephine watched as he pulled out the piece of paper she'd tucked inside. "Read it aloud."

"'Dearest Thomas, I turned twenty-one at the first of this month. Now, at the end of the month, I discover I have a lot of money in the bank. Money I can claim, since I turned twenty-one. If you will let me stay married to you, love you and make a family with you, I'd like to give you all the money that belonged to my father. I love you. Josephine.'" Thomas looked at her with moist eyes. "When did you write this?"

She smiled. "Right after the doctor brought me my letter." Josephine took his large hand in her smaller one.

"I can't take your money, Josephine."

Josephine had known he'd say that, so she smiled. "All right, look inside the envelope."

Thomas frowned. He pulled the envelope open again and pulled out a smaller piece of paper.

"Read it."

"'I, Josephine Young, do hereby give my husband, Thomas Young, a ranch, a bank full of money and my undying love for Christmas. He is not allowed to refuse any of the three. Josephine Young.'"

The smile that tugged at her lips broke free. "It's a Christmas gift. You can't give it back."

Shock filled his face.

Did he feel tricked? Or did he understand the depth of just how much she loved him? "Now, are you going to marry me today? Or not?"

Thomas scooped her up into his arms and kissed her soundly. "I better marry you before you give me another Christmas gift," he whispered against her lips. "I love you, Josephine Young."

Epilogue

Thomas paced the floor. How much longer would he have to wait out here? The doctor had said it could be any moment, and that was a couple of hours ago.

"Thomas, stop pacing. You're going to wear out that fancy rug, and then Josephine is going to kill you." Philip yawned and reclined on the settee.

"What is taking so long?" Thomas demanded, scowling at the closed bedroom door.

Seth answered, "Babies take time." He juggled his three-month-old daughter, Katie, in his arms.

"Besides, Ma and Hazel are in there with her. She's fine," Andrew said from his spot by the fireplace. He had been reading Charles Dickens's *A Christmas Carol*.

Thomas looked about the room. It was only fitting that Josephine would have their first child on Christmas Eve. He looked around the farmhouse. She'd decorated it from top to bottom. The place screamed *Christmas*.

Clayton and Benjamin played a game of checkers at a small side table while Joy watched. Andrew continued reading his book and Seth jiggled Katie until she slept peacefully in his arms.

His own baby was struggling to enter the world. Thomas had wanted to go with Josephine to the bedroom, but his adoptive mother and Hazel forbade him to come in. They claimed it was women's business.

The sound of someone being slapped split the air. A sharp cry followed. Thomas headed for the door. The baby's cry continued.

"I wouldn't go in there yet." Seth's deep voice stopped Thomas in his tracks.

He stood as if frozen in front of the door. The baby stopped crying. Only the sounds of shuffling feet could be heard.

A few minutes passed. The room behind him was silent, as if his family was listening, too. Why didn't someone come tell him what was going on? Didn't they know he'd be waiting to see his wife and child?

Just when he'd decided to barge in anyway, Ma opened the door. She and Hazel stepped out, grinning like two possums.

Ma hugged him and said, "The doctor says you can go in now."

Thomas hurried into the dim room. Doctor Bridges was cleaning up his hands and smiling at the mother and child resting on the bed. "How are they, Doc?" Thomas asked.

"Both healthy and awake." The doctor slipped out of the room and left Thomas alone with his little family.

"Come see your son." Josephine's voice sounded soft and warm.

He walked to the bed and looked down upon her. Her

long red curls framed her face. The baby rested on her chest. "He's beautiful." Thomas touched his small head.

"He is, isn't he?" Her tired eyes looked up at him and a soft smile graced her sweet lips.

They'd decided that if the baby was a boy, they would name him John David Young. John after the man who had adopted Thomas, and David after Josephine's father. "Do you still like the name we decided on?" he asked, looking at the dark hair on the baby's head.

"I think it is a good strong name. But if you would rather name him Thomas, after you, we can." Josephine yawned.

He stroked the side of her face. "No, I like John David." Thomas bent down and kissed his wife's forehead. "I love you."

"I love you, too." Her eyes drifted shut.

Thomas eased the baby from her arms and cradled him close. He checked all the baby's fingers and toes. John David was perfect in every way. He sat down in the rocker beside the bed and rocked his baby.

As he rocked, Thomas thanked the Lord for his new family. How different and empty his life would have been without Josephine in it.

He loved her more than he loved life itself.

She whispered his name from the bed. "Thomas."

Immediately he hurried to her side. "I'm so glad you married a Pony Express rider and made her a mother."

Thomas laughed, then gently kissed her lips. "So am I, Jo. So am I."

* * * * *

Don't miss these other
SADDLES AND SPURS *stories*
from Rhonda Gibson:

PONY EXPRESS COURTSHIP
PONY EXPRESS HERO

Find more great reads at www.LoveInspired.com.

Dear Reader,

When I was researching the Pony Express, I came across a letter from a little girl who asked if there were any girl Pony Express riders. The gentleman who answered her letter said, "not that history recorded but that doesn't mean there wasn't one." That got me to thinking, and Josephine's story was born. I enjoyed telling Thomas and Josephine's love story.

Thank you so much for reading *Pony Express Christmas Bride*. I hope you are enjoying reading this miniseries as much as I am writing it.

Warmly,
Rhonda Gibson

COMING NEXT MONTH FROM
Love Inspired® Historical

Available January 3, 2017

MONTANA COWBOY FAMILY
Big Sky Country • by Linda Ford

When cowboy Logan Marshall and schoolteacher Sadie Young discover three abandoned children, they are determined to help them. But working together to care for the children while searching for their missing father might just leave Logan and Sadie yearning to make their temporary family permanent.

HIS SUBSTITUTE WIFE
Stand-In Brides • by Dorothy Clark

Blake Latherop must marry if he wants to keep his store, so when his fiancée weds another and her sister arrives in town offering her hand instead, he has no choice but to accept. But will their marriage of convenience lead to true love?

FOR THE SAKE OF THE CHILDREN
by Danica Favorite

Silas Jones needs a mother for his daughter, and marriage could help his former sweetheart, Rose Stone, repair her tattered reputation. The single mother, wary of trusting Silas with her heart again, refuses his proposal. But she *is* willing to be his child's nanny...

RESCUING THE RUNAWAY BRIDE
by Bonnie Navarro

On the run to escape a forced engagement, Vicky Ruiz is injured while rescuing a rancher from harm. Now can she find her way past language barriers and convince Christopher Samuels to return the favor by not taking her home?

LOOK FOR THESE AND OTHER LOVE INSPIRED BOOKS WHEREVER BOOKS ARE SOLD, INCLUDING MOST BOOKSTORES, SUPERMARKETS, DISCOUNT STORES AND DRUGSTORES.

LIHCNM1216

REQUEST YOUR FREE BOOKS!

2 FREE INSPIRATIONAL NOVELS
PLUS 2 *FREE* MYSTERY GIFTS

Love Inspired® HISTORICAL

YES! Please send me 2 FREE Love Inspired® Historical novels and my 2 FREE mystery gifts (gifts are worth about $10). After receiving them, if I don't wish to receive any more books, I can return the shipping statement marked "cancel." If I don't cancel, I will receive 4 brand-new novels every month and be billed just $4.99 per book in the U.S. or $5.49 per book in Canada. That's a saving of at least 17% off the cover price. It's quite a bargain! Shipping and handling is just 50¢ per book in the U.S. and 75¢ per book in Canada.* I understand that accepting the 2 free books and gifts places me under no obligation to buy anything. I can always return a shipment and cancel at any time. Even if I never buy another book, the two free books and gifts are mine to keep forever.

102/302 IDN GH6Z

Name	(PLEASE PRINT)

Address	Apt. #

City	State/Prov.	Zip/Postal Code

Signature (if under 18, a parent or guardian must sign)

Mail to the **Reader Service:**
IN U.S.A.: P.O. Box 1867, Buffalo, NY 14240-1007
IN CANADA: P.O. Box 609, Fort Erie, Ontario L2A 5X3

Want to try two free books from another series?
Call 1-800-873-8635 or visit www.ReaderService.com.

* Terms and prices subject to change without notice. Prices do not include applicable taxes. Sales tax applicable in N.Y. Canadian residents will be charged applicable taxes. Offer not valid in Quebec. This offer is limited to one order per household. Not valid for current subscribers to Love Inspired Historical books. All orders subject to credit approval. Credit or debit balances in a customer's account(s) may be offset by any other outstanding balance owed by or to the customer. Please allow 4 to 6 weeks for delivery. Offer available while quantities last.

Your Privacy—The Reader Service is committed to protecting your privacy. Our Privacy Policy is available online at www.ReaderService.com or upon request from the Reader Service.

We make a portion of our mailing list available to reputable third parties that offer products we believe may interest you. If you prefer that we not exchange your name with third parties, or if you wish to clarify or modify your communication preferences, please visit us at www.ReaderService.com/consumerchoice or write to us at Reader Service Preference Service, P.O. Box 9062, Buffalo, NY 14240-9062. Include your complete name and address.

LIH15

SPECIAL EXCERPT FROM

Love Inspired® HISTORICAL

*When cowboy Logan Marshall and schoolteacher
Sadie Young discover three abandoned children, they
are determined to help them. But working together to
care for the children while searching for their parents
might just leave Logan and Sadie yearning to make
their temporary family permanent.*

*Read on for a sneak preview of
MONTANA COWBOY FAMILY by Linda Ford,
available January 2017 from Love Inspired Historical!*

"Are you going to be okay with the children?" Logan
asked.

Sadie bristled. "Of course I am."

"I expect the first night will be the worst."

"To be honest, I'm more concerned about tomorrow
when I have to leave the girls to teach." She looked back
at her living quarters. "They are all so afraid."

"I'll be back before you have to leave so the girls
won't be alone and defenseless." He didn't know why
he'd added the final word and wished he hadn't when
Sadie spun about to face him. He'd only been thinking of
Sammy's concerns—be they real or the fears of children
who had experienced too many losses.

"You think they might have need of protection?"

"Don't all children?"

Her lips trembled and then she pressed them together
and wrapped her arms across her chest in a move so self-
protective that he instinctively reached for her, but at the
look on her face, he lowered his arms instead.

LIHEXP1216

She shuddered.

From the thought of him touching her or because of something she remembered? He couldn't say but neither could he leave her without knowing she was okay. Ignoring the idea that she might object to his forwardness, wanting only to make sure she knew he was concerned about her and the children, he cupped one hand to her shoulder. He knew he'd done the right thing when she leaned into his palm. "Sadie, I'll stay if you need me to. I can sleep in the schoolroom, or over at Uncle George's. Or even under the stars."

She glanced past him to the pile of lumber at the back of the yard. For the space of a heartbeat, he thought she'd ask him to stay, then she drew in a long breath.

"We'll be fine, though I would feel better leaving them in the morning if I knew you were here."

He squeezed her shoulder. "I'll be here." He hesitated, still not wanting to leave.

She stepped away from him, forcing him to lower his arm to his side. "Goodbye, then. And thank you for your help."

"Don't forget we're partners in this." He waited for her to acknowledge his statement.

"Very well."

"Goodbye for now. I'll see you in the morning." He forced himself to climb into the wagon and flick the reins. He turned for one last look before he was out of sight.

Don't miss
MONTANA COWBOY FAMILY by Linda Ford,
available January 2017 wherever
Love Inspired® Historical books and ebooks are sold.

www.LoveInspired.com

Copyright © 2017 by Linda Ford

LIHEXP1216

SPECIAL EXCERPT FROM

A promise to watch out for his late army buddy's little brother might have this single rancher in over his head. But he's not the only one who wants to care for the boy...

Read on for a sneak preview of the fourth book in the
LONE STAR COWBOY LEAGUE: BOYS RANCH
miniseries, THE COWBOY'S TEXAS FAMILY
by **Margaret Daley**.

As Nick settled behind the steering wheel and started his truck, he slanted a look at Darcy. "So what do you think about the boys ranch?"

"Corey is much better off here than with his dad. He's not happy right now, but then he wasn't happy at home."

"He's scared." That was why Bea had brought him to the barn first to see Nick. "He'll feel better after he meets some of the other boys his age."

"What if he doesn't?" Darcy asked.

"He's confused. He wants to be with his dad, and yet not if he's always being left alone. He doesn't know what to expect from day to day and certainly doesn't feel safe." Those same feelings used to plague Nick while he was growing up.

"I've dealt with kids like that."

"In a perfect world, Ned wouldn't drink and would love Corey unconditionally. But that isn't going to happen. Ned isn't going to change." He knew firsthand the mind-set of an alcoholic and remembered the times his dad promised to stop drinking and reform. He never did; in fact he got worse.

"How do you know that for sure?"

"I just do." He didn't share his past with anyone. It was a part of his life he wanted to wipe from his mind, but it was always there in the background. He never wanted to see a child grow up the way he had.

"Then I'll pray for the best for Corey," Darcy said.

"The best scenario would be the state taking Corey away from Ned and a good family adopting him. I wish I was in a position to do it." The second he said that last sentence he wanted to snatch it back. He had no business being anyone's father.

"Because you're single? That might not matter in certain cases."

"I'm not dad material." How could he explain that he was struggling to erase the debt that his father had accumulated? If he lost the ranch, he would lose his home and job. But, more important, what if he wasn't a good father to Corey? It was one thing to be there to help when needed, but it was very different to be totally responsible for raising a child.

Don't miss
THE COWBOY'S TEXAS FAMILY
by Margaret Daley, available January 2017 wherever
Love Inspired® books and ebooks are sold.

www.LoveInspired.com

Copyright © 2016 by Harlequin Books S.A.

LIEXP1216

Turn your love of reading into rewards you'll love with
Harlequin My Rewards

**Join for FREE today at
www.HarlequinMyRewards.com**

Earn **FREE BOOKS** of your choice.

Experience **EXCLUSIVE OFFERS** and contests.

Enjoy **BOOK RECOMMENDATIONS**
selected just for you.

PLUS! Sign up now
and get **500** points
right away!

Earn **FREE** REWARDS
Join Today!
HarlequinMyRewards.com

MYR16R